When The Fat La

Karen Anstee originally trained as a violinist at the Royal Academy of Music. She then continued her studies in Boston USA before embarking upon a successful career playing for many symphony, opera and ballet orchestras, alongside working as a backing musician for artists such as Sting, Take That, Goldfrapp, Dame Shirley Bassey and Kanye West.

Karen has used her many hours travelling from city to city on tour to write fiction inspired by her years in the music industry. Her short story, *Symphony of Sighs*, starring Hugh Dennis, aired on BBC Radio 4 and was named a 'Pick of the Week' by *The Telegraph*.

She graduated from the London Film School with an MA in screenwriting and recently wrote and directed her first film *Rachel* which won Best Foreign Film at the New England Indie Fest, USA. Her latest short film script, *Approval Needed*, was the Audience Award Winner at the 2017 IMDb Script to Screen Awards.

Karen lives in London and, when not working, she enjoys spending time with her family & friends, yoga, battling weeds on her allotment and fencing, of the sword-fighting variety.

With enduring thanks to my family and friends.

You know who you are but cannot possibly begin to imagine how very much I love you and appreciate all your support and encouragement.

Special Thanks To

Nathaniel, Zachary and Gabriel

Celia, Lori, Beth, Lorraine and Margaret

KAREN ANSTEE

When The Fat Lady Thins

CONTENTS

FEATURED MUSIC

LITANIAE LAURETANAE K.195 (1774) Wolfgang Amadeus Mozart.

TOSCA (1900) Giacomo Puccini.
Libretto by Giuseppi Giacosa & Luigi Illica
(Publisher Casa Ricordi)

SALOME (1905) Richard Strauss.
Libretto by Richard Strauss, based on Hedwig Lachenmann's
translation of play by Oscar Wilde.
English Translation Peter Gutmann.
(Publisher G.Schirmer Inc.)

DIALOGUES des CARMÉLITES (1956) Frances Poulenc.
Libretto by Frances Poulenc.
(Publisher Casa Ricordi)

MADAME BUTTERFLY (1904) Giacomo Puccini.
Libretto by Giuseppi Giacosa & Luigi Illica.
(Publisher Casa Ricordi)

LA BOHÈME (1896)   Giacomo Puccini.
Libretto by Giuseppi Giacosa & Luigi Illica.
(Publisher Casa Ricordi)

COVER IMAGE
PIANO SERIES: THE SINGER III
© September McGee PSA, CPS, PSWC NPS,
www.septembermcgee.com

Motif - violin, crossed with sword and quill - designed by
Meticulous Ink, Bath, Somerset UK.

For

Mum and Dad

WHEN THE FAT LADY THINS

chapter one

OVERTURE

'Shit, shit... shit,' said Olivia Tarrent under her breath, feeling the heel of her shoe descend into, and lodge in, the heating grate as she walked down the aisle of St. Paul's church. That she was stuck was certainly irritating, but it was actually the sight of the choir eagerly awaiting her up at the altar that had caused her outburst. A quick look told her that there were less than forty of them, which would have been fine had they been professional singers, but they were not. So, here was the typical mismatched, top-heavy assembly that sent shivers down Olivia's spine. No surprise then to see only a few, overly done up and no doubt overly pleased with themselves young women amidst the jolly flock of middle-aged sopranos, who naturally outnumbered the altos two to one. The tenors were a sorry bunch; only seven of them, with one woman and three pubescent boys in their midst. And, of course, at least one corpse amongst the five ancient basses.

It's a fantastic choir. The concert will be fabulous exposure for you. As far as Olivia could recall, that was what her agent had said. Just how many times would she have to go through a gig chanting *never again, never again* before she'd learn to stand up to Laura's bullying? Fabulous exposure indeed - only if she were referring to the missing panes in the stained-glass windows through which the dank, cold draughts of an early Autumn were flowing freely. Not surprisingly, there was no hint of heat billowing up from the vent as she slid an already ice-cold foot free and tugged at her shoe.

Her infuriated *oh fuck* silenced the prattling choir immediately and echoed about for some time. Olivia couldn't care less as she examined her ruined stiletto - the leather was puckered along the length of the heel, revealing its white plastic innards. There went her pay cheque if, that was, she got one. Terrence Danvers - director of the choir - was notorious for trying to persuade the musicians and solo singers that the church's need was greater than their own. A quick, disparaging glance around told Olivia that the previous concerts in this series of restoration fund-raisers had yielded little or no profit. The once ornately carved stone pulpit was roped off, just in case the rusty supporting metal rods were not clue enough to its unsafe state, and the sound of a permanently flushing toilet could be heard coming from the robe room behind the organ.

Terrence pounced on her before she could take evasive action.

'Ah my *dear* Olivia, so good to see you again. It's such an *honour* to have a soprano of your calibre in our humble midst.'

He was her least favourite of all the mini führers she suffered on these wretched dates. A tall, spiderish man, who still clung to his youth by dressing as he had back in the seventies, though his love of cravats made it clear that he had taken Basil Fawlty rather than Mick Jagger for a style guru. Tonight he would sport his velvet dinner jacket, with a large burgundy bow-tie and matching cummerbund (also velvet), and the ladies of the chorus would swoon. Didn't they see that vulturous face? Olivia was amazed by the admiration that Terrence inexplicably inspired. The flutter of hearts could almost be heard as he took to the podium with that flirtatious smile they had waited months for. It was a wonder they didn't all faint when he ran a hand back through his hair, with practised fatigue, before taking his bow when the performance was done. That wiry, grey thatch wasn't a toupee but it certainly did a good impression of one.

Terrence could do no wrong, though he showered his ardent admirers with hurtful insults at every rehearsal. Olivia was sure that Terrence had had a horrible childhood at the hands of his mother and was now enjoying this chance to play with the tender emotions of those women who had joined the choir in order to abate the boredom of marriage or widowhood. All appeared entirely unaware that his unrelentingly cruel criticism was a ruse, a smokescreen to hide his own lack of talent.

3

'Hello Terrence,' Olivia said, with teeth grinding behind her smile. She fought to remove her hand from his cloying grasp, only to find his arm come to rest about her shoulders so that he could propel her to her place in front of the many chairs and stands that were crammed into what little space there was between choir and front pew. How the hell was the orchestra supposed to play in such a confined space?

'Is there somewhere to hang my dress?'

'Oh dear. I'm afraid the vicarage is all locked up just at the moment. Of course Mrs. Davenport will be there to welcome us, as usual, for tea before the performance, so... if it can wait till then?'

'Of course,' agreed Olivia, dismayed at the thought of all those little sausages on sticks, semi-defrosted quiches and neatly triangled mystery meatspread sandwiches to come.

'Ah, *wonderful*! Here are our other soloists.'

Laura had clearly rounded up all the usual suspects for this concert. Brendan O'Leary was the tenor, which was unfortunate because it was Mozart's all too rarely performed *Litaniae Lauretanae* that was to be massacred tonight and there would be more flying about than he could pull off with that strangulated hernia of a voice he was so proud of. Terrence loved him though - pert, with monstrously big blue eyes, tight blond curls, and a cute little arse. Barry Bosworth had been a great bass in his youth but the audience, on this evening, might be forgiven for thinking that the soloist had been a no-show and replaced by a brave member of the chorus. And then there was mezzo, Julia 'Jameson' Jarvis, whose love of whiskey could be seen in the tremendous bulk of the woman and heard in her diction.

Olivia lifted her eyes from the sight of them advancing cheerfully towards her and stared up at the depiction of the crucifixion in the arched window above the main portal. How often, in her childhood, had she been told that He had died on the cross so that her sins might be forgiven? Often enough to think it ironic that she should now find herself in this earthly hell. Just what had she done to deserve this? But then she remembered and quickly turned her attention to her score.

'Good afternoon everyone,' said Terrence, tapping an excessively long baton impatiently against his stand. 'Ladies, *ladies* can we have a little peace, *please?*'

The twittering in the sopranos immediately ceased and every last one of them turned adoring eyes upon their maestro.

'That's better. Now there's lots to do before this evening's performance but before we get started, I'd like to extend a warm welcome to our *illustrious* soloists.'

The chorus clapped enthusiastically and *hear, hears* were to be heard from the men. Olivia dutifully gave a little nod in their direction and wished wholeheartedly that their warm welcome had included the loan of a fur coat. It was going to be a long, miserable afternoon.

By the announcement, at rehearsal's end, that tea would be served over in the vicarage, Olivia could hardly have discerned which would be the preferable - to go ahead with the concert or to top herself and face eternal damnation. Sure enough, the preceding three, interminable hours, had been a perfect example of how to mismanage time. Thanks to Terrence's faffing about with last minute tempo changes and screaming matches with string players, there had been no opportunity to rehearse the final of the five parts that made up the *Litaniae Lauretanae*. The *Agnus Dei* was Olivia's chance to shine, untarnished by the other soloists but, with no rehearsal, there was no telling what Terrence and his choir would do to sabotage her efforts.

In the quiet of an upstairs vicarage bedroom, which typically housed a vast assortment of things collected for church bazaars, Olivia perched on the edge of a battered Lloyd Loom laundry basket and attempted to meditate. It was something she did, to absolutely no effect, before every concert. She could not remember the last time she had walked out in front of an audience, however small, and not found herself shaking so violently that she could barely keep her music in hand, let alone stand.

Olivia gave up and set about glamming herself up before Julia arrived. Two fat ladies - and one of them drunk - trying to crowbar themselves into evening gowns whilst manoeuvring between the lampshades, coats, crocheted poodle toilet roll covers, china and stacks of fragile '78s; it didn't bear thinking about.

By the time Julia squeezed her way into the room, Olivia had been looking at herself in the mirror on the back of the door for so long that she was close to tears. Months of dieting and yet she could still see the fabric of her bodice forming little folds where it pulled at the seams. Julia saw immediately, from the way Olivia was pulling at her dress, that she was losing her nerve. What was new? She wasn't exactly fond of Olivia; she was like all those kids back at school who swore they were going to fail their exams and then came out top of the class. Every time she sang with Olivia she'd have to coax the stupid cow out of the dressing room. *The rehearsal was great, You've got a beautiful voice, You look stunning.* Never changed and, worst of all, every word was the bloody soul-destroying truth.

Julia recognised that Olivia's lack of confidence could not actually be put on, for who in their right mind would knowingly waste a voice like hers? Olivia pissed her off anyway. When you had a voice that fitted in just fine with a crap choir like tonight's, and a body to make all those ladies feel really good about their corset-bound flab, it was no joy to see Olivia looking for all the world like a 'fifties movie star. So what if Olivia would never make it into a Calvin Klein underwear ad - at least *she* could back away far enough in this piddling little room to actually see her whole body in the mirror. Well, tonight the vicar had tried to have a quiet word with Julia about AA counselling, so she wasn't in any mood for playing supportive friend; Olivia could take her blonde hair, big brown eyes and swanky, forest green taffeta number and piss off.

* * *

With the choir in place and orchestra tuned and resigned to missing last orders at the pub, Terrence strode forth and Olivia followed, all semblance of calm disintegrating as the first ripples of applause met her ears. The church was packed; they must be really hard up for entertainment around here. The urge to turn and run was only tempered by the insurmountable Julia, following close behind like fast-flowing lava in a voluminous cacophony of red and orange chiffon.

This wasn't one of those works where the soloists got to sit out the first few numbers. Olivia eyed her chair and wished to God that she might be allowed to sink down onto it now but, instead, the choir arose with impressive synchronicity as Barry took his place, suddenly distinguished-looking in bowtie and tails, with silvery beard combed and beer gut smoothed out by his cummerbund. To his right stood Brendan looking down his delicate nose into his score, back incredibly straight, head tilted back just a tad, as if he had shot up after sitting on something very sharp.

For a while Terrence appeared loath to start. He fiddled with his stand as if it hadn't been at exactly the right height all afternoon, and turned over the corners of certain pages in his score. By the time he was ready, rather than waiting in the silent, awed anticipation he had hoped to create, the audience were chatting amongst themselves, putting coats back on having realised that the heat was not on, and rustling programmes as they tried to read about the soloists in the dim candlelight. Terrence was in his element, turning upon them with disapproving eyes. When the shushing had ceased, only Olivia's gasps for air could be heard echoing about - or so she thought.

Now the baton was in hand and violins were raised. Terrence looked down the line of soloists, gave a little nod and smiled. All returned the gesture except Olivia, who stared at her music as a tide of anxiety bore the sea of swirling black notes to and fro. For a second there was hope. Terrence had failed to give the agreed four beats in. They would stumble to a halt, she would not have to find her voice after all.

The gentle throbbing of the second violins, supported by a luxurious cello line brought goose bumps up over Olivia's entire body, the first violins' introduction of the tune that she would soon be singing, numbed her to her fingertips. A lump rose into her already dry throat as she realised that the orchestra was mutinying - they were in control and there was no turning back.

Kyrie.

Kyrie.

Kyrie.

First Barry, then Brendan, then Julia came in in close succession.

But where was the soprano?

Shit! She was the soprano. Olivia couldn't believe that she hadn't joined them. She had not even taken a breath. They were singing on without her.

Kyrie eleison.

As if she were half way down the aisle, Olivia could see herself standing there, not a sign on her face of the turmoil within, whilst the panicking Terrence slapped a smile on his face and tried to spur her into action without letting the audience know that there was something wrong. Olivia knew it was a wasted effort; if the punters had not gone screaming from the church when they'd heard those opening entries, the one more out of tune than the other, then they would hardly be likely to notice Olivia's absence. And, if that appalling intonation *had* caused aural discomfort, as it bloody well should have, then they must only be thankful that a fourth dischord was not added to that unholy trinity.

Now the choir joined the fray. *Christe eleison!* The sopranos opened up their attack on Olivia. *They* hadn't forgotten to sing, *they* weren't going to let the maestro down. With voices oscillating in wide vibrato, just to prove they could do it, and a couple standing out loudly from the rest, just to prove that they were the best - which they certainly weren't - they sang bravely on. They'd gone this far without her, so clearly she was not indispensable, thought the disembodied Olivia, virtually on her mental way out of the church as the slow intro dragged to its conclusion.

And then she saw them all hiding there in a neat little row at the back, hoping not to make her nervous. Her sister Katriona, with husband and four children, all in Sunday best, hassocks placed beneath their bottoms so that they would be able to see; four little pairs of eager eyes all waiting for Auntie Olivia to sing like the angel that taught the birds to sing - their grandfather never tires of telling them that she can.

Now what? Her disembodied self turned from them to see the enraged Julia, by now an unflattering shade of purple, muttering something out of the side of her mouth. Silly woman, didn't she know that Olivia was back here, almost out the door already? And what had Julia been thinking when she'd bought that gown? If she could see herself. On the other hand, thought Olivia, I look pretty hopeless too; completely vacant, just waiting to be assassinated by the chorus. On cue, there they went again, those odious sopranos sending forth shrill high notes into Olivia's back, jaws gyrating with their efforts to achieve yet more volume and wider vibrato, eyes looking lovingly to Terrence, uncharitable minds locked on the unfortunate soloist.

Kyrie.

Julia almost jumped clear of her volcanic dress as Olivia decided that the kids could not leave disappointed and came in bang on time. *Kyrie*, echoed Julia, surprised that she had not lost her own voice in shock, and then she and Olivia joined forces, singing an unaccompanied, fast rising scale in perfect harmony. It was triumphant and nothing short of a miracle, as was proven by the

11

second time the phrase came around and Julia's intonation reverted to its usual unpredictable self. Olivia was bitterly disappointed; momentarily she had been able to believe that she had been returned to a body in a different church, where a brilliant performance, memorable for something other than the conductor's plush dinner jacket, was taking place. The rest of the evening stretched out ahead of her like a path of white hot coals. She wished she had got out while she could.

The *Sancta Maria* did not begin well. Still reeling from the *Kyrie*, Olivia couldn't settle and knew that her voice would not be carrying, even though her fellow soloists and the chorus were silent for several pages worth of music. Then, coming up against a phrase wherein she was supposed to run twenty-one notes smoothly into a single elegant breath, she found herself running out of puff. She sensed Julia's mouth twitch into a minuscule smile at her appalling lapse of control. Thank God her teacher, Dame Cecilia Jones, wasn't here to witness such an embarrassment to her reputation; she'd probably waltz tut-tutting up the aisle (her heel would never get stuck), a cloud of French perfume settling in her wake along with a gregarious hat and billowing pashmina, wrest the baton from Terrence and put a timely end to this shambles. The ensuing masterclass would be better than any concert on offer in London that night, and the audience would have got their money's worth.

But that was a dream and in reality, Julia and Brendan were going for it, and missing in a big way.

After that, so astonished was the orchestra that they lost it too; the violins parted company with the cellos and they refused to make up until the violas chose a side. Unfortunately, they chose incorrectly and disaster was only narrowly averted by Terrence suddenly yelping a bar number at them - unaccountably he had actually guessed right. The audience politely didn't bat an eyelid between them, though only because the majority had deficient hearing, surmised Olivia - well, they must have.

Salus infirmorum. Safe haven for the weak. Hardly. Brendan and Barry made sure of that, the passage they had to themselves being more a battle of wills than the sonorous duet it should have been. However, they did rouse the most senior of all the citizens in the church from his pleasant dreams in the second row. Olivia could only think that what was to come would finish him off.

'Jesus wept,' murmured Julia as Brendan took off in the *Regina Angelorum* without, it soon became apparent, taking adequate notice of the safety card. By rights he should have gone with oxygen and a parachute at close hand, so long and high were the phrases, but Brendan thought of himself as the Errol Flynn of tenors; a flying ace, a swashbuckler, a Gentleman Jim and unfortunately his was none of the above nor, in fact, anything even close to what might be called a tenor. He reached for the sky and tumbled like Icarus. All that could be said in the end, was that everyone should be thankful that his suffering was over, and that it had been a mercy that he had never known what was happening to him. And he hadn't. Just as he deluded himself into thinking he was heterosexual, he couldn't grasp the fact that his voice was dire. Insanity could be the only explanation for his obvious conviction that he sounded bloody marvellous. Only the likes of Terrence, who held out hopes that he would one day recognise the fact that he was in the closet, kept Brendan working.

Olivia wondered if she were suffering the same affliction. Dame Cecilia had claimed her as her protégé and been proud to send her to her own agent, yet now Olivia couldn't bring herself to call up for a lesson, for fear that the diva would turn her away in disgust.

As her eyes drifted back up to the stained glass window, she prayed silently to be delivered from the purgatory that her life had become. And then she grew aware that Terrence was awaiting some sign from her that she was ready for the *Agnus Dei*. How appropriate it was that she should have to sing these sacred words, she thought. Then, filled with a desire to communicate to anyone who might be listening just how desperately she wanted those words to be heard, she stood slowly and smiled first at Terrence and then to the lead violinist.

French horns and oboes combined to bring a sensuous richness to the opening melody that was exquisitely echoed in Olivia's voice as she began her public prayer. *Agnus Dei, qui tolis peccata mundi* - Lamb of God who bears the sins of the world. In stark contrast with what had gone before, there were no skids up to the top notes, no desperate gasps for air, no wavering of certainty to mar the clarity of intonation that Mozart commanded. Just pure and simple mastery of her craft.

Agnus Dei, qui tolis peccata mundi. No hair in the church was not raised by the perfect phrasing that Olivia found for those words as she sailed from low notes to high, descended the weaving path of music and then, without taking a breath, rose effortlessly again, her voice arching like a rainbow. Everyone was held in suspended animation, unable to inhale unless Olivia did, as she repeatedly conquered the melody's heights and depths with a grace that brought attention solely to the beauty at its heart.

Parce nobis Domine - Spare us Lord. Terrence nearly dropped his baton as his chorus, moved by the majestic honesty of Olivia's interpretation, bowed to her sovereignty and paid homage by continuing her line with hitherto undiscovered restraint and sensitivity. No longer forced, mellowness permeated the sound and each note became true to itself. Tears welled up in Terrence's eyes, he knowing that something wonderful was happening, and that he had nothing whatsoever to do with it.

Exaudi nos Domine - Hear us Lord, pleaded Olivia over and over, her eyes closing out her surroundings, her music falling into Julia's lap as her hands came up to clasp one another for strength.

Amdist the transfixed audience, Katriona reached out for Patrick and held on to him, knuckles white as Olivia climbed the final peak and began her concluding trill, dominating the alternating notes, beginning very slowly and then increasing the tempo so that her voice blossomed into something glorious and ethereal which reverberated around the church as the chorus took over with the final words of the Agnus Dei. *Misere nobis* - Have pity on us.

For a while there were only the harmonics left over from the closing cadence to be heard circling in the rafters, and then there was a magical, awed silence.

* * *

When Olivia saw the clock tower in Crouch End she breathed a sigh of relief, although it still took some time to get home because the trendy restaurants were emptying out and stylish, contentedly full and drunk revellers were crossing the high street without a care for oncoming traffic. Olivia envied them their Friday night out - as a performer she was always someone else's night out and even if she had a night off, she had no-one to go out with.

And no-one to go home to. There was no welcoming light beckoning from her tiny flat on the top floor of a formerly grand Edwardian house.

'Hello you two,' she said to the cats that came rushing to her side as soon as she stepped over the threshold. They followed her to the kitchen, ever hopeful, and then sat mewing pitifully by their empty dish.

'I suppose I'm meant to feel sorry for you, am I? At least you ate twice today,' she muttered, draping her long dress over the back of a chair.

She went into the living room. As per usual her heart sank at the sight. Under the orange shag-pile carpet there was probably a lovely wooden floor, behind the wall-mounted gas fire and pine tongue and groove, there might be an original fireplace and, above the white polystyrene tiles, possibly an ornate ceiling rose and some cornicing, but she had barely enough money to pay the mortgage, let alone decorate. She pressed the play button on her answer phone and thumbed her way through the junk mail she had scooped up on the way in.

'Hello Miss Tarrent, I'm afraid *Amanda* won't be able to make it to her lesson tomorrow. I know that *technically* this is rather short *notice*, and that we *really* should pay you, but I *can't* believe you won't make an exception for *Amanda*. See you next Saturday.'

'Hi, it's Dominic. Do you know when Calli's getting back? She asked me to feed that bastard cat of hers and I can't find him anywhere. Hasn't touched his food in four days. Do you think he's all right? Should I be leaving the country now, or do you think plastic surgery will be enough to throw her off my trail? Call me. *Please!'*

'Can't come to my lesson Saturday, got Beyonce tickets... what? WHAT? Oh, mum says to tell you this is Joe.'

'Olivia darling, it's Laura. Just wanted to remind you that they'll be expecting you at Il Dolce Momente tomorrow night as usual. And I've got a simply marvellous gig lined up for you with the North London

Singers, week after next, at that church in Muswell Hill. It's a *fantastic* choir. The concert will be *fabulous* exposure for you. Talk to you Monday.'

'Olivia, I wish you'd tell me when you're coming down our way. Saw your concert advertised in the local newspaper, so I'm bringing the kids and Patrick, if his train gets out of Waterloo on time... but you'll know that by now! Hope you've forgiven me, love you, bye.'

'Come to the phone, Olivia. I know you're there - screening that bitch Laura's calls, I hope. Pick up! It's me, Calli... Olivia, how dare you be out! If you're doing another of those crappy concerts, you'll suffer when I get back. Piss off! Not you Olivia; some idiot romeo just pinched my arse. God, I love Italy. Can't wait to tell you all about it. Miss you. How about lunch Tuesday, after I get in? One o'clock, Harvey Nicks. See you then.'

Great, two cancellations and a lunch date at Harvey Nicks, just one of life's little jokes. Still, hearing Calli's voice raised Olivia's spirits greatly. It wasn't much fun when her best friend was off on tour. No one to leer at waiters with - actually, no reason to even go to a place where there might be a lust-worthy waiter - and no one to berate her for accepting those ghastly gigs Laura kept offering. But Calli *was* outrageous; why Dominic should think that he was supposed to be feeding Scarpia, Olivia didn't know - perhaps Calli was extracting her revenge for one of Dominic's practical jokes - but Scarpia was alive and well, here in Crouch End. Of course he'd been here for three weeks now, which rather begged the question, just who or what was eating his food up until the last few days? She put her hand on the telephone to call Dominic and then thought better of it. It would be more fun to let him go through the hell of telling Calli that he'd killed her cat - well, Olivia couldn't help suspect that Dominic hadn't really made an attempt to feed Scarpia until four days ago.

Instead she flipped on the TV. *Die Hard* was on again. That'd do. She turned up the volume so she could hear the rapid-fire weapons from the kitchen, and went in search of a snack.

'You... you...' Olivia was lost for words as she was met by the sight of a very satisfied Scarpia arching, with his talons sunk into her concert dress. She could hear the fabric ripping as he flaunted his ultimate control of the situation, a frisson of pleasure vibrating the length of his body as he enjoyed one more stretch for good measure. Then he dashed out the cat flap and down the fire escape before Olivia could rouse herself.

'Thanks a bundle Tosca, you're a big help,' she snapped at her own cat, as if she could understand - her contrite expression as she sat on the kitchen table did indicate that she might. Olivia didn't even bother to examine the dress, she knew it was ruined and could only push it with disgust onto the floor, sit down and rest her head on the table.

'God, didn't you hear a thing tonight? Don't you ever listen to me?' she murmured.

Eventually, Tosca plucked up the courage to come over and nuzzle against her ear. Olivia took a deep breath, wiped away her tears, sat up with as deep a sigh, and went to the fridge. Quite deliberately there was not much to choose from. She looked at the clock. Twenty to one. The convenience store down the road would still be open. No lite this or that tonight. Hot chocolate with a shot of brandy and loads of whipped cream on top, garlic bread, pizza, crisps, a variety pack of Mr. Kipling's cakes, a box of chocolates; she didn't really know what she was going to buy, she'd see what took her fancy when she got there, but it was going to be comfort food. Sod the dress, it was too tight for her anyway. Sod what they'd have to say at Weight Watchers next week. Sod the fact that she had no career. Sod life.

Did He hear that?

chapter two

ACT ONE

Whenever Calliope Syrigos walked into a room you knew it without having to turn your head – not thanks to that mystical aura that seems to radiate from the great and famous, but rather because she enjoyed an entrance off stage as much as she did on stage, and never failed to make one to remember.

Even as Olivia continued to thumb through the contract that the Opera House had asked her to sign, she knew from the very sound the door made as it closed, that Calli had arrived and that she would now be struggling valiantly to close her huge Hermes umbrella, shaking it noisily to get the faint sheen of London drizzle off it as if she'd actually been caught in a monsoon. And there was little doubt that her passage to Olivia's table at the back of the restaurant would be a treacherous one. Clad in something red and bodycon, her svelte frame, balanced precariously in a fabulous pair of Louboutins, would have to arch to its best advantage as she wove her way between tables. Tables that suddenly appeared far closer to one another than they did when the waiters paraded easily amongst them, though burdened with far more than an umbrella and an alligator-skin handbag.

But, closer they suddenly were. And so, no wonder that Calliope would have to stop and apologise to some poor man for nudging his drink into his lap, no wonder that her hand would come to rest on his shoulder and he would find himself looking down her fine cleavage and protesting happily against her offer of a replacement, no wonder his girlfriend looked hopelessly unglamorous and sadly deflated at this moment. And, of course, no wonder that by the time she had reached Olivia, everyone in the restaurant would know that Calliope Syrigos - the Lady Gaga of opera - was in their midst.

When Calli sank into her chair, she appeared to be as drained as if she had hacked a path through the Amazon jungle, but a nano-second later, hearing the tell-tale sound of footsteps on her trail, she revived to her most radiant, effervescent self. Olivia smiled wryly, grabbed a passing waiter, ordered a martini for her friend and then continued to peruse the deliberately confusing document until just about every patron had swiped the flowers from their table and exchanged them for the diva's signature on their napkin.

'Good God, when's a girl supposed to relax?' sighed a breathless Calliope, bending across the table to kiss Olivia her customary three times.

'You love it really.'

'You know me so well,' laughed Calli, rubbing with her thumb at the lipstick marks she had left on Olivia's cheek. 'Darling, you look wonderful.'

'Not as fantastic as you do - Italy and *Carmen* obviously agreed with you.'

'You think so?' replied Calli, long-red-nail-bedecked fingers playing with the black curls that cascaded to her shoulders, before choosing a rose from the pile before her and planting it in their midst.

'Oh come on Calli, you know you look great. I can tell you've had more than your fair share of sun, Chianti and handsome men.'

'When in Rome!' offered Calliope with a wickedly suggestive smile, less for Olivia's benefit than for the waiter's as he placed a martini before her.

Olivia laughed as he snatched his hand away and fled into the kitchen.

'What are you laughing at?'

'I've just missed having you around terrifying all the waiters.'

'*Moi?* Scare waiters? Do you really think I frightened him? Oh dear, I suppose I should apologise. Oh waiter. Oh waiter!' she called with delighted evil intent, 'I need to talk to you.'

'Calliope Syrigos, don't you dare,' hissed Olivia as, with urging from the *maitre d'*, the poor man found himself forced to return. Calli ignored her, naturally, and pulled the waiter close by his tie so that she could whisper in his ear.

Olivia watched with discomfort as his face grew flushed under his tan. Then he was let free and disappeared even more speedily - if that was at all possible - than before.

'It's OK Olivia, you can calm down. All I did was order us a little *antipasti*.'

'Right. And the rest!' laughed Olivia, feeling happy to have her partner in crime back.

'So how was Italy?'

'Oh all right I suppose, if you don't mind spitting out a mouthful of mosquitoes after every aria. Singing at midnight in some ancient ruin of an amphitheatre, filled with real opera-loving Italians, sounded so bloody romantic when Graham sold the tour to me.'

'But?'

'But the schedule made no sense. We went up and down the country like we were trying to lace that damn boot up, and then there were the insects, thunderstorms, no toilets, enough encores to tie my vocal chords in knots and a tenor who jumped into the mould for Pavarotti's body before they broke it, but didn't get there in time to nab the voice as well.

'And the *orchestra!* I don't know where they got her from - probably screwing the conductor - but there was this harpist who couldn't even tune the bloody instrument. Every night she'd find an opportunity to balls up the performance. One night she came in early on a big *glissando*, then when the conductor cued her entry in the right place she just sat there and refused to play. So he pointed his baton at her again, and she sat there, and he shook the baton at her, and she sat there. The stubborn, macho idiot just wouldn't go on without her. And she, of course, thought *I've played it and I'm buggered if I'm going to do it again.* Anyway, you're not going to believe this, but they ended up having a huge great argument.'

'Out loud screaming and shouting?' asked Olivia incredulously.

'I mean he actually got off his podium and went over to have it out with her, so to speak, and in *my* bloody aria too! The strings could hardly get their bows near their instruments for giggling. Then there was the night my wonderful tenor nearly broke his bloody neck. You know when Don Jose comes to arrest Carmen at the factory? Well, he gets to the door and finds it won't open - I'm sure it was some bastard stagehand arsing around. Anyway, after a couple of pushes, he throws his entire substantial weight behind it, comes flying through and can't stop. I swear he somersaulted ten times down the staircase and would have kept on going into the pit if he hadn't landed on one of the extras. Of course everyone corpsed; chorus, orchestra, conductor, even me. The only one who wasn't laughing was the extra.'

'So, no good crits for the scrapbook?'

'Hardly!'

'Well at least you got the tan.'

'Oh, and this,' said Calliope placing a small box on the table. 'For you,' she said with a cheerful eagerness that came from knowing that she'd got the perfect gift for her friend.

'It's beautiful,' came the expected reply, as the cameo brooch was revealed.

'I found it in Florence. On some bridge with lots of jewellery shops.'

'The *Ponte Vecchio*.'

'I don't know, maybe. Isn't it amazing? The only problem was that by the time I got there we'd already done Milan and Rome, so I was virtually cleaned out. The credit card bills will probably bankrupt me!'

'Well, it's gorgeous.'

'And so's this waiter,' mused Calliope as the food arrived and wine was poured - and spilled - by a nervous hand. 'Really, I don't know why I bothered going to Italy when we've got all the best ones here.'

Olivia wasn't sure but, from the way he jumped, she thought Calli had pinched the waiter's arse as he left. Calli was apparently innocent, busily tearing the wrapping off a box of cigarettes. On second thoughts, Olivia *was* sure - with Calli one only had to watch your back, or your husband for that matter, when she appeared to be otherwise engrossed.

'I thought you'd kicked those. You know, just because Carmen works in a cigarette factory...'

'Oh, give me a break, Liv. It's not so long since you scandalised all the proper little madams in the Academy bar yourself. If you'd been on that tour, you'd be joining me, believe me.'

There was no denying it was their joint responsibility that the bar at the Royal Academy of Music had been constantly out of gin, and that fog lights were needed by any student wanting to traverse the room safely. But that was then. It was one thing to be an instrumentalist; most of their studying was already done by the time they got to the Academy, but singers didn't mature till nearing thirty.

So, for Olivia and Calliope, it had been three years in the Academy bar, a couple in the College Bar and a few more sampling the delights of various Irish-American bars, discovering that Guinness tastes different when poured in Boston versus New York – the usefulness of that piece of knowledge only became truly apparent once they had actually got their careers under way and realised that in order not to be hung, drawn and quartered on stage, you had to get along with those best of friends and worst of enemies, the stage crew and musicians, off stage. How many Queens of the Night had been lost to that top 'E' thanks to an impossible tempo? And how many Toscas had jumped off the battlements only to find a trampoline awaiting them and hear an audience's tears replaced with laughter as they rebounded over and over?

It was not a fate any singer wished to suffer, but how Calli managed to keep up the pace, Olivia just didn't know. She herself had had to miss only one golden opportunity thanks to a hacking cough to know that she couldn't. But, Calliope Syrigos was a rule unto herself. Beautiful, slim and with a voice like an angel, no matter how she had abused herself in her thirty-something years. Invulnerable. Why should she change? Olivia gave her a *fine, do what you want look* and left it at that.

'So what's next?'

'Well, if Graham's got anything to do with it, ruining my bloody career,' responded Calli, knocking back her drink in one. 'You won't believe what that little shit's got me lined up with now - a season with E.N. bloody O.! Some agent he's turned out to be.'

Olivia could see the problem immediately. English National Opera sang in English and generally employed British singers. Calliope, better known to Olivia, the one friend who would still recognise her from B.C. (Before Calliope) as Caroline Smith, wanted to be anything but boring old English. Perhaps not the Lady Gaga of the opera world after all, but the Eliza Doolittle. A fraud. Maybe from Palmers Green, known to north Londoners as Palmers Greek, but certainly not of that sensuous stock, nor from the conveniently unnamed Mediterranean isle she had so often alluded to when interviewed. In any case, Caroline Smith was not a name to be seen next to sultry photos and such adjectives as 'exotic', 'temptress' and 'enigmatic' on the cover of *Opera Monthly* and *Classic FM Magazine*. Caroline Smith had done everything in her power to wipe out herself and become Calliope Syrigos, a woman with an intriguingly mysterious past, not a human history complete with trauma and disappointment.

'I suppose there's no way out?'

'If only! But you haven't heard the best of it yet,' said Calliope, thinking that at least her friend would get a good laugh out of this disaster and thoroughly relishing the opportunity to revel in her misery. She paused for effect, an iniquitous smile playing on her lips. Now the bombshell. 'They're resurrecting *Dialogues des Carmélites!*'

There was time to order a bottle of wine and drink the better part of it before Olivia had regained some control. Calliope handed her a mirror so that she could fix the tragedy that was now her makeup.

'Yes darling, Calliope *thrown-out-of-Catholic-girl's-school-in-disgrace* Syrigos is going to play a bloody nun! I mean what the hell is Graham thinking?'

'Christ knows!' laughed Olivia.

'I'm sure he does.'

'Sister Marianne will be turning in her grave - this is too perfect.'

'Well, I'm glad you think it's funny,' said Calliope with feigned hurt. 'But what about my reputation?'

'And more importantly, what about your beautiful nails?'

Calli groaned. Unusually, she hadn't even thought of that.

'Don't worry darling, it won't hurt a bit,' smiled Olivia, placing a soothing hand on Calli's.

'I'm going to have to kill Graham. Slowly. The death of a thousand cuts. I'll wear red nail-varnish so his secretary won't notice the blood dripping off my fingers as I leave.'

'What a lovely thought.'

'Yes, and it'll be good practice for *Salome* too.'

'Huh, just when I was beginning to feel sorry for you, you drop that one in. You've landed *Salome* too?'

The responding smile was answer enough. The cat had not only got the cream off the top of the milk, but had managed to get away with the pint of double cream hidden at the back of the fridge too. Everyone had been waiting for that juicy role to come around again and ENO's production was phenomenal. Olivia should have known that Calli would get it - if anyone had the voice for it, and the body for the dance of the seven veils, it was her.

'That explains why Graham got you into that other mess. All or nothing, I suppose? Well, at least now I don't have to feel so awkward about my news. Take a look at this.'

Calliope's smile never faltered as she read the contract that Olivia had passed to her with excited hands but, try as she might to hide it, try as she might to force her friendship-inspired feelings of joy to triumph, her voice was still tainted with bitter envy when she finally forced herself to speak.

'This is *amazing*. I'm so happy for you. Haven't I always told you it'd all come right in the end? But how?'

'It's ridiculous, completely ridiculous! If I saw it in a film I'd laugh. I was on my usual Saturday night gig at Il Dolce Momente, warbling away for the post-performance, champagne-guzzling set from the House, when in walks Angelo Verasano. Angelo Verasano! Can you believe it? It was all I could do to keep singing. Just one look at him took my breath away - he's even more gorgeous in the flesh than I imagined,' sighed Olivia and then proceeded to extol his virtues with quite sickening breathlessness.

For once Calli did not want to have their usual leeringly appreciative conversation about said tenor. The *dérigeur* contemplation on whether his dick was as big as his incredible voice and whether the rumour that he had bedded the entire chorus for *Aida* last season was true or not, seemed wholly unappealing right now. But if Calli listened a little too quietly, uncharacteristically Olivia didn't seem to notice, which was annoying in itself. All Calli really wanted to do was tell Olivia to bloody well cut out the swooning and get on with explaining how in hell this had happened to her, a singer who'd stupidly blown her only ever chance at success and been doing time ever since, singing in front of endless amateur choirs as they squawked their way through *The Creation*, *The Messiah* and *B minor Mass* after B minor bloody Mass. Just how had Olivia Tarrent bagged a contract to sing

Tosca opposite Angelo Verasano at the Royal Opera House, Covent Garden? Calliope had a good idea, if that heaving bosom across the table was anything to go by.

'So?' she interjected.

'I know, I know, get to the point. Well, of course I couldn't actually stop singing, even though I wanted to. Got to pay the mortgage. So I sang. You know, all the obvious stuff that the punters will recognise so they'll feel knowledgeable. After a while I even forgot he was there and then suddenly, I'm singing an aria from *La Bohème* and out of the crowd comes a voice.'

'Angelo singing Rodolfo to your Mimi?' offered Calliope, reluctantly acknowledging to herself the tremble of excitement that travelled down her spine at the image of that scene. How electric must the atmosphere have been. She could just hear the silence fall on the restaurant as the most ludicrously improbable miracle had actually happened.

Olivia went silent for a moment, eyes bright as she stared into her drink, clearly enjoying the memory, irritatingly insensible to her friend's mood.

'Well, as I said, it's just ridiculous and laughable. And this contract, even more so.'

Calli felt sick.

'Oh, really Liv, how can you say such a thing, after all you've been through? No, it was meant to be. No-one deserves success more than you do, darling.'

'You've no idea how much it means to me to hear you say that Calli. You've always stood by me, but there aren't many friends who could rise above rivalry and be pleased in a situation like this.'

'Oh, I have to admit that I'm just the teensiest bit jealous that you got to spend a night in with Angelo Verasano. Was he as good as they say?'

'Spend a night with Angelo Verasano? If only! When we were done singing, he just kissed my hand and went right on back to his friends. And, of course, afterwards everyone was so busy talking about it that I swear they didn't hear another note I sang. I felt so disappointed. *Used* really. I went home thinking he was an egocentric arsehole; not content with getting all the attention at the Opera House, he had to come and steal my show too.'

'Well, he *is* a tenor darling; it's to be expected.'

'True. But then this morning I was weighing out my *Special K* - don't even ask about the diet - when the phone rang and I found myself talking to the Director of the House.'

Calli felt sicker.

'Sir David Langley called you himself?'

'I know, I couldn't believe it either. Anyway, he says in this pompous as hell voice, 'Madam, our soprano for *Tosca* has somewhat inconveniently pulled out and Angelo Verasano, strange fellow that he is, has insisted that you be her replacement. Of course you've taken some finding - dear chap had a few too many glasses of champagne and couldn't remember the name of the restaurant where he discovered 'his' Floria Tosca - so the notice is short. *Sitzprobe* is ten, Friday. Will send a bike over with the contract. Incidentally my dear, you *can* sing can't you?' To which I said a far from convincing 'yes' and he hung up. This contract showed up a few hours later.'

Why couldn't Olivia just make it easy, like all the other 'friends' who'd got the lucky breaks over the years? Why couldn't she have lured Angelo home for a night of sex like any other self-respecting diva would have done? Why couldn't Calli feel good about the bile that was mingling so enthusiastically with the booze in her grinding stomach? Good friends were to be relied upon always, and this whole 'situation' as Olivia had called it, was not following the accepted rules of their friendship.

'*Sitzprobe* on Friday. This week? No mention of coaching or a rehearsal with the music director? It's outrageous. And he just assumed that you'd be willing to do this? Just assumed that you'd have nothing else worthwhile to do? Bloody cheek!' said Calliope indignantly as she turned the pages once more, looking for some sign that this was just another one of Dominic's elaborate practical jokes.

'Why? Is there something wrong with the contract?'

'No there's nothing wrong, that I can see. I just think Angelo Verasano and old Sir David are presumptuous gits. Who do they think they are, expecting you to show up just like that?'

'But I haven't got anything else to do, have I? To be honest, even if you told me that the contract says I have to sell my soul, I'd sign it if it means singing with Angelo again.'

'Well, I've already advised you to do that once before and it certainly didn't bring you success, or happiness. Maybe you should get someone else to look it over before you make a mistake.'

Olivia's entire countenance seemed suddenly to turn inside out. The glow of anticipation immediately dulled satisfactorily, the balance rectified.

'I'm sorry, Liv. I shouldn't have made you think of that. Not at a wonderful time like this. God, I'm an insensitive bitch.'

'Don't say that. It's OK. I'm fine, see?' said Olivia, forcing a smile, even as she struggled to suppress the cold shudder which visibly thrust up through her.

'No you're not,' insisted Calli, placing a concerned hand on her dear, dear friend's shoulder and feeling that reassuring shivering she knew so well. 'So what if it's six years? You can be honest with me. I understand what you went through, what it took to make that decision. Knowing that I was right doesn't help when I see how it's hurt you. But, I *was* right. And now you've got this opportunity to prove it.'

'Looks like I sold my soul for this already then, doesn't it?'

'That's not what I meant,' Calli reprimanded as she dutifully offered her handkerchief to Olivia.

If there were no tears before, the sight of that inviting white cotton was enough to provoke them.

'Really, Olivia, you mustn't torture yourself like this. Don't turn what should be a wonderful celebration into a mire of self-recrimination.'

'You're right, you're right,' sniffed Olivia. 'What would I do without you?'

'Oh I'm sure you'd do just fine,' said Calli, blissfully unaware of just how true that was.

'No, no. I'd always be making myself feel bad about the past instead of getting on with the present. Thank God I've got you to pull me together.'

'Well that's what real friends are for. You can always count on me to be there when you're in trouble.'

Olivia looked buoyed up by her words and Calli felt good that, even when her friend had made the singing coup of the century, she was still capable of rising above petty jealousy and being there for Olivia when the past unaccountably reared its nasty head.

'I know what'll really cheer you up. Let's order some of that fantastic chocolate mousse they serve here,' she suggested, nausea quelled and enthusiasm for the meal renewed.

Olivia danced with uncertainty.

'Oh come on Liv, anyone'd think you're the size of an elephant the way you carry on!'

'Oh all right,' laughed Olivia, even though she felt more than a few portions of mousse away from being the new style, slender soprano that Calliope Syrigos was.

'And while we're at it, we should have some champagne to celebrate,' decided Calliope without the slightest thought to calories or cash. Then, after narrowing her green eyes, clearly considering something of extreme importance, she purred, 'Definitely by the glass, so we get to call back that delicious waiter, over and over, and over until we're satisfied...'

- chapter three -

'Bloody hell, he's got me again. Darling, you should have this wretched cat put down,' cried Dominic, desperately attempting to stem the flow of blood that the monster itself had just drawn with a vindictive swipe, before sauntering off to find its mistress in the kitchen.

Dominic knew it was more than his life was worth to allow a drop of blood to fall in Calli's heavenly, white drawing room, so he followed the nasty creature.

'Got any plasters?' he asked without hope of an affirmative reply. If you didn't cook, you didn't use a knife, you didn't need plasters - Calliope could never understand why everyone else didn't see the obvious, didn't make the only viable choice economically and save money by eating out. Not that a passing chef would have found the kitchen bereft of even the most obscure gadget. From sieves so fine water could not pass through unhindered and forks for fishing out the meat from lobster claws, through Sabatier knives, copper mousse moulds, fish-descalers and saucepans of all sizes and metals, to an eagle-crowned espresso machine, it was all there in a kitchen whose pristine maple and stainless steel had so often been pictured in fashionable decorating magazines. However, if the present losing battle she was fighting with the coffee machine was anything to judge by, it was just as well Calli ate out.

As red nails went flying and Dominic bled, the Siamese cat slithered in a figure of eight about Calliope's legs, eyeing him with insulting nonchalance.

'Sorry, what was that? Plasters?' responded the defeated diva finally. She spoke the word as if she didn't know what they were.

Dominic had long before resigned himself to bandaging his hand with the taupe silk handkerchief which had, until that moment, been the ultimate finishing touch to his Armani linen suit - his not by virtue of the income to support such a purchase but merely thanks to the fact that he had been wearing it when its owner had thrown him out in the midst of a jealous tantrum. Though the jealousy had not been entirely unjustified, Dominic could not bring himself to do the expected crawl back; the suit was, in the end, a better catch than the lover.

'Yes, plasters... for the cut... on my hand,' he said, waving his hand about petulantly in front of her.

'You can buy some while we're out.'

'Out? Won't Olivia be here soon?'

'We'll leave her a note.'

'And where exactly are we going?'

'For coffee, of course.'

'Oh for heaven's sake darling, I'll make the coffee and you search the bathroom cabinet for plasters. Every time I come here that tyrant attacks me; I must have left a hundred boxes of the things around.'

'Scarpia's not a tyrant.'

'So why did you name him after one?'

Calliope was gone on her futile quest but, as if in response to his question, the cat circled Dominic in her absence with an obvious view to intimidation, giving him a sense that Scarpia must have been to a performance of *Tosca* and studied his evil namesake well.

'Leave me alone or I'll snip off that tail of yours,' said Dominic bravely once he was armed with a pair of scissors that lodged with the coffee in a steel canister. But, though they were apparently specifically intended for opening vacuum-packs, he could neither complete the task at hand nor keep a firm hold of them, so insistent had the cat's hissing and growling become at his threat. Just at the crucial moment, his taunter leapt onto the work surface and skidded along its shiny length towards Dominic with claw festooned paws flailing.

'See, it's not just me!' laughed Calliope as Dominic catapulted the coffee all over the slate floor in his effort to evade certain death. 'Why don't you leave that and we'll have some champagne instead.'

'Suits me,' he smiled as he happily stepped over the mess he had created and swanned back to whence he'd come. He loved Calliope's living room. It was a room to be seen in, a backdrop against which not only Calli but also her guests, who were often as gregarious and gorgeous as herself, could relax in the knowledge that they and not the room were the star. Only the Steinway grand in the bay was allowed its own personality. Not *nouveau riche* white but beautifully, boldly black. For all Calliope's faults - and in Dominic's opinion they were both plentiful and endearing, as were his own - she could not be accused of having bad taste. But neither could she be accused of being able to play a note on that instrument, or any other. Before fame had arrived, there seemed to be little that gave her more pleasure than telling people that she had gone to the Royal Academy of Music and upon receiving the expected, impressed, 'Oh, you're a musician', replying, 'Heavens no, I'm a singer!'

'It has to go.'

Caught indulging in a little self-appreciation, Dominic jumped as Calliope suddenly appeared next to him in the mirror over the fireplace and passed sentence on the goatee that he had been sporting for some weeks, along with his slightly over-long waves of chestnut-brown hair all swept blithely to one side and a quirky, thin moustache.

Her judgement was not to be argued with, at least not while he shared the same mirror with her. Five foot eight, with at least another six or seven inches to add for heels, hair and personality. She made Dominic feel like a latter-day Toulouse Lautrec - not in fact on the imposing side of six foot, but a fake, likely to fall off a box if he took a step in any direction. As it happened, he had just been thinking the same anyway. His foppish, Oscar Wilde phase was surely on the wane; his latest conquest, a rather esoteric, depressed and depressing young architect who came from Berlin, had inspired him to reach Isherwood off the bookcase and contemplate the merits of hair smoothed back, Liza Minnelli-like. Life is a cabaret, and all that.

'You're right, as per usual my dear; I do look a little *passé.*'

Calliope's wide mouth smiled. 'We'll go down to Charlie's later and get him to make you over,' she said, giving the tiny beard a playful tug and winking one Cleopatra's eye at him. Then she sighed, 'If only you were straight, darling,' and blew his reflection a kiss before turning her attention to the bottle of champagne.

Dominic stood watching for a moment, admiring her latest incarnation; charm bracelets joyfully tinkling against the bottle as she attempted to untwist the wire, hoop earrings caressing bare shoulders, full black skirt somehow serving to emphasise rather than obscure the long lines of the legs beneath. Indeed, if only he were straight, he thought regretfully.

'If I were straight we'd fight like dogs - too much alike, you and me.'

'As it is we fight like cats!' laughed Calli and thrust the cantankerous bottle into his expectant hand.

'I wonder what's keeping Olivia.'

'London Transport, I should think,' said Calli as she and Dominic sank, perfectly synchronised, into facing, feather-filled sofas. The ice-cold bottle smoked next to a plate of McVitie's dark chocolate Digestives on the glass coffee table between them. 'I wish she'd just give up on the suburbs and move to the river. Really, what is she thinking of living out there?'

Dominic eyed the plate, secretly amused. Even the most platinum of fake blondes couldn't hide their roots all the time. Of course, only Olivia knew the truth about their friend and she wasn't talking, which irritated him greatly, but it was fun to theorise when the clues presented themselves. Away from the press and operatic rivals, Calli's phoney Greek accent gave way readily to one that belonged right here in Chelsea, so one couldn't help wonder if that were a fiction also. And McVitie's biscuits - how middle class!

'Money I should think. Besides, if you'd ever actually been there you'd know it's not exactly Timbuktu we're talking about. Crouch End's bloody expensive and totally on trend - restaurants, cafes, theatres, cinema, music... *bohemians* even.'

'And it isn't here? She spends most of her time here anyway.'

'That's only because you flatly refuse to go North and 'most of her time' is very little when you consider how often you're out of the country.'

'I'll thank you not to start trying to stir me up. You just love to paint me as the selfish bitch don't you? But seriously darling, I can't see what's wrong with wanting to have her nearer. We've always been together and nothing you say can change the fact that Olivia's my closest friend and I love her.'

'If only you were gay!' drawled Dominic.

'I might have known that's all you'd have to say on the subject. The nearest you, or any other man for that matter, gets to understanding the bond we have, is to be jealous of it. Men never do have a clue about real friendship. Hardly surprising when you think how unreliable you all are.'

'Well I'm not the one who's late, am I? Perhaps she's chickened out. Maybe there's no need for her to go through a practice run with us after all.'

'I wouldn't blame her. The orchestra's notoriously hostile and the conductor's a real sod too.'

'Who he?'

'Alexander Petrov.'

Dominic tossed his head back, ran a hand through his hair, narrowed his eyes and pursed his lips seductively before snickering, 'You mean Alexander *Call me Sasha* Petrov,' with as slimy a Russian accent as he could manage.

'Poor Olivia doesn't stand a chance this afternoon. It's been years since she's done anything but sing in half empty churches with naff choirs who think the sun shines out of their duff conductors' arses. The worst thing she's had to face has been the obligatory tea in the church hall before the performance.'

'You mean, darling, you don't think that withstanding an onslaught of fairy-cake-bearing old biddies is preparation enough for a *sitzprobe* at Covent Garden? And really, with some of the crits they've been getting recently, you could be forgiven for thinking that Olivia's going to feel right at home.'

'That may be the case, but she's got to show up to find out. You know Olivia - she's been a complete wreck all week; my phone's white hot from all the hours I've spent trying to calm her down and convince her that she's up to the challenge.'

'And is she? She's not exactly the queen of self-confidence. Not at all suited to being a singer, really.'

'No, I suppose not, except for the fact that she's got one of the most beautiful voices you or I are ever likely to hear - there are still a few people who think that how one sings actually matters,' snapped Calli.

'Sorry. You know I didn't mean that she doesn't have talent. But she hasn't been able to stand the pressure in the past and I was just wondering, with *entirely benevolent* and friendly motives, if you think she's going to be able to deal with it this time,' said Dominic, thinking all the while that the ease and speed with which Calliope had risen to her friend's defence was as sure an indicator as any that she was definitely not expecting Olivia to triumph over her paralysing self-doubt.

'With our help, I'm sure she will. Anyway it's a long time since that dreadful business with Guy. Things are different now and if Laura wasn't such a useless agent, she'd have realised that one embarrassment didn't need to mean never putting Olivia up for a decent role again. Honestly, it just makes me sick to think of Laura getting all the credit for setting this *Tosca* date up, and I'm sure she will find a way to take credit. Bitch!'

'You really think Olivia's over the thing with Guy? Doesn't the fact that you still have to refer to what happened as 'that dreadful business' tell you something, if only that your mutual lapsed faith isn't quite so unimportant to you as you'd both like everyone to think? I mean call a spade a spade, why don't you?'

'That'll be Olivia now, so just shut up about all that will you? Not a word, you understand?'

Really! As if he would do such a thing, thought Dominic shirtily as Calli rushed off to answer the door. As far as Olivia was concerned, he didn't know a thing about the 'dreadful business with Guy' and he certainly wasn't about to calmly drop it into conversation. No, if it were to be mentioned on today of all days, and there was a damn good possibility that it would be, it wouldn't come from his lips.

As expected, Olivia was a grey-green shade of pale when Calli shepherded her into the room,

'Olivia my lovely, how are you? Nervous?'

Calliope shot him a completely unnecessary cautionary look.

'Petrified.'

'Well sit down, have a glass of champagne and you'll feel like a new woman.'

'Champagne? It's only eleven!'

'I'm afraid Scarpia and that too-flash-to-use coffee machine won the day again.'

'And we wanted to celebrate your success,' added Calli.

'I'm not going to celebrate till I've got through this afternoon,' said Olivia, heading for the kitchen, trailled by her friends, glasses in hand. 'If I do that, then you can open a whole case of champagne and watch me drink every last drop. Right now though, I need a coffee and I mean to have it whatever it takes. Scarpia doesn't scare me and as for that ridiculous machine... I'm a desperate woman and I'm ready for combat.'

'That's the spirit,' said Dominic, noting the faint waver in Olivia's voice. 'Just keep it up and the *sitzprobe* will be a breeze. Just got to think of Alexander Petrov as a cappucino - all hot air and froth - and you'll be fine.'

'Fine, just so long as I can tear my tongue off the roof of my mouth.'

'I don't think there's a one of us who feels any different before we go on, is there Calli?'

'No,' Calli responded with a little too noticeable a hesitation - well, nerves were hardly a problem she knew anything about. She then delved into her stock of interview replies to find the appropriate response, 'Of course we all feel like that. It's only natural, but success comes at a price; even if every performance means using up a little bit of yourself just to get past the terror, you have to do it or you might as well give up, accept failure and...'

'Sing three *Creations* at the Muswell Hill Methodist next week,' interjected Olivia, staring hard at her friend, dark eyes shining black with unshed tears. For an uncomfortable time the only sound was the angry noise of espresso sputtering onto the work surface.

'That's not what I was trying to say, at all.'

Dominic doubted that, although he recognised the 'quote', loved it and knew that Calli had actually been about to sigh, as dramatically as possible, *die*.

'Yes it is, and you're right. Absolutely right. If I don't pull myself together, that's where I'll be next week. Back on the pile of could have beens, waiting for Laura to throw yet more crap on me. What's wrong with me Calli? I just seem determined to be a failure. You know, I haven't even had the guts to call up that idiot conductor and tell him to get himself another soprano. Why bother coming here today, let alone going to the Opera House if I'm that confident I'll screw up again and be free to do his stupid concerts?'

Stunned, Olivia paused momentarily to consider what she had said and then smiled.

'But the thing is,' she then said perkily, 'I am here. Which means that deep down I must believe in myself. Thanks Calli, you always know just the right thing to say. You know, I think I'm going to call that conductor now, then you can listen to me sing and tell me that I haven't just made a huge mistake!'

Dominic thought that Calliope was starting to look a little grey-green herself now.

Calliope hung back in the kitchen, ostensibly to hide any evidence that it had actually been used. It took significantly longer for her to complete the task at hand than it would a person with less unmanageable nails and emotions. As she patted a stilletoed foot gingerly at the paper towel she had dropped with little accuracy onto the espresso-damp floor, she listened to Olivia's heated conversation with the sorely disappointed and unco-operative conductor. The boldness and unbridled sarcasm with which she directed the annoying little man back to her agent was unsettling to someone who was used to having to get Olivia out of all those free gigs she just didn't have the heart to say no to.

'How dare you call me unprofessional?' Olivia said and then staggeringly continued, 'I'm not interested in hearing about our contract. Sir, intimidation is not going to work; sue me if you want, but remember that it is the Royal Opera House you will be dealing with. I'm sure that Laura will be more than able to find you a singer who can meet the exacting standards you have for your choir.'

Calli's eyes widened as the telephone was then hung up with a firmness that was reminiscent of the closings of most of her own calls with conductors, agents and lovers.

The whole was underscored by Dominic running long fingers with fluid ease up and down the keyboard of the Steinway. It was strange to hear him warming up for someone else, though they had always shared his accompanying skills back in their college days. Recently however, Olivia had had very little work that justified the expense of having a coach - a friend maybe, but Dominic, not always able to secure an Armani man, still had to eat, pay the rent and fund his frequent makeovers. Calliope on the other hand, could not function without his remarkable talent for bringing out the best in a singer.

Calli was a fine example of that breed of singers who could neither read music nor speak the languages in which she had the audacity to sing. Calli had been blessed with a gorgeous voice, a positively thespian talent for misrepresenting herself and balls enough to consider the fact that she had - to put it mildly - bugger all musicality in her veins, of no importance whatsoever. Nothing had surprised her music teacher, Sister Marianne, more than seeing her least willing, least capable student rise to stardom on the operatic stage. And that surprise gave Calli reason to smile when she might otherwise have been crying at the remembrance of the years she had spent in that hellhole of a Catholic girls' school.

Of course she had been a troublesome teenager, but wasn't that the way it was supposed to be? Did the fire of her rebellion have to have been fuelled and stoked to such all-consuming intensity by those so-called sisters of mercy? How many times, at the sight of scarlet nails, did a ruler have to come down onto already bruised knuckles for Caroline Smith to stop preparing with lipstick, jewellery and scent for her lunchtime liaisons with boys from the local comprehensive, to stop that alter-ego Calliope Syrigos taking shape? As it turned out, more times than even the most dedicated of punishers could manage. It is hard to douse the symptoms of anger when one pours on rage.

The nuns' rage came from jealousy, or so Caroline Smith thought. Why not, when she was so lovely and young, and they so thwarted? It made her angry to see them claim contentment in their unyielding belief in God, to see them reject all the wonderful gifts that their God had given them, in pursuit of some higher realm. It made her angry because every time her chance at redemption came, every time the nuns sent her regretfully bearing her sins to the confessional box, it was she and not Father Timothy who heard a confession. He would speak to her of his desire for her, in words that made even her soul blush, and then he would ask for forgiveness, leaving her burdened with the sins of two.

And when finally the Father could not contain his yearnings any longer and replaced his imagined self that caressed her silken, milky-white thighs gently, with a physical self that spread them violently right there in the confessional box and tore through resistance and innocence, Caroline Smith discovered that the rage, that had so often been turned upon her, was in fact founded in a knowledge of what had been said to her as she chanted Hail Marys to drown out reality. But, it was a rage directed only at her, the guilty party who had flaunted herself shamelessly and attempted and tempted the seduction of Father Timothy.

When they found her, the nuns did not believe what she told them - didn't she realise that they knew all about her meetings with boys and did she really think she could cover up her sins in this way? Caroline Smith's parents did not believe her either. Father Timothy had introduced them at a church social, wed them, christened her and put them all in fear of the eternal fires every Sunday since; to lose Caroline was to lose a part of themselves but to lose Father Timothy was to lose their entire selves. The other girls saw what happened when Caroline Smith dared to confess the truth and could not believe her. No-one believed her and Caroline Smith found herself destined for a very demoralising sort of life, dismissed from her school without so much as a GCSE and discarded by her family without considering that, through their actions, they might be securing themselves that feared place in hell. Caroline Smith hoped it was the case, yet could not help but think that God's omnipresence was somewhat in doubt.

The 'ten items only' check out at Sainsbury's, running a faulty bar code over and over the beeping machine, was where she was and thought she would probably always be, when she had looked up wearily one afternoon to find that amongst the everybody who loved to shop there was Olivia Tarrent.

'Hello. Remember me?' Olivia had said with what sounded like compassion in her voice.

Caroline was surprised to hear so friendly a tone from this girl. How could she not remember Olivia? Cheery, fat, horrible goody-two-shoes Olivia. Caroline had been less than kind to Olivia during all those years in class together because she was not the type you wanted to been seen with if boys were your prey, and because she had also hated her for just that reason - no silken, milky-white thighs there. If she had been Olivia, thought Caroline, she would have gone to the back of even the longest queue rather than have to be civil.

'Olivia, right?'

'How are you?' Olivia smiled warmly.

In answer, Caroline cast a grim look about her depressing surroundings.

'How about you?'

'Oh good,' Olivia said awkwardly, clearly embarrassed to admit it.

'Don't suppose you know how much this is?' questioned Caroline, as she passed the packet of biscuits over the red beam just one more time.

'Sorry. No.'

Caroline pressed the little button that set the light above her till flashing for assistance and a difficult silence fell between them.

'I've just started at the Royal Academy of Music,' smiled Olivia, when just too much time had gone by for comfort. 'I'm studying to be a singer. An opera singer.'

She has the figure for it, thought Caroline.

'Wow, an opera singer. So all those music lessons paid off. Sister Marianne must be thrilled to death, the old cow. Make up for me, I guess. *Caroline Smith, you'll send me to an early grave. If only I could train your personality to be as beautiful as your voice, God might forgive your sins to date.* An early grave! Chance'd be a fine thing.'

Goody-two-shoes Olivia didn't look at all shocked, which was shocking for Caroline.

'One pound ninety-five,' said the customer service assistant.

Caroline held out her hand for the money.

And then Olivia did it.

She took hold of Caroline's hand and held it.

Held it tight and didn't let go.

'I'm sorry for what he did to you, truly I am.'

The words had been whispered and Caroline thought for a second that she had conjured them up herself. But Olivia's eyes were full with tears.

'Thank you,' Caroline responded quietly, feeling a huge sense of relief rush through her.

'Excuse me, I haven't got all day to hang about while you two gossip,' said the embittered looking woman behind Olivia, as her brattish daughter began to whine like a sulky two-year-old.

'All right. All right,' muttered Caroline, taking her time about sorting the coins into their proper homes.

'You know,' said Olivia, 'you should consider singing yourself. Sister Marianne was right about you having a beautiful voice.'

Caroline laughed. 'I can't even read music!'

'It doesn't matter. That's what coaches are for.'

Caroline laughed some more but Calliope's interest was piqued.

'No, really. Look, here's my number. Give me a call and perhaps you could come and sing to my professor.'

'I don't think so.'

'Well it can't be any scarier than sitting here, now can it? Just think about it - call me any time.'

'Are you finished?' interrupted the woman again.

'Quite,' said Olivia with a smile and disappeared off, waving as she went.

'Oh, I'm sorry,' said Caroline sweetly after she'd gone, 'you can't come through this check out, madam. You have eleven items.'

'Oh for heaven's sake don't be so stupid girl. You've kept me waiting long enough, so I suggest you let me through or I'll talk to your supervisor and make sure you have no job.'

Caroline dutifully began to add the eleven items and when she was done she smiled at the woman's daughter, all decked out in a nasty bottle-green and burgundy uniform.

'I see she goes to Saint Jude's.'

'Yes, we want her to have the very *best* education. It's a *wonderful* school.'

Her judgment upon Caroline was implicit and Calliope took exception to it.

'I know,' she smiled, triumphal as a horrified look met her comment, 'I went there myself.'

If it were not for Olivia, Caroline Smith might still be there in Sainsbury's, pale and insignificant under the fluorescent lights, at the mercy of every superior bitch who was having a bad day and needed someone to punch. Calliope shuddered at the thought and felt a renewed desire to make sure her friend went to the Royal Opera House prepared and confident.

But, as she stood just outside the drawing room and Olivia's voice joined Dominic's accompaniment, Calliope could not be sure whether the goosebumps that spread up her arms were there for the splendour of that voice or the jealousy of it. When Calliope rehearsed with Dominic it was so that he could literally coach and coax every last note out of her. He would have to play each phrase over and over to her, tell her when she was sharp or flat, help her with not only the fine tuning of her enunciation but also the very basic pronunciation of the words and, when all that was done, she could rely on him to help her interpret the music. All this, so that Calliope could walk on stage where she belonged and have all the world believe in the greatness that she had created. Yet here Olivia was, filling Calliope with the need to weep at the sincerity of her *Tosca*, and without the slightest interference from Dominic. He played, she sang and Calliope, fearing that she might not be adequate in controlling her urge to destruction, went to her four poster bed, lay down under the weight of her misery and listened.

'What do you think?' asked Olivia when they were finally through.

Calliope jumped at the sound of her voice - Dominic was still playing in the other room and somehow the fact that it was jazz and not *Tosca* had failed to filter through Calli's defences. She sat up quickly, with her back to Olivia, and went immediately over to the dressing table.

'You've been crying,' said Olivia, seeing the tell-tale mascara marks on the antique quilt. 'What's wrong?'

'Nothing. Nothing at all. You just sing so beautifully, it makes me tearful.'

'I think that's the nicest thing anyone's ever said to me,' said Olivia, going over to give Calli a hug.

'So, are you ready for this afternoon?'

'I think so. I'm still shaking, of course,' Olivia said, holding up her hands for Calli to see for herself, 'but Dominic's amazing - he's so good at restoring my faith in my singing - it's going to be great to actually have enough money to work with him as often as I want.'

Calli could not help but feel a little annoyed at the thought - good coaches were hard to come by and her need for Dominic was greater than her friend's - what if he were suddenly unavailable when she needed him?

'So, what are you going to wear for the *sitzprobe*?' she asked.

'Well this,' responded Olivia, suddenly questioning her choice of dress.

Calliope looked her friend up and down. Olivia had lost some weight recently and though not skinny, by any means, she really didn't look bad in the dress she was wearing. Nonetheless, Calli did not think it was right at all.

'Charcoal grey for a *sitzprobe* with Angelo Verasano? No, I can't let you do it. You should be wearing something vibrant. Splashy. Your clothes should say *Look everyone, I'm here and I belong here, so don't even think about giving me any crap this afternoon!*' said Calli, and she meant it.

'But I haven't got time to go home before the rehearsal.'

'It's O.K., you don't have to look so dismayed. I've got just the outfit. It's in here somewhere,' she assured

Olivia, her voice muffled as it came from the depths of her walk-in closet. 'I bought it in a hurry a few weeks ago and picked up the wrong size. It's way too big for me... but it should fit you perfectly.'

Calliope emerged carrying a cherry red suit which turned out to fit anything but perfectly.

'I can't believe it didn't work for you. There's no way you're bigger than a fourteen - it must be cut wrong.'

Olivia had been disappointed but now she felt huge and disgusting; though she could have sworn that the divine suit was a twelve, not a fourteen. And she knew that even if had been a size fourteen she shouldn't have attempted to put it on.

'Never mind,' smiled Calli, 'I've got a better idea,' and she fished a glamorous, long silk scarf out of a drawer and draped its luminescent length about Olivia's shoulders. It was lovely, but it wasn't an adorable red suit and it would probably be a nightmare to keep in place. Olivia smiled anyway, thanked Calliope for sorting her out and, looking at her watch, realised that she had better get going or risk infuriating the conductor on her first day.

Just as Olivia stepped out of the front door, Calli put her hand out to stop her.

'Olivia, there's something I feel I ought to tell you before you go,' she said hesitantly. 'I think it's important that you know, that I warn you...'

'Warn me? Warn me about what? If it's Alexander Petrov, don't worry. I've heard all about him, I'll be OK.'

'No, Olivia, it's about Guy.'

'Guy? What about Guy?'

'He's in the Opera House orchestra.'

Calli watched the colour drain out of her friend's face. 'I'm sorry,' she said.

'I know. I know,' was all that Olivia muttered as she turned away.

Calliope closed the door quietly behind her, deep in thought.

'I thought Guy wasn't to be mentioned,' commented Dominic from his vantage point down the hall, making Calli's heart skip a beat.

'I had to tell her.'

'I'm sure you did.'

- chapter four -

'Excuse me! Excuse me, you can't just go wandering through there like that. Passes only.'

The stage doorman was as camp as Christmas and his shrill voice caused all eyes to turn. Olivia was forced to come back to the front desk.

'I'm sorry, I didn't realise.'

'Clearly!'

Smug titters erupted behind her. Of course this had never happened to any of those people waiting; they belonged here, they knew someone to wait for. Bugger the fact that she was about to rehearse *Tosca*, Olivia felt like a nobody.

'And you would be?'

She had to think for a moment.

'Olivia Tarrent... I'm here for the *Tosca sitzprobe.*'

His *and I'm the Queen of Sheba* look as he took up his clipboard, told her that she obviously looked like a nobody too. If Calli had walked through that door, they'd all have jumped up for her autograph, whether they recognised her or not; she just looked like you'd want her signature. Instead, Olivia was now faced with the yet greater humiliation of finding that her name hadn't been added to the list.

'God, I'm sorry,' she said contrite, her mind blank. 'This is so embarrassing... I just don't know why I came in here.'

'That's OK pet. I'd get yourself a drink, if I were you,' he responded, giving her a concerned little pat on the hand. Then he looked meaningfully to the stage door.

It was only when she dropped her musical score in her fluster to get out of there, and saw the words 'Property of The Royal Opera House, Covent Garden' emblazoned across its cover under a royal coat of arms, that she woke out of her stupor and realised that it was the doorman, not she, who was in error.

'Still here?' He was playing to the gallery.

'Please can't you just call someone? I'll be late for my rehearsal.'

And she *would* be late. Two o'clock was rapidly approaching and the thought of what torture she'd be inviting if Alexander Petrov were to be kept waiting by her, fuelled her resolve not to be put off this time.

'Look for yourself. I'm sorry love, you're not here,' he insisted, pursing his lips self-righteously and turning the clipboard so that she could have a gander –

did she think he was born yesterday? He hated it when these nutters were persistent. But, he had to concede that Angelo Verasano was hot as hell, so maybe it was just lucky that this was the only crazy-stalker-girlie he'd had to deal with today.

Olivia looked from the doorman to his clipboard, overwhelmed with a sense that she'd woken up in one of her recurring nightmares – and this was just the beginning; any minute now she'd realise she wasn't wearing any clothes and she was lost at the back of the auditorium while the curtain was going up on the show she was supposed to be in. She could hardly breathe and tears started to well up.

'But... but...'

She woke up on the floor, being fanned with the musical score, surrounded by the concerned assistants to various people, who'd been sent looking for her and then found this embarrassing mess at the stage door.

Helped up, forced to drink water, vehemently apologised to, and calmed down - sort of - Olivia now stood with her fingertips resting hesitantly against the heavy grain of large, wooden swing-doors. She could tell that the studio beyond was huge - its echo enhanced the sound of the chattering chorus, the clamour of the orchestra warming up. One push and this nobody would be through the looking glass, into a world she had dreamed about every sleeping, every waking moment. But then what? What if this door should turn out to be the revolving one of her nightmares?

Minutes ticked by. The hubbub before her was lost in the hue and cry to the rear - voices from her past crowded in, wound about her, tightening and tightening until her ribs cracked with the effort to breathe...

...*'Olivia dear, that was beautiful. I think it's time you sing to my agent. Not ready?! I'll have none of that from you. How many years have you been studying towards this moment, how many people have put their time and energy into getting you here? This isn't just about you, you know - a voice like yours just has to be shared sometime and, in my judgement, now is that time. You've got an eagle of a talent, so make that leap from the nest and let it soar up where it belongs, let it strike terror into those twittering sparrows beneath. Don't let fear clip its wings, Olivia, you're too good for that.'*

...*'How many times do I have to tell you, she means nothing to me? You're the one I love. I can't believe you've done this. After all that crap I've had to take for not sharing your beliefs. You didn't even give me a chance to make things right, did you? How can you say you love me when it's always Calli you turn to. Every bloody time, she's there sticking her nose in, giving you advice, telling you lies. Oh you think so do you? And just how would that bitch know anything about me? She's never stopped causing trouble long enough to have a civil conversation with me, let alone get to know me, but Calli knows best. Oh right, I was in the pub with my mates when she was 'supporting' you, 'being there' for you. Well yes I was, because surprise, surprise I'm not a fucking psychic. This isn't just about you, you know. How was I* supposed to pass the test when you didn't even tell me the problem? Fine, have it your way, I should have known. And you know what, you should have known that this would mean something to me, that I would actually care. But we both know now, don't we? We're finished and we probably always were.'

...'Glyndebourne, Olivia. I get you Glyndebourne and this is what you repay me with. Jesus Olivia, how many times have I told you to quit smoking? What makes you think it's all right to party till you've got no voice? Did you really expect them to cut you some slack? You're not at college now, this is the real world, there's no place for the kind of amateurish attitude you're clinging to. Do you understand what it took to get you that role? An outsider, a nobody to them. But I convinced them. 'You've got to hear this voice, you've never heard the like of it, the beauty of it. Trust me, I said.' Trust me! Ha. This isn't just about you, you know. This is my reputation you've fucked up ....Well that's noble of you Olivia, but I don't need you to promise me that it'll never happen again, cause there's no chance whatsoever that you'll be in a place where it'll actually matter, ever again. You want to act like an amateur, that's fine by me, amateurs are all you're going to get from now on. Just be grateful you've got an agent at all. This'll be all round the profession by now - there's only one thing worse than having a nobody on your books and that's having a nobody called Olivia Tarrent.'

...'What are you going to do? Never sing again? I can't let you do it darling. You didn't sneak off to another check out when you saw me festering in that wretched supermarket, did *you? And now you're telling me to leave you alone to drown yourself in self pity. Well darling, no can do. If you're going to play the tragic heroine let it be Madam Butterfly, and let it be centre stage at La Scala, Milan. For Christ's sake darling, I can't even read music and I'm booked there next month! Are you listening to me? Sod the lot of them, Olivia, and pull yourself together. This isn't about me or your parents or Dame Cecelia, this isn't about Guy and this certainly isn't about that cow Laura. It's about you, and only you. You are the one you're letting down if you do this. You!'*

The door nudged Olivia as it swung to behind her. The violent, vibrating jangle of a cymbal hitting the floor, greeted with heckles from every corner of the orchestra, immediately confirmed what Calli had told her. Guy MacLaren was here. But Calli was right about many things. *This isn't about him, this is about me,* Olivia repeated over and over to herself, refusing to look in the direction of the percussion section, from whence she could hear the inevitable laughter. She lurked at the door, as if it were her first day at a new school, hoping that they could not see what she had now become aware of - her trailing scarf was caught in the door.

'Guess I shouldn't have had those last five pints,' laughed Guy, affecting a drunken slur for his fellow percussionists' amusement and to rile a disapproving violinist nearby, but even as he playfully staggered about in retrieving the cymbal and deliberately missed in his attempts to get it back in its stand, his eyes never strayed from Olivia. Why he was surprised to see her here, he wasn't sure. She was a singer and if you played for the Royal Opera, you were liable to bump into singers, especially when they had a voice like Olivia's. He could have listened to that voice forever, for the rest of his life.

'Hey Guy, isn't that Saint Olivia over there?'

'Yes,' he agreed with Frank absently. Did she know he was here? he wondered. Was that why she looked so petrified? He hadn't given her a second thought in as many years as had passed since their break up. Five years, two hundred and fifty-eight days and not once had he recalled those deliciously inviting curves, the way her perfume lingered deep in that river of blonde hair, those enormous, mahogany eyes. Just look up here, he thought, see how little I care.

'So Guy, how many sopranos does it take to change a light bulb?'

'Sorry? Oh right... I dunno. How many sopranos does it take to change a light bulb?'

'One – to hold the light bulb while the world revolves around her.'

The night they'd met, Olivia had loitered in the doorway of the Lamb and Flag just as she was doing now, clearly uncomfortable, not sure if she was in the right place. Frank had said she was out of his league, but that hadn't stopped him. Her eyes had only met his for the briefest moment, but not so brief as it should have been if she weren't interested, so he'd winked a bold, blue eye at her and abandoned the lads.

She hadn't been at all what he expected. He had gone over with a thought to a one night stand and had, at first, felt well and truly put in his place by her complete refusal to take his cues to flirt. But, never one to walk away from a challenge, or to be seen to fail by his mates, he'd persisted and, in doing so, discovered that the real challenge came from her being so unaware that she was out of his league as to make it a task and a half just to convince her that he was interested in her. The big nervous eyes were not an attention-attracting ruse after all, but a reaction to not finding her best friend waiting in the pub where they'd agreed to meet - from the description, Guy had immediately recognised the friend to be the fabulous, and contrastingly not backwards about coming forwards, brunette who'd slinked out half an hour earlier with a stagehand.

Lucky Calliope; no matter how many times she left her friend in the lurch for a night with some sleaze or other, she always got forgiven - well, if God could forgive her then who was Olivia to do otherwise? He, on the other hand, without a telephone to the all-fucking-mighty, had to pay over and over for the mistakes he made. Confess and repent all he liked, it was always the same, he could never mean it the way those two did. Sure, he knew what he'd done was different but how could she judge him so harshly and then respond to his actions with what must, by her standards, make his crime pale into insignificance? And then to assume that just because he didn't share her religious convictions, that it would mean nothing to him. Even now, he felt his blood rushing angrily at the hypocrisy of it all. And all for what? For a career that had gone nowhere. So, she'd finally made it into the chorus here. Big deal - it was nothing compared with the dizzy heights she'd been expected to reach. He'd heard about her 'debut' at Glyndebourne. He'd been glad that she'd screwed up. And he'd hoped that her wretched voice turning out to be not so fantastic after all had made *her* feel as guilty about her choice as she'd made *him* feel about it.

'Holy shit - looks like Olivia's playing Tosca!' remarked an amazed Charlie, as Angelo Verasano hurried over to Olivia, who was busy disentangling herself from her scarf, and kissed her hands repeatedly before placing a possessive arm about her waist and taking her over to meet their arsehole of a conductor.

Guy believed it. Who was he kidding? It had always been just a matter of time before this happened. She had got what she'd wanted, she probably didn't feel anything other than as 'right' about everything as she'd always been.

'Can we borrow your earplugs?' he jested to a viola player, who generally did less playing than expostulating about the deafening volume of the percussion section. 'Looks like we're going to get treated to a rendition of the *Cat's Chorus* this afternoon.'

Only Frank, who knew fully the history between Guy and the woman whom Angelo Verasano was clearly already in the early stages of seducing, heard past the joviality to the reality. Charlie and Dave were just falling about, finding anything their always comical principal said all the funnier for the liquid lunch they'd imbibed.

'You OK, mate?'

'Yeh, Frank. Why wouldn't I be?'

Why shouldn't he be? Did Frank really think he'd give a damn that Angelo was all over Olivia like sauce on spaghetti? The man had got every soprano and contralto that came within his cologne's reach into the sack, not to mention a few baritones, and yet regardless of his reputation they kept on falling into bed with him, one after another, as if it just wouldn't do to be the only one left out. If Olivia was fool enough to fall for that little shit's line, that was fine by him. Let her sample the kind of punishment one of her compatriot Catholics could hand out, it might do her some good. No, Guy wasn't bothered one iota.

'Hey, don't you think we should warn old angel face that he's wasting his time with the Virgin Mary?' joked Charlie, immediately wishing he hadn't as Frank elbowed him sharply in the beer gut and Guy's face darkened threateningly.

'Charlie,' said Guy.

'Yes?'

'Just shut the fuck up.'

* * *

'So this is the great Olivia Tarrent.'

So said the not so great conductor, Alexander Petrov, not bothering to get down from atop his high stool. Olivia guessed that this was because he was far shorter in person than his publicity shots betrayed and he wanted to maintain his terrifying image. He needn't have bothered, it was in his very nature to be intimidating - perhaps fifty, maybe seventy, with a thick mane of white hair resting on his shoulders, he had a face like chiselled granite that would have been unquestionably handsome had it not been for the harshness in his eyes. Eyes which narrowed, Clint Eastwood-like as they considered Olivia.

'Hardly great, Mr. Petrov,' Olivia said with embarrassment, the sarcasm in his voice having not missed its mark.

'Please, call me Sasha,' said Alexander Petrov, taking a hold of Olivia's hand and squeezing till it hurt and not letting go while he exchanged unpleasantries with his well-loathed star - though the words were spoken to Olivia, they were clearly addressed to Angelo. 'Angelo tells me he has discovered you in a restaurant. I hope he has not been taking too much champagne again - it is prone to make a man hear voices where there are none at all.'

'Maestro, how can you say such a thing? Olivia has the voice of the angel. Angelo's angel,' smarmed Angelo, taking hold of Olivia's other hand, overjoyed to see Sasha close to snarling mad. If he was honest, he had had too much champagne and too much grappa - he really couldn't remember much about that evening at all but, all pinked at his flattery, Olivia was certainly a pleasant reminder and Sasha was suitably pissed off, so he was more than satisfied with his handiwork.

'Ah, but angels are such elusive things, are they not, my friend? God does not usually loan them to us for so humble a cause as a night at the opera.'

Olivia smiled through the pain Sasha was inflicting - quite deliberately she suspected - and thought wryly back to Dominic's earlier assurance that if she could conquer the coffee machine, she could easily take on the maestro. Unfortunately, the man's reputation had prepared her not for this dismissive attack, but to be lavished with sticky-as-Sasha-torte sexual innuendo and then only when she had refused to sleep with him, to find herself at the wrong end of his baton, so to speak. She should have been feeling relieved that he was not interested in her - she knew it, and yet felt the slight deeply, seeing clearly that there would be no honeymoon period in which she could prove herself to the rest of the company, and thereby gain their support, before Sasha set about robbing his soprano of all self-possession as was his habit when his powers of seduction failed him. But Olivia wasn't even worth seducing. She thought ruefully of Calli's little red suit, a coincident roar of laughter from the percussion section, making her almost believe that they had seen into her mind and glimpsed the horror of the skirt's waistband stuck firmly at her fat, bulging thighs.

'*Mia bella,* do not listen to this Stalin. He is a bear with a sore head because Luciana Carmosino did not go to his bed before leaving for Italy!'

'Senor Verasano, you go too far. It is just like an Italian, to think everything is about sex,' snapped Sasha, furious to have been discovered. He'd had great plans for Luciana; she'd already fallen foul of this Latin upstart during the spring production of *La Traviata* and was therefore ripe for the picking but alas, Angelo had been such a bastard then and was so entirely impenitent now, that she could not remain in the same room with him for more than a minute without recourse to either tears or tirades. Thanks to Angelo, Luciana had scarpered back to Milan, leaving Alexander Petrov to face a season of professional and sexual frustration - not only had this unknown soprano been foisted upon him with no notice but, worse still, she was all a flutter at every word the little creep had to say.

'Let us not forget Senor Verasano, that it is your bed that Luciana Carmosino has left empty... but maybe not. Perhaps poor Luciana left us to the perils of an untried soprano because she found this 'angel' watching over you one night.'

'Now you go too far!' retorted Angelo to the great joy of the orchestra. Pistols at dawn seemed imminent. One shot, good and true, and the way would be clear for management to set about poaching the guy from New York's Metropolitan Opera - well, they could dream.

'Gentlemen, gentlemen. Please! I'm not surprised you're all fightin' over this young lady here, but she'll come clean in half if you don't let go'a her tiny hands. That's better now. Really, what fine gentlemen these European men are. I guess you'll be Olivia Tarrent. I am Marshall Lincoln Small.'

Olivia hadn't even thought to ask who the baritone playing Scarpia would be. The awesome Marshall Lincoln Small's arrival spread a ripple of applause across the entire studio, his deep voice with its Harley-Davidson purr caused Angelo and Sasha to immediately let her hands free.

Now Olivia was really scared. Here, actually so close to her that she could feel the air between them stir as he breathed, was all six-foot-five of arguably the best baritone of all time. He had been born in America's deep south when a black man couldn't sit on the same bus, learn in the same school or sing hymns in the same church as a white man, let alone hope for a future on the international opera circuit. But, by the time he was a grown man, things had moved on and now the voice, that would once have been consigned to Sunday services, could be heard the world over although, sadly, the predominantly white audiences in opera houses across the globe were a confirmation that cultural segration was still alive and kicking.

Never in her wildest dreams had Olivia pictured herself on stage at the Royal Opera House with this man; to her, the collective talents of the 'three tenors' couldn't eclipse the greatness of Marshall Lincoln Small.

Marshall recognised in Olivia's unblinking eyes, and the coldness of her hand as it disappeared into his cavernous grasp, the 'fear of God' that he seemed to strike all too often in young singers. He gave forth a bellowing laugh that set music stands vibrating and music fluttering to the floor.

'Miss Olivia, you all calm down now. This ain't no masterclass, though I'm sure I'll learn plenty from you.'

That was *so* ridiculous that even Olivia found herself laughing.

'OK everyone,' interrupted Sasha, looking at his watch, 'we have much to do and as usual, very little time. Maybe not everyone is aware that Luciana Carmosino has left us and so I must introduce and welcome our new Tosca, Olivia Tarrent.'

There was polite applause all round, though pointedly more from the orchestra than the chorus, some of whom Olivia recognised from student days, and if that didn't make her uncomfortable enough, wolf whistles erupted from both the percussion and brass sections. Olivia cast an embarrassed smile about the place and gratefully took the chair that Angelo offered her. With her legs giving way beneath her, she could not have been more relieved that this was a *sitzprobe*; a seated rehearsal that would be not much more than a run through to test the waters and see how work to this point would gel when the orchestra was added to the mix. But, for Olivia, there had been no work up to now and, although that meant that for today at least the strain of attempting to memorise stage directions on top of everything else would not be an issue, she still feared the dangers that lay ahead - without the slightest idea of what the already antagonistic Alexander Petrov had in mind for even basic *tempi*, let alone what nuances of interpretation he might then desire, Olivia did not doubt that this afternoon would test her to her limits.

She was not to be proven wrong.

The rehearsal got under way and Alexander Petrov confirmed that conductors were the same everywhere by almost immediately screaming abuse at the brass and accusing them of being drunk, which they probably were, but his subsequent segue into levelling the same reproach at the flutes brought guffaws of incredulity from all sides and rendered the former complaint less valid. It mattered little to Sasha though, and he was swift to move on to Angelo. It was clear to Olivia where he was headed. Without ever hearing her voice he had allowed his dislike of Angelo Verasano to make his mind up and was now warming up for his dismantling of her performance, preparing the scene a little so that his behaviour towards her would not stand out. All these years she had screwed up performance after performance because of imagined foes, so how, if she hadn't been able to surmount those, was she now going to conquer the very real and out for blood Alexander Petrov?

And then there was the chorus. For the most part, the amateur choirs she'd sung with had been more desperate to worship the ground she walked on than anything else. Generally they were genuinely disappointed by her failures, but here was a chorus of rivals, glaring at her with undisguised jealousy and a transparent desire for her to prove an undeserving recipient of Angelo's admiration - they made the Valkyries look like girl scouts.

Olivia tried to put herself back in time to that morning, when Dominic had played the score with such joyful exuberance due, he had told her, to the immense pleasure he got from accompanying a voice of such distinction as hers. And, if she doubted his claim, she had only to think of her dear friend's tears when she was done to believe that she was capable of silencing Petrov. And why shouldn't she? How could he call himself a musician when he was so little interested in music that he was prepared to be judge and executioner of her voice, without even granting her a chance to put the evidence before him? No, Alexander Petrov was nothing but an over-inflated Terrence Danvers.

Bolstered by her internal dismissal of the maestro's own talents, Olivia began to believe that she could break with tradition. If she could keep to the fore of her mind, the memory of all the times she had pulled herself together mid-disaster and sung like a star, and use that image now to make her opening phrases as impressive as her last usually were, then Alexander Petrov would indeed be undone.

And Sasha was astounded by the sparkling clarity of Olivia's voice when she first entered, and could not deny to himself the warm throb of arousal that her beautiful rendering of Tosca's first aria set aglow, but she had underestimated the measure of his malevolence. If she had sung with the mediocrity that he had expected, then he might happily have let her make his point herself, but now he was livid and without the slightest hesitation, harnessed his rancour in pursuit of wiping the self-satisfied smirk off Angelo's face.

'Stop, stop, stop,' he screamed in the midst of a particularly gorgeous note. 'What are you thinking woman? This is Puccini, not Rodgers and Hammerstein. You are supposed to be seducing Cavaradossi into a night at your country cottage, not inviting him to a clambake. Where is the passion? Do those words mean nothing to you? *Arde a Tosca nel sague il folle amor!* In Tosca's blood burns the madness of love! I say again, where is the passion? You sing like a virgin.'

To which came the inevitable chorus of Madonna's *Like a virgin, Oo...* from the ranks of the orchestra. Olivia could guess where from and felt the double humiliation keenly as giggles were barely stifled all around. The ferocity of Petrov's tone had surprised her. Not only had she actually managed to surmount her fear of that first entry but, for once, she had felt like she was giving a good account of herself. And yet she'd met with unequivocal dissatisfaction.

From her right and left Angelo and Marshall offered hushed words of reassurance and Olivia raised a weak smile. This was merely Petrov's way of working. It meant little about her voice, she mustn't let her confidence be shaken so easily.

'Now, once more,' said Sasha, even as he spoke summoning up in his mind the next put down. At first he just grunted occasionally and fidgeted around on his stool, as if she were making him uncomfortable, and thereby took a little of her mind from what she was singing. Then he stood up and glared at her from the podium as she struggled on. Finally he threw down his baton in a rage and allowed the orchestra to stumble to a cacophonous halt.

'My dear child. Do you not know anything of Tosca? Anything at all? Here we have a woman who will *kill* for her man, who will *die* for her man and yet you cannot even sing for your man. Senor Verasano obviously fails in his nightly duties, if you cannot bring to us here the jealousy that Tosca feels over Cavaradossi, even when the man playing him is your bedfellow!' he said, wholly pleased with himself for managing, with one blow, to make it clear to everyone in earshot why he thought Olivia had got the role, and to cast aspersions on Angelo's sexual prowess. 'Again,' he barked, before either of the offended parties could muster a retort.

Nothing disturbed Angelo's performance; with a string of vindictive *prima donnas* to his name, whose tongues were far more creative in their fury than Sasha could ever be, he was used to this and more. Though irritated to find it so, Petrov was soon basking in his success as a slight quiver developed in Olivia's voice, urging him on his destructive path. He stopped over and over, poking and prodding at her with complaints about her breathing, her intonation, her apparent inability to follow his beat, until what had been products of his imagination became all too real and Olivia was doing more apologising than singing.

As Sasha let an ever-decreasing number of bars pass before complaining about the fact that this run through was turning into a masterclass, so the rest of the company grew more fractious. The chorus had nothing to do till the end of Act One and started first to shift about in their seats and then to get up and wander out of the studio to the drinks machine in the hall, the thud of cans and clatter of change punctuating the rustle of newspapers in the orchestra. It no longer seemed worth it to sit up and go to the hassle of putting a violin under a chin, or raise a French horn to lips - by the time the deed was done the maestro had stopped and, besides that, he didn't seem the slightest bit interested in the fact that half the band weren't playing. There were crosswords to be done, scarves to be knitted, bassoon and oboe reeds to be scraped.

Before long, the memory of Olivia's first, gorgeous notes had been quite submerged under the deluge of criminally wrong and excruciatingly unpleasant notes she was now forcing out. Alexander Petrov pressed on nonetheless. To one side Marshall Lincoln Small was thinking that if this was what he'd have to put up with, then it might be a good time to retire. To the other side Angelo was wondering if he could have been *that* drunk. To the fore a host of sopranos whispered snide remarks about the no-hoper who'd got their chance. And, to the rear, Guy couldn't think of a better example of why the orchestra referred to Opera as 'song shouting', nor could he justify silencing his colleagues as the soprano jokes came thick and fast.

And in the midst of it all was her harshest critic. Olivia knew what they were all thinking and saying. She wasn't deaf, she could hear her voice for what it was now. Hardly something worth destroying a relationship for. Guy was back there somewhere, knowing what she had done, and all in the name of not wasting her precious voice. A voice more precious even than the life of a child. Olivia's shoulders curled over under the weight of her thoughts, head falling forward as if ready to receive the blade of the guillotine, tears pattering upon her score.

'Stop this now, you bastard. Look what you have done. Is this your Russian gallantry?' Angelo suddenly burst out, conceiving that however disastrous she had turned out to be, if he didn't defend his choice of Tosca, it would mean he himself looking as foolish before the company as Olivia did.

'I am a musician not a *gigolo* Senor Verasano. I have no time for pampering the ego of this inexperienced and untalented woman, when there is a production to make ready. This is not my doing, but yours. Listen to her Angelo, now that you are sober, and tell me that I am mistaken.'

'When she came in here today she could sing. The voice I heard was the same one that has crept into my heart when I sing with her in the restaurant,' responded Angelo, realising only as he said it that he was speaking the truth. 'You say she sings like a virgin... well yes, she is a virgin, inexperienced in this corrupt and bitter world of ours, but what could be more beautiful than taking that virgin voice and caressing it into passion, gently bringing it to flower and then fruit as God intended when he put this woman on the earth. Instead you rape her with your jealousy and destroy what is beautiful. Well, I will not stay here a moment longer and neither will Miss Tarrent. Sir David will hear of this and will not be happy to hear that you have lost another two stars,' he said with a triumphant laugh and, with that, he then gathered Olivia into his arms and ushered her swiftly out of the studio, leaving a stunned silence in their wake.

It was only momentary, for Petrov then stormed after them, sending his baton flying into the violin section, and the orchestra errupted with hoots of joy and restored instruments to cases, thrilled at the prospect of time off for bad behaviour.

- chapter five -

Guessing that Petrov would be hard on their heels, Angelo didn't stop till he'd got Olivia well clear of the building. In fact, she sobbed inconsolably all the way to a little French patisserie that had stood him in good stead on previous occasions - the waiters there were no strangers to the spectacle of Angelo arriving with one his desolate divas. For Angelo this was however a unique experience. He, for once, was not the cause of the misery and his motive was not merely to get out of the public view. Consequently there was even a hope that the cafe's exquisite desserts might stand a chance of cheering the damsel in distress. The thought was some solace to him as he saw yet another silk handkerchief bite the dust in a torrent of mascara and felt the familiar sting at the back of his neck that alerted him to the accusatory stares their fellow patrons were giving him.

'I'm *so* sorry,' sniffed Olivia, the aroma of the cafe mocha that he'd ordered for her finally bringing her a little to her senses. And not before time, thought Angelo, sincerely hoping that those around them could hear that it was she, and not he, who was doing the apologising.

'There is no need for apology,' he said.

'Really, you think so?' she said with sarcasm. 'I'm not an idiot Angelo, I know what I did this afternoon. Believe me, you deserve my head on a platter for that performance. It's nothing for me to make a fool of myself - I do it all the time - but to let you down in this way is unforgivable. You gave me a wonderful opportunity, and look what I have done to thank you. I should have been honest with you. I should have admitted that I wasn't up to the job, instead of humiliating the both of us like that. I was just so enamoured with the thought of singing with you at Covent Garden that I let myself believe that I could do it.'

'But of course you can. You forget that I've heard you do it; we did sing together. If you think that I will be disappointed because you are not able to do battle with that pig Petrov, then you are wrong. You are punishing yourself for something that is nothing but refreshing to me after all my years in this hateful profession. Any singer who can remain unmoved by a tyrant like him cannot possibly have the emotion in them to sing *Tosca*.'

'I didn't see you rendered incapable of sounding a note. You sang like the great tenor you are and I sang like the loser I am.'

'But I have had more experience than you. With experience you can hold your hurt inside, use it to make your voice better and men like Petrov more angry than they could ever make you. This will come to you, Olivia, it will come with time.'

'You're very sweet Angelo, but I don't have time. Singing *Tosca* just a few weeks from now? I'm not up to it. However much I want to be, I'm just not.'

As Angelo drew breath to mount a counter attack, off Olivia went again, much to his chagrin.

'Maybe once upon a time I had the potential and if things had gone differently for me then perhaps I could have made it, but as it is, even if I had all the time from here to eternity it just wouldn't be enough. I'm never going to do any better than I did this afternoon. I can sing in a restaurant, when nobody's interested enough to stop talking even, but when it counts, when someone might actually be listening, I screw up. That's life, or at least that's *my* life and I've got to accept it. I let you down, I'm truly sorry and I won't let it happen again,' she said, making to stand up with the intention of leaving.

'Where are you going? You haven't touched your coffee.'

'I'm going to Sir David now. If I'm lucky, Petrov won't have got to him yet and I'll be able to hold on to what little dignity I have left after this afternoon, and withdraw from the contract before I get fired.'

This was not what Angelo wanted to hear at all. Have Alexander Petrov get the better of Angelo Verasano? Not an option; the man would be insufferable

- not that he wasn't already - and who knew what he'd replace Olivia with? Probably one of those monumental divas who dwarfed him no matter how many lifts he crammed into his shoes, and with whom love scenes became so laughable as to warrant him being awarded an *Oscar*, just for keeping the alarm off his face as it was swallowed up in the embrace of a vast bosom.

'I cannot hear of this, Olivia. It is out of the question,' he said with evident desperation, grabbing her before she could flee. 'Please, stay a while and think this over,' he pleaded, 'It would be a dreadful mistake to give up now.'

'Haven't you been listening to a word I've said? The point is that I should have given up long before now. Look at me. I'm a mess.'

That much was certainly true, Angelo admitted to himself as he eyed her across the table, keeping a firm hold of her hand while he considered what to say next, if he were not to agree with her.

'Give up? This would be a crime against opera. You say that you can only sing when no one is listening, but this is rubbish, complete rubbish! In the restaurant there was not even a whisper when we sang together.'

'Oh for God's sake, that's because they were all listening to you, not me!'

'To me?' said Angelo with astonishment, 'No, my foolish one, to us. Us! Hearing Angelo and Olivia singing as they should always be heard - *together.*'

Olivia almost laughed. Such an Italian, such a tenor - a dangerous combination if you hadn't spent years watching them making a profession out of playing the romantic hero. For heaven's sake, he'd probably lifted that line right out of an opera.

Mistakenly pleased to see her lips flirt with the possibility of a smile, Angelo refused to allow Olivia to disentangle herself from his grasp and went about bestowing a wealth of tender kisses upon her fingers, between words spoken in his most beseeching and infatuated of voices, 'There can be no escape for you, until I have your promise that you will be my Tosca.'

'Oh, you're good,' she smiled, 'Really good!'

'Good? I do not understand.'

'I think you do,' she retorted, feeling herself flush despite her determination not to let that velvet voice and those persuasive lips get the better of her. 'You're wasting your time, I know all about your reputation for being, how shall I say it, persuasive? But it won't work on me, and to be honest, I can't for the life of me think why you're bothering.'

'Reputations are not always deserved and if I believed what you say about your voice then I must have dreamed its beauty. But, I did not and I am bothering because you are meant to sing at my side. To find you in that restaurant was no accident and I tell you again, they were listening to us, not me. So, Fate has given you to me and you have no right to walk away from me now,' he insisted, feeling the sudden racing of her pulse against his lips as he turned her small hand in his and caressed her perfumed wrist. No matter what she had to say, he was on the road to seducing her into continuing as Tosca and, possibly, into his bed.

Olivia was unimpressed by his romanticised talk of Fate and yet, to her great discomfort, found that she had to clear her throat before she could respond.

'Well, maybe you are right, maybe they were all listening to 'us' and not you alone, but what matters is that I thought they weren't listening to me and that's why I could sing.'

Her self-deprecation was incessant and irritating.

'So pretend always that the audience is listening to me,' he suggested flippantly, immediately regretting betraying his impatience as Olivia suddenly snatched her hand away and sat back in her chair, safely out of reach.

'And how am I supposed to achieve that state of denial after the attention Petrov paid to my every note today?' she snapped with frustration. 'And am I really to make myself believe that a theatre full of people, some of whom will have paid over *two hundred pounds* for the pleasure of hearing *Tosca*, aren't actually going to pay any attention to the soprano singing the role?'

Now Angelo too retreated back into his chair to regroup. Playing *dashing romantic hero to the rescue* wasn't working. Clearly he had underestimated the obstacles in his path, the issues being more complex than the jitters that inevitably accompanied an inexperienced singer's inaugural clash with Sasha. Perhaps, he reflected as he sipped his espresso, if she really did find it impossible to perform under pressure - and she was quite convincing in her assertion of that fact - it would be wiser to admit defeat now. But even *she* had conceded that once upon a time she had had the potential to deserve her place as Tosca today.

If things had gone differently...

What things? he wondered.

It seemed inconceivable that so lovely a woman, in possession of a voice to match, could be reduced to this state. She certainly appeared ready to admit defeat but, even as he saw that right now she wasn't capable of getting her cup back onto its saucer let alone singing an opera, Angelo's thoughts could not help but return to the early moments of the rehearsal when her voice had resonated about the studio until the air itself seemed alive with it, making a mockery of the many complaints the House got from singers such as himself when they had to rehearse in the room's voice-crushingly dry acoustics. There had been nothing short of terror on her face when he'd spied her at the door, yet she had pulled herself together and sung. Deny it all she liked, Olivia did have it in her to conquer her fear and Angelo, ever one to fall for that enticing blend of beauty, talent and vulnerability, would just have to approach the battlements from another angle.

'I am sorry,' he said, in such a way as to somehow imply that he recognised himself to be the lowest of the low, as crass and insensitive a man as had ever walked the earth.

Olivia immediately felt guilty for having been so ungracious in response to his encouragement.

'No, no,' she replied, 'I know that you are only trying to help me and it's truly appreciated. Really, it is.'

'But... I should leave you to be. Of course I must, Olivia. You are right to distrust me. I have been selfish beyond belief - thinking only of the difficulty I will now have to face with Petrov. I am an Italian man, always too proud. I know it and I am sorry to think so little of your feelings. Can you forgive me?'

'You're the last person who should be apologising,' sighed Olivia.

'Then we can agree that neither of us have anything to apologise for and let us forget all about it. There is so much more to life than opera and all its hideous sides, so many other things for us to speak of. Let me order you another coffee.'

With Angelo now apparently agreeable to her breaking her contract, Olivia had been planning to make a swift exit, but his tone was so reassuring, so coaxing that she could not find the words to facilitate her escape. How could she refuse the invitation when he had been so gracious about the humiliation she had caused him, not once making her feel that he agreed with her own assessment of her performance? She wasn't fooled though. This was an act of incredible generosity on his part, given what she had heard of his egocentric attitude and, not surprisingly, there was something very flattering about that.

'And, of course, you must try one of the delicious cakes.'

'Oh, I couldn't possibly,' she said, casting a fearful eye over the vast array of gateaux, pastries and flans in the glass-fronted cabinet under a marble counter that ran practically the length of the cafe.

'But Pierre will be very hurt if you do not, won't you?' he directed to the proprietor who was busy putting a shine on his display of deco coffee pots.

'*Mais oui*. Of course!'

'And I will be very fat if I do.'

'You, fat?! Surely you cannot tell me that you are on a diet?' said Angelo with pleasing incredulity.

Her smile of confirmation brought that engaging laugh from him that she had so often seen burst forth to dazzling effect when he was interviewed on TV. He really was very handsome, she thought. She liked the boyishness that his tightly curled black hair gave him despite his forty-something years, for it was more than balanced by a physique made powerful by years of training and a dangerous smoulder in his heavily lashed eyes. No wonder every time he performed it was impossible to get within fifty feet of a stage door - there were always so many women anxiously awaiting his appearance, that the average passer-by might be forgiven for thinking there was some famous rock star in the vicinity. Some had even been known to faint at his feet, though nothing had come close to as amusing as the infamous occasion when Angelo had appeared on *This Afternoon* and turned his charm upon Gina with such impact as to leave her virtually panting with desire when he sang the show out, in turn causing the producer to have to physically remove her husband and co-host, John, from the set. The tension that ensued had rendered the show unwatchable for over a week and it had taken nothing less than a six-strong, fawning girl-band to restore John's good humour.

At the time, Olivia and Calliope had thought Gina rather a pathetic specimen for responding to the slathering of flattery Angelo had given her, but sitting here with him at such close proximity (he had already managed to shift from opposite to next to her without her perceiving the move) she was beginning to sympathise with Gina and see just why old John had felt so threatened. She knew he was turning on the charm and supposed that if she were a fly on the wall she might find it all rather ludicrous and amusing, yet it felt really good to have him pay all this very public attention to her. Even now, noticed Olivia with satisfaction, there were a few faces pressed to the cafe window for a peek at him. She was no stranger to this kind of attention; it happened all the time when she was out with Calli, but it felt gratifyingly different to be seen with a gorgeous man, enhanced rather than diminished by the association.

'Finally a real smile,' said Angelo, 'and it is as beautiful as the rest of you. Tell me, what are you thinking about?'

'I was thinking that, for a man who supposedly doesn't deserve his reputation, you're doing a bloody good job of living up to it.'

'Ah, it is the tragedy of my life, this reputation of mine. To be a famous tenor, you must not only have the voice but also the character for the opera houses and the record companies to sell. Why is it that the public do not believe everything they read in *The Sun* or *OK!*, but if it is printed in *Classical Music*, then it must be the truth? And now, it has come to this - you are a beautiful woman but I cannot say it without being accused of lying.'

'So what else have they made up for you?' asked Olivia, intrigued and, dare she admit it, just a little hopeful that he might genuinely find her attractive?

'Maybe everything. Sometimes it is hard for Angelo to know what is truth after all these years. Perhaps I am not even Italian.'

'I hardly think that's likely!'

'No, you are right, I am Italian through and through. You only have to meet my darling mother to know it, and to know, dear Olivia, that you do not need to diet - my mother, she is as round as this table!'

'That's not a very nice thing to say about your mother.'

'You are right again, but then it is true and she would not deny it. I think Mama is quite pleased with herself. In my village it is normal to become tremendous as soon as you are a wife and a mother. There is no shame, no loss of beauty, and maybe even some pride - it is a sign that there is plenty of good food and many children in the house, something we Italian men value highly. If you ask an Italian man what he considers most important in his life, he will tell you this: family, food and sex. We have our priorities right, I think!'

Maybe, thought Olivia, but she knew from bitter experience that if looked at the wrong way, those same priorities could for some people be anything but right. Whatever, she still laughed, agreed with him and tried not to visibly flinch when the waiter placed a huge slice of chocolate tart down next to her coffee, which she should also have been refusing on the grounds that it was certainly made with full fat milk.

'So, where exactly are you from?' she asked, idly trailing her spoon back and forth through the dreaded froth. 'You mentioned a village just now. I always thought you were from one of the big cities - Rome or perhaps Milan.'

'You see, so much is fiction. What is it they say about me? That I was discovered singing in my father's pizzeria in Milan, I think. With no training, a simple waiter became an international star. A wonderful story.'

'But not true?'

'Not one word. I am from Tuscany. I grew up in a small village just outside Lucca, playing football with my five brothers and dreaming of playing for Italy in the World Cup one day. Yes,' he said with reverence, 'now I think about it, I should say that football comes very close to being as important as sex is to the Italian male!'

'Five brothers?! What a life your mother must have had with all of you playing football and no washing machine, I bet.'

'Or girls to help her. She is still waiting for me to find the right woman and add the daughter she always wanted to our family,' he said meaningfully.

'So what went wrong?' asked Olivia swiftly, 'Why aren't you striking goals for a living?'

'I couldn't kick a football, as you say, to save my life! That is the truth. It is the greatest disappointment in my life. Without my voice, I would have been finished in here, no use to anyone,' he said, placing his hand somewhat dramatically over his heart, though the words were spoken with sincerity.

'And how did you come to find your voice? Football to opera seems a rather big leap.'

'No, not really. You know, opera is seen quite differently in Italy. Of course, there is La Scala which, like that place,' he said gesturing dismissively in the general direction of the Royal Opera House, 'is all about money, but elsewhere you will find no sign of this elitism that comes to the profession in other countries. In Italy, ordinary families take baskets of food, bottles of Chianti and every one of their screaming *bambinos* and go to the opera festivals. My family would make the pilgrimage to the festival in Florence every year. Do you know it?'

'Of course, I spent a few months in Florence some summers ago, studying Italian.'

'So, I must apologise for my patronising words. You understand then - the atmosphere is fantastic - not really so different from watching a football match. Yes?'

'Well, I can't actually say I've ever been to a football match,' admitted Olivia sheepishly.

'Never been to a football match?! No! Really? Then I will have to take you to Italy as soon as *Tosca* is over with.'

Olivia could not help feeling pleased that Angelo didn't seem to see her withdrawal from *Tosca* as necessarily meaning the end of their acquaintance. Angelo could not help feeling pleased that he'd been able to mention the opera without her turning into a quivering wreck.

'OK,' she responded, more enthusiastically than she had intended. Realising it, and not wanting to sound too desperate, she quickly steered the conversation back to Angelo's voice, 'but don't think you're going to stop me finding out the truth behind Angelo Verasano's pizzeria discovery by getting me onto the subject of football. This is a much better story than the one they print in the programme notes. So tell me, how did you get from football to opera?'

'Simple! I realised that what I wanted more than to score a goal, was to hear the crowd cheering as I did it. In Florence I hear the crowd roar for a good top 'G' as loudly as if Italy had won the World Cup and so I decided to try that instead.'

'So, here you are. And what about your father's pizzeria?'

'My father grew courgettes and tomatoes on a hillside, my mother made lace. Nothing more. They worked hard, and my brothers did without so that I could go to Milan and learn my trade. My success story was not anything like the miraculous stories my press cuttings tell; there was no immaculate conception. It took years of learning, just as it should. Oh, it is true that I sang in a pizzeria in Milan, but that was to help pay for my tuition... and I needed it! I was lucky to find that my vocal chords had the natural talent that my feet missed, but it took many years for me to mature and begin to understand that this was not enough, that if the music is not in the heart, then there will be no fans to roar when you hit the high notes. Only when I understood that the music must be more important than my *self*, did I get discovered - and not in a pizzeria, but auditioning at La Scala.

'So, now I can repay my family for all they have sacrificed for my voice. But, even though I could now give him that pizzeria and fill it with opera enthusiasts, my father, he is still happy to grow his tomatoes and courgettes and my mother still sits in the village square making lace with her friends and talking about the terrible things the gossip columns have to say about her little Angelo.'

'And your brothers?'

'They,' Angelo said with a resigned chuckle, 'like to drive red sports cars, wear Armani suits and remind me of what they did without, if I complain! And you Olivia, what is your history?'

Olivia was taken aback. Angelo Verasano was not noted for being interested in much other than himself, but she could hardly lay much store by what the press had to say about him after what she had just heard both in the substance of his story and the warm, sincere tone with which he had relayed it. No, they'd hardly painted a very accurate picture of him if she were to believe the famed lothario to be deserving of her softened mood. And she must believe it, she concluded with surprise at her foolhardiness as she found herself responding when good sense and her customary reserve might otherwise have led her to ask for the bill.

'What do you want to know?'

Now *there* was a question, thought Angelo, but he declined to use it to its full potential for the present.

'No more than I have told you.'

'Well, I grew up here in London. Nowhere near as picturesque as a Tuscan village, I'm afraid. A very boring, middle-class, suburban life is what I had. No opera festivals and definitely no Chianti, though we did occasionally get dragged over to Kenwood House for the summer lakeside fireworks concerts, but you know England, rain cancelled play more often than not.'

'We?'

'We? Oh, I see. Me, my sister and... well there was my brother Michael, but he was killed by a drunk driver when he was just seven - he was riding his bike up and down outside our house when a car mounted the pavement. And that was it, gone forever.'

Olivia saw that he was shocked, perhaps more by the almost matter of fact way she had said it than the actual fact itself, and didn't know what to say.

'I'm sorry,' she said, 'It's such a long time ago now and I've had to tell the story so many times over the years. In the end you can't let yourself keep feeling the pain, though I still miss him. He had a great personality - he would have been a great man - you know, the really important things - generous, thoughtful, honourable.'

'To hear you speak of him, I can honestly say that I now feel his loss too; there are very few good men in the world. They are not as deserving maybe, but it is only when I hear a story such as that, that I can know how lucky I am to have my brothers. Were you there when it happened?' he ventured gently, hopefully.

'No, I wasn't. I was at my singing lesson when it happened.'

Angelo had to bite his tongue to prevent himself exclaiming 'Ah, ha!' in a Holmesian fashion, he having been wondering if this traumatic event was the significant factor preventing her from using that voice of hers. And yet, when the possibility seemed to have been confirmed, he immediately doubted the validity of his theory, knowing that it was highly unlikely that she would reveal herself so early in his interrogation - women were never that simple. Still, he was willing to give the idea a go.

'How old were you then?'

'I'm the middle one. My sister was twelve and I was ten.'

'That must have been very difficult for you; you must have blamed yourself for not being there. It must have affected your singing.'

'No, it was my sister who really suffered; she was in the house and I think she's never forgiven herself for not taking care of Michael. I had an excuse; there was no opportunity for me to save him.'

Oh well, thought Angelo, he was not done for yet.

'A true tragedy - sometimes, when our work is all about making one ridiculous tragedy after another believable to an audience, we forget that in the world outside our opera houses the disasters are very real and no less heartbreaking for their... how do you say *semplicità?*'

'Simplicity,' she offered, surprised at this philosophical side to Angelo, little knowing that much of his 'wisdom' could be gathered under the banner *Things talk show hosts and their guests have said on just about any subject*. Angelo had passed many a hotel-bound afternoon on tour watching and learning.

'Thank you, my English often fails me.'

'If only my Italian were as good as your English,' sighed Olivia.

'This afternoon, it was so perfect I could believe you are Italian,' flattered Angelo and then seeing her eyes dart off, gleaned that his return to the subject of the rehearsal was pre-emptive, followed quickly on, 'I am only happy to know that it was your lovely voice that saved you from the same sadness that your sister lives with. It is a truly wonderful gift. Did you know always that you were destined for life as a singer, or was football also your first love?'

'Well, ask my father, and he'd say I was singing from birth but, in fact, if it weren't for Julie Andrews in *The Sound of Music*, I doubt it would ever have entered my head to sing. I was just your average little girl who wanted to be a ballet dancer, but unfortunately, even then I was built like an opera singer. I just didn't belong in a tutu and the girls at my convent school made sure I knew it. It's amazing how cruel good little Catholics can be. Anyway, I was miserable and I just didn't fit in. Then I saw that daft film and it changed everything. My silly head was immediately filled with dreams of miraculously becoming acceptable, lovable and, of course, pretty enough to get the handsome man, just by singing. My poor parents had no choice but to give me singing lessons though it was, of course, far too early to be of much relevance - I think they were just grateful to see me so happy about something. It only dawned on me that I could actually sing when I got my place at the Royal Academy of Music - that part of my dream world, at least, was a reality.'

'And much more, I think,' said Angelo, 'Even without your voice you would be both beautiful and charming, and yet you sound so disappointed when you speak of your childhood dreams. Why is that, I wonder? Is it perhaps the handsome man? I see there is no wedding ring on your finger - I am surprised that you have not been claimed before now. Are you surprised too, maybe? Was that the most important part of your dream, Olivia? Is there something more your heart needs than the music?'

How had he got from Julie Andrews to that?

'This silence is very loud, Olivia. I think I have my answer. No?'

'No... well maybe,' she found herself uttering, despite herself.

'But with your beauty, I cannot believe there has been no-one in your life.'

'Oh for heaven's sake, stop telling me I'm beautiful,' she snapped, more out of self-preservation than true irritation.

'I had wished that you would learn something about Angelo this afternoon - you can believe in this man who is sitting here with you now. It is not that other man they photograph and write about in the magazines, but *I* who am Angelo Verasano. And, however you complain, I will say what I wish. You are beautiful - so there! And now tell me who was the man who made you doubt what I see?'

'A musician.'

'Why am I not surprised that it would be a *musician* to do such a thing?' he said, having about as low an estimation of that beer-swilling bunch of philistines as they did of him, 'And what did this 'musician' play?'

'He's a percussionist.'

Suddenly, Angelo recalled the sound of a cymbal crashing to the floor as Olivia entered the studio, saw her resolve crumble at every burst of raucous laughter from the back of the orchestra, felt the thrill of discovery. Now this was something he could understand and work with. The one who had left her in this state was in the orchestra and she was still in love with him. To make her forget this percussionist, to make her sing again. Nothing could have appealed more to Angelo's

103

romanticism, or his narcissism. That she had shared this much with him was enough to convince Angelo that he could do it.

Outside the patisserie the majority of passers-by were heading wearily in the direction of the station, burdened with shopping bags, sunglasses occasionally reflecting the burnt umber sun as it sank between buildings in a yellowing end of day sky. Only persuade Olivia to share one more coffee with him and the path to a candlelit dinner for two would be at their feet. And, if he could charm her into that, then it was certain Olivia would be succumbing to a lot more than singing *Tosca*.

- chapter six -

'*Love* that dress!' thrilled Dominic as Calli came towards him up the sweeping staircase, her every curve visible through a clinging gown of beaded black lace.

'*Love* the escort,' purred Calli, catching sight of a dashing young man who was casting possessive glances towards her friend from within the Crush Bar.

'Hungarian. One of those dressage horsemen.'

'Handy with a whip then, you lucky boy! Really darling, where do you find them?'

'Tell *you*, the seductress *extrordinaire*? I don't think so,' he laughed and motioned to his Hungarian stallion to procure an extra glass of champagne. 'So, how's she doing?'

Calli gave him a puzzled look and then, well timed, the penny dropped, 'Oh, you mean Olivia. I really don't know. It's been days since we last spoke. I tried calling, but she's not replied to my messages.'

'How very rude.'

'Not at all. She's been busy, what with costume fittings, publicity shoots and stage rehearsals. You know how it is.'

He did. But that was not how it was with Olivia. Of course Olivia hadn't been in this situation before, but it didn't sound right nonetheless. Olivia, suddenly stop calling her best friend, when for year upon year there had been numerous occasions when Calli's behaviour might justifiably have caused her do so and yet had not? Perhaps, for the first time since he'd known her, he heard hurt in Calli's voice. It was strangely shocking to Dominic, so incongruous was it with the picture of invulnerability before him.

'Come on, admit it, I can tell you're fed up with her. At a time like this, I'd expect her to be round at your place every night looking for some reassurance and encouragement. Did you argue?' he asked.

'Certainly not.'

Dominic just looked at her then, waiting patiently until Calli gave in and let out a miserable sigh.

'No, we didn't argue. It's just the oldest story in the book - where there's trouble there's a man.'

'A man?'

'Don't look so surprised, Olivia's no virgin.'

'So who is it? Tell me more.'

'I will not,' she stated, to his immense frustration, but the answer dawned upon him immediately despite her restraint. Who else could cause such a chink in Calli's gleaming armour?

'My God, darling, it's Angelo Verasano, isn't it?' he gasped, completely ignoring his returning Hungarian as if he were just one more anonymous waiter.

'Yes, if you must know. She's been spending a lot of time with him - too much time, if you ask me. To be honest, I'm really worried about her. I think she's actually falling for all that charming crap he dishes out.'

'No! Surely she knows better than to get caught out like that.'

'Well, you'd think so, wouldn't you? I mean, you only have to look to the chorus of the Royal Opera for about forty reasons why not to trust the man, but it's as if he's cast a spell over her. I've tried talking to her, reminding her of all the times we've nearly died laughing over the list of our rivals who've added their scalps to his belt, but she just gets all bent out of shape and defends the little bastard. *You don't know him,* she says, *that's all lies from the publicity department,* she says.'

'The publicity department wishes!' laughed Dominic. 'They'd be over the moon to have that kind of creativity - it's all they can do to put out a release with all the names spelled correctly.'

'This isn't a laughing matter Dominic. Olivia's going to get hurt if she doesn't snap out of this soon.'

'Do you think she's sleeping with him?'

'I don't think so - Angelo's not known for sticking around once he's got his end away. As I've heard nothing from her in the last couple of days, I assume she's still adrift in a pink haze of stupid infatuation and he's not charmed her into bed so far. But, it can only be a matter of time and Christ knows what will happen then.'

'She's really that far gone?'

'Completely brainwashed; all memory of his reputation wiped away.'

'Do you think this is a reaction to Guy being in the band?'

'Of course it is. It's pure denial if I ever saw it and when Angelo lives up to his notoriety, there will be Guy MacLaren and all the attendant memories staring up at her from the pit. Then the shit'll really hit the fan.'

'And you say you've tried to talk some sense into her?' asked Dominic, unable to rid himself of the suspicion that Calli had done no such thing. He had guessed full well the emotions that had lead Calli to tell Olivia of Guy's presence in the orchestra the other day - in her position he might well have done the same. But now, with Angelo on the scene... well, if that vile charmer could keep up his charade long enough, there was every chance that Olivia would sing well tonight.

'Yes I have. But frankly, if the fact that he's screwed every soprano in the business plus a few of his own ilk doesn't ring some alarm bells, then nothing I can say will make a difference.'

On the other hand, mused Dominic, the very opposite could be the case - to date, Calli hadn't got between the sheets with Senor Verasano, so perhaps the jealousy he could hear in her voice came in the oldest form in the book. In which case she would hardly be likely to allow herself to be outdone.

It all amounted to the same thing in the end though - with or without Calli's help, Angelo would no doubt run true to form and then, as Calli had said, the shit would really hit the fan. Poor Olivia, he thought as the bell for the first act rang and they took their seats in the Dress Circle. The best he could hope for her was that for tonight, at least, Olivia would be granted her moment of transcendent denial and supreme success.

'Peter, will you *please* sit still. You're making me nervous. Here, look at the programme,' Olivia's mother urged her husband.

'You'd think that you'd at least get a comfortable seat for your hundred quid,' he griped in response, gloriously unaware of the surprised looks his comment had raised from those around them in the Stalls, as he tried to manoeuvre his long legs, which had become painfully wedged against the seats in front. 'It's like flying economy class. When do you think they'll be around with the dry roasted peanuts?'

'Oh really dad,' hissed Katriona as her children giggled and her husband visibly flinched at the mention of the vast sums of money it was costing the family to be here tonight. It seemed wholly unfair that the Opera House had not considered Olivia worthy even of a couple of complimentary tickets or invitations to the after-performance party for her guests. Katriona thought ruefully of the credit card bill that was to come and what Patrick might have to say when he discovered that the tickets had in fact cost a *lot* more than the hundred pounds a head she and mum had admitted to.

Not that either Patrick or her father would have missed this for the world, but they might perhaps have thought better of bringing the children along too, especially as the unspoken fear that Olivia might be overcome by nerves stalked the back of their minds. But Katriona could only countenance the thought that this evening would bring Olivia out of her exile and that to look back on this night and know that the kids had missed such a momentous occasion, just for the sake of money, would be terribly sad. Of course, with fidgety Michael kicking at the chair in front of him and the girls complaining that the collars on the dresses they'd been bought especially for the event were itching their necks, Katriona was shrinking under intolerant glances into her less than comfy seat and doubting her sanity.

Little Aidan was the only one of them who seemed content with his lot. He could not fathom every word within, but was enthralled by the satisfyingly weighty programme he'd been given; its shiny red cover, embossed with the royal crest, just begged to have small hands run over its glorious smoothness time and time again, and inside there were reproductions of the set designs and even photographs of his Auntie Olivia rehearsing. When the novelty of that had worn off he had used his big, doleful eyes to wring a pound out of his grandmother and then liberated a pair of opera glasses from its holder in order to gaze about the theatre in blissful wonder. What a thrill to focus on the lights that ringed the Grand Circle and find, at the centre of each pair, the naked torso of a beautiful alabaster girl with flowing locks - at home, the appearance of bare breasts on the TV sent his mother diving for the remote control, at the Tate he was discouraged from staring too long at Rodin's *Kiss* and yet here, with the rest of his clan so fraught with nerves, he was left to peruse unhindered. Above these lovely lights, sat lavishly dressed women chatting to partners in evening dress, diamond-laden hands resting on red velvet, often clutching a fan or a fine-stemmed champagne glass. The expectant hum with which these people filled the already hot, stagnant air, had Aidan on the edge of his seat with excitement. To think that all these important people were here just to see his Auntie Olivia sing. When would they get started? he wondered, scanning his little red binoculars quickly from the huge crystal chandelier that unnervingly hung directly above him, to the vast scarlet curtains in hopes of a twitching sign that the lights might soon dim.

Nothing. And so he begged to be allowed to go and have a look at the orchestra. He took the lack of acknowledgment of his request from his anxiously twittering family as an OK, they not even noticing his escape when an audible trail followed him as he used the line of evening shoes that marked the path to the aisle as if they were stepping stones.

Cute kid, thought Guy, winking at the little tike whose chin rested atop the pit wall as he struggled to focus a pair of opera glasses on him. Must be about six or seven - just about the age... best not to think about that, tonight of all nights, Guy decided and contorted his face into a series of apparently hysterical characters for the little boy's entertainment.

'I'd say *careful or you might get stuck like that*,' sniped a sarcastic violist, 'but really it'd be an improvement.'

'Thanks Fran, you're such a good sport. I never thought I'd get such a *Frantastic* critique of my impression of you!' returned Guy with the prerequisite punchline *ba-dom-bom* on the side drum. 'So Fran, come the revolution, who's going to be the first against the wall - the violist or the conductor?'

'I don't know, do tell me,' she replied with a resigned sigh of disapproval, which was supposed to camouflage the all-consuming crush she had on the arrogant bastard.

'The conductor,' he laughed, 'because it's *always* business before pleasure!'

'Oh ha bloody ha,' she returned, pleased that he had spoken to her at all. Perhaps the little backless number she'd invested in would pay off at tonight's party.

He should have stayed in the pub with the lads, thought Guy. There really wasn't anything to do here but wind up Fran and he could see the signs of interest in her manner and really didn't want to go down that road - she was just too, too... well, too unlike Olivia.

Shit! he thought and then, when heads turned, realised he'd said it out loud, and so fiercely it had been at considerably more than a whisper.

Olivia had been on his mind as consistently as sex normally was - basically ever since that first rehearsal. No matter how much he fought off thoughts of her with memories of all the things that he despised in her, he could not escape the image of her contented smile as she slumbered beside him, the self-effacing way she dropped her eyes from his even as she was persuaded to sing to him, the silent tears that had met his final rejection of her some six or so years earlier. She'd been avoiding him, he knew it.

He knew it because he had unaccountably found himself walking corridors he'd no reason to be in, reading the newspaper from cover to cover by the stage door, and even risking his good name by being seen to turn down the pub in favour of the House canteen, and all for a chance to have their eyes meet and see what there was to see, see what was really left of 'them' now. But not once had their paths crossed, save for the several occasions he had glimpsed her from the upstairs bar at the Marquess of Anglesey, going into the little café across the street on the arm of Angelo Verasano, the pair of them seemingly always sharing a private joke that had their laughing heads leant together in happy collusion.

'Arsehole.'

Despite the growing numbers in the pit - all tuning noisily to their own version of an 'A' ahead of the oboeist's intervention - everyone turned to eye Guy again.

What on earth was wrong with him? Guy asked of himself, feeling seized with an almost overwhelming desire to send every cymbal, tubular bell, snare drum, triangle and tambourine flying across the pit. Why did he feel so fucking regretful all of a sudden when he had sweet, scatty, straightforward nurse Emma cooking a meal for him back at her flat tonight? There were no complications there; night duty to save them from getting into the habit of always sleeping together, guilt-free sex without strings attached - unless they were in the mood for them - and no questions asked when he'd been off on tour or she'd gone to a Christmas party with some rich surgeon. Emma was everything a man might dream of. His friends were jealous and until now he had been more than happy to believe they should be. But the dress rehearsal had shocked him.

That first unqualified disaster that had masqueraded as a rehearsal had left Guy swaying between a sense of guilt for possibly having been the one to destroy Olivia's voice, and a triumphant feeling of pleasure at hearing that he had been right to accuse her of murdering their child for no reason whatsoever. But yesterday he had heard a different Olivia, a soprano with a voice that was neither destroyed nor worth silencing for him. She had not caved under the continuing pressure from Sasha, nor failed to recover after making a mistake - and there had been many. OK, so she'd not been Renée Fleming or Montserrat Caballé, but neither had she been an embarrassment to listen to. There was potential there and it angered Guy to hear it because every time she got it right, he was back in the Marquess of Anglesey watching her share an umbrella with Angelo, allowing Angelo to carry her bags, smiling as Angelo kissed her cheeks in that irritating continental fashion.

He wanted her to screw up, Guy realised, and if she didn't, he wanted it to be because of him, not that horrendous cocktail of styling gel and aftershave. The thought of what might be happening in her dressing room, right this minute, caused him to stand up suddenly to leave the pit, unfortunately forgetting that the stage was just above his head.

'Fuck, fuck, *fuck*,' he exclaimed through his pain, the laughter of his section just sneaking in as darkness fell upon the audience, and the ripple of applause that accompanied Sasha Petrov onto the rostrum.

Olivia felt a prickle in the back of her neck as the general orchestral uproar that was relayed through a crackling speaker in her cramped, subterranean dressing room, suddenly fell away to expose the oboe sounding the 'A'. The familiar shaking of her legs greeted its plaintive call to arms before the ringing in her ears crescendoed to take its place and deafen her to the world outside her own fear-filled reality.

She had made so many errors during the dress rehearsal that there had not been hours enough for her to hear all the stage manager's notes, let alone those of director and, naturally, Sasha. Even the wig master had been none too pleased by her efforts. The large paste and glass encrusted rings she was wearing had got caught up in her hair during a particularly harrowing scene for Tosca and they'd had to stop the rehearsal to extricate them, or face Olivia completing the opera with her hands on her head. The stagehand who'd come to her assistance left her in a right mess, with bits of hair flapping about like a bald man's comb-over caught in the wind. The only saving grace of the whole afternoon was that it was not he, but Peggy from wardrobe, who'd rushed to her aid when her boobs had come close to popping out of her dress a little later.

Everything was in its place now though. She barely recognised herself. Floria Tosca had cascading dark hair adorned at the back with a fine lace veil, her eyelashes were so heavy that Olivia could hardly keep her eyes open, her lips were ruby red, her nails long, her breasts lifted and pushed together, as if to mock the crucifix that nestled there, in a pale blue Napoleonic style dress with a plunging square neckline, from just under which flared the skirt into a small train behind her. The woman staring out at her from the mirror might have been Calliope observed Olivia with a wry smile, but *she* wouldn't be holding onto the dressing table as if it were a life-raft, now would she?

Only now did it strike Olivia that Calli had not been backstage to see her. She was surprised, less by the fact that Calli hadn't come backstage, than by the realisation that she herself hadn't noticed till now. Under normal circumstances she would have been in desperate need of her friend's help, but tonight she was glad that Calli had stayed away. Not that she couldn't have used her when her agent had *Just dropped in to wish you good luck,* which roughly translated into *Just dropped in to check that you've not been at the fags and booze.* But then, she wouldn't have been alone when Angelo came to her bearing three dozen red roses and a bottle of champagne which he had said, in just about the sexiest of tones she'd ever heard, that they would share together later - in private.

Every time she'd spoken to Calli over this rehearsal period, she'd had to listen to a list of Angelo Verasano's faults and warning after warning about the disaster that would surely befall her if she fell under his spell. Olivia was sick of hearing it, tired of defending Angelo. But, if she had to, she would defend him to the ends of the earth because though she was petrified of making an arse of herself out on stage tonight, still not being convinced of the merits Angelo attributed to her voice, she had not *ever* in her life felt as beautiful as she did when she was with him. For the first time in years she was looking in a mirror and seeing herself as shapely rather than obese.

For as long as she could remember, she had thought to her first night with a new man with dread, always allowing the fear that revulsion would flicker across his face when he saw her naked to steal away any pleasure, and sometimes to even cause her to break off an affair before she had to face the possibility of sex. Yet there was no denying the yearning she now had to make love with Angelo. Olivia touched the petals of one velvet bloom to her lips and felt the nervous twinges in her back swept away by a wave of tingling expectation surging up and down her spine.

'You're still here? Oh my God, we'll have hellfire raining down on us if you don't get your arse stage-left this minute,' stammered the out-of-breath assistant stage-manager as he burst into the room, 'Petrov told Randy not to give the green light till he's seen you in the wings - seems to think you're about to make a break for it. Anyway, the orchestra's tuned *three* times already, the audience is getting restless, management are worried they're going to get stuck with a massive overtime bill and our Petrov's about to blow a bloody fuse, so hurry. For God's sake, hurry up! *Please.*'

- chapter seven -

Nothing could be more satisfying than the throb of almighty power that coursed through Alexander Petrov as he swept his baton upwards and its decisive downbeat brought forth an orgasm of sound from the brass section. A dark, menacing fanfare that built defiantly upon seemingly insurmountable volume to a climax that had Guy bring together the gleaming steel of a vast, heavy pair of cymbals before raising them away from his chest, opening out their vibrating surfaces to send the sound shimmering into the auditorium.

Now the rest of the orchestra joined them in a swiftly descending scale that diminished till only the clarinets and bassoons remained as the curtains pulled back into the wings, releasing a heady scent of incense into the air as the interior of a magnificent Italian church, the church of *Sant'Andrea della Valle*, was revealed in all its grandeur. The pews were empty but there were obviously plenty of worshippers – a multitude of candles burned to the honour of the saints and angels whose statues nestled in shadowy alcoves. To the left, with an ornate iron gate across its entrance was the Attavanti family chapel, to the right a scaffold towered high where an artist had been at work, the massive painting now draped in white cloth and flanked by awesome marble pillars that launched towards a vaulted roof. And to the rear, in perfect perspective, more columns buttressed huge, gothic stained-glass windows through which came fans of light, their dusty iridescence seeming so like the reality of sunlight pouring in through the roof of the House, as to immediately draw the audience into this world created by carpenters, painters, electricians and make it more real than the seats they were sitting in.

Little Aidan let his much-prized opera glasses drop to the floor with a gasp of astonishment. Opulent though the Opera House was, his surroundings had not prepared him for the splendour that had awaited behind the teasing curtain. There was no need for binoculars; the scene seemed to expand far beyond its confines, disappearing into the distance, reaching forwards to pull him in, as deceptive as Doctor Who's police box. There was only a fleeting moment of impatient wondering as to when his Auntie Olivia might appear, before he was sucked into the plot as the shadowy figure of the escaped prisoner Angelotti darted nervously on stage and went about his desperate search for the key that his sister, the Marchesa Attavanti, had left hidden for him. His voice trembled as he sang, his eyes looked constantly for his pursuers, taking Aidan to the edge of his seat to sigh with audible relief as, just in time to avoid being seen by the elderly sacristan (there to prepare the church for the service) Angelotti gained entry into the family chapel.

Now the aged sacristan was confused. He could have sworn that he'd heard Cavaradossi return and yet, he noted a little ruefully, the artist's basket of food remained untouched. For a second it looked as though the sacristan might actually be tempted to steal some of its contents but instead he knelt to sing the *Angelus*. And just as well, because almost immediately Cavaradossi appeared out of the shadows.

A glimpse of the great Angelo Verasano, and the audience burst instantaneously into applause, thoroughly ruining the ambiance and drowning out both sacristan and orchestra.

'Jesus, is the opera over already?' muttered Guy, always incensed by this disruptive display of hero-worship at the expense of every other poor sod who was performing their heart out for this bunch of plebs. Still, it could be worse - when the Royal Ballet was on, the bastards usually talked over the music if there wasn't a dancer on stage to hold their limited attention. Not surprising, with companies buying up blocks of tickets and handing them out to clients who'd have much preferred a day at the races. *Classic FM* might have popularised opera, but the true devotees couldn't afford a ticket and, for those who just thought that opera was what one should like, having to sit through bloody hours of nonsense before they got to hear *Nessun Dorma*, had to be a bit of a shock. Guy often thought the audience applauded before the event, for fear that they might not be awake to do it at the end.

Angelo, meanwhile, was basking in the adoration and feeling moved to reflect it back in his performance tonight. And more so, because he'd just left Olivia in the wings, that shadowy no-man's land between fact and fiction where everything seemed possible. There had never been a leading lady he hadn't fallen for and this woman was only an exception in that the hot ember of desire she'd set smouldering in his gut had yet to be fanned into the all-consuming fire that would inevitably mean its extinction. As Cavaradossi looked upon his painting of the Madonna, whose features he was supposed to have taken from the Marchesa Attavanti on her secret visit to leave the key for her brother, the taste of Olivia's lipstick lingered with him, the besotted gleam of her eyes as they'd looked up into his haunted him, and suddenly the great aria found its truest expression. Cavaradossi sang of the magical way in which art could blend the diverse beauty of the Marchesa Attavanti and Tosca, and Angelo thought of Olivia; with her blonde hair and dark eyes, she was indeed the personification of these two characters.

...ma nel ritrar costei, il mio solo pensier, Tosca tu sei! - but while I paint her, my only thought, Tosca, is of you!

Until now, Olivia had been incapable of picturing herself out on the stage singing - she would surely find herself facing a thousand dinner jackets in silence, if by any chance she could even overcome the fear that had been threatening to freeze her to the spot, unable to move an inch out of the womb-like security of the wings. And yet, as she listened to Angelo sing, the words given life with more meaningfulness than she had heard in any performance previously, it was as if he were saying that while he was 'painting' Tosca with Puccini's music, his only thoughts were of Olivia, telling her that she was the only woman for him. A tingle of excitement spread through her as an overriding desire to be at his side took hold of her and told her that enough fortitude to get out there and go for it might well be lurking within her, if only she had the courage to look.

She was visibly shaking as the sacristan left the stage and with a sympathetic wink, told her to break a vocal chord - he didn't hold out much hope of this poor girl getting through the evening on her feet. Olivia saw him whisper to a stagehand and before she knew it she was handed a glass of water and a paper bag, should she begin to hyperventilate, but she assumed that they expected her to throw up into it and just the thought made that option a possibility. Only moments now to her first entry, as Angelotti revealed himself to his friend Cavaradossi, telling him of his escape from the evil chief of police, Scarpia. Cavaradossi promised him his help to escape and then, from off stage...

Mario!

The collective sigh of relief from Olivia's family did not go unnoticed by the critic who was sitting in the row in front, but he could not comprehend its cause as just that single word sent a shiver of expectation down his cynical old spine and had him yearning to set eyes on this new soprano everyone had been speculating about.

Calli too felt a shiver of expectation as she heard Tosca's voice calling out again and Cavaradossi gave Angelotti his basket of food and ushered him into hiding again, lest the jealous Tosca hear another voice and suspect him of infidelity. So this was it, thought Calliope, Olivia had found her voice at last. She wasn't going to fuck up tonight; it was all there to hear in that opening entry, and when Tosca came on stage and went to Cavaradossi's waiting arms, it was all there to see. So what if she was unheard of and was not met with rapturous applause? It did not matter, because that would never again be the case. Calli rolled the pages of her programme up, one by one as the story of love and betrayal began to unfold.

It was not a difficult task for Olivia to project Tosca's jealousy; she had only to look to the feelings of insecurity in her own past to find her inspiration. No sooner had she gone to Cavaradossi, than she pushed him away and asked suspiciously why the door had been locked, and to whom had he been whispering. Cavaradossi was amused at her active imagination, laughed off her mistrust and tried to kiss her. It was all Olivia could do to stay true to the character, so intense was the memory of the reassuring kiss she had received from Angelo before he went on stage, but Tosca, for all her faults was quite the devout Catholic and so she first took the flowers she was carrying up to the altar and knelt to pray.

However, it was not long before she was cosying up to Cavaradossi, her head upon his shoulder, eyes upturned to his handsome face as she told him that she was singing tonight, but that he should meet her at the stage door after the performance, from whence they could retreat to his country villa.

Angelo received the message loud and clear and smiled to himself as he feigned Cavaradossi's distraction. There was something very enjoyable tonight about making Tosca work for her night of passion. Olivia had not been the easy lay he had hoped for. Interested yes, but clearly more deeply damaged by her musician fellow than he had expected. Now here she was, reaching her hands over his shoulders, running them around his neck and on downwards into his shirt to caress his chest and score his flesh with teasing nails as Cavaradossi sat on a pew, trying to think how to refuse her offer so as to be free to help his friend Angelotti.

Non la sospiri la nostra casseta che tutta ascosa nel verde ci aspetta? nido a noi sacro, ignoto al al mondo inter, pien d'amore e di mister? - Do you not long for our little house, waiting for us, hidden in the trees, that nest sacred to us, unknown to all the world, full of love and mystery?

If Angelo were Cavaradossi, heroics other than of the five times nightly variety couldn't be further from his mind as this Tosca turned her sweet voice around the seductive words with such delicious appeal.

...Ah, piovete voluttà, volte stellate! Arde a Tosca nel sangue il folle amor! - Ah, rain down rapture, ye starry

vaults! In Tosca's blood burns the madness of love! sang Olivia, moving her hands up to cup his face, then turning him to her.

Angelo rose a little out of his seat, unable to resist the temptation to rest his cheek against her breasts and close what he considered to be his masterful arms around her, so that he could almost feel the awakening desire in her pelvis as she was arched against his chest.

Ah! M'avvinci ne' tuoi lacci! Mia sirena, verrò! - Ah! You have caught me in your snare, my siren: I will come! responded Angelo, thinking through his list of romantic retreats for the one best suited to the fair Olivia - oh, if only they were in Italy now; he did indeed have a country villa to his name.

O mio amore! replied Olivia, wondering if her flat in Crouch End could pass for a 'sacred nest' and whether she'd left her underwear strewn about the place or forgotten to sort out the cat's litter tray before coming out. Oh, what the hell!

Now Alexander Petrov's blood was burning with madness as Tosca pulled Cavaradossi into a kiss to set the House on fire. On and on it seemed to stretch, until it struck Sasha that he might actually have to signal an urgent repeat to the orchestra, which was only likely to be followed by half the musicians, if he were lucky and would surely, by some abhorrent miracle, be noted by one of the tone deaf musical philistines in the audience who might do well to call themselves gossip columnists, if they hadn't already knighted themselves opera critics.

The reluctance with which the couple parted lips left no doubt in anyone's mind that Angelo Verasano and Olivia Tarrent were heading to the same bed that night. Her mother felt herself blushing, her father suddenly had the urge to thumb noisily through his programme and Dominic squeezed Calliope's forearm in recognition of her accurate surmisal of the situation.

Calli was, to her shame, relieved when Olivia left the stage after the subsequent scene, which had Tosca getting upset about the resemblance Cavaradossi's painting bore to the Marchesa Attavanti. Calli wanted very much to believe that the tension in the back of her neck was borne out of nerves on her friend's behalf, but Olivia was unshakably resplendent tonight. Tomorrow her voice would be compared with the greatest, she would be daubed *the new Callas* as Calli, despite her success and her agent's best efforts, had never been. And how could she expect Olivia to doubt Angelo's intentions when she, Calliope, felt so convinced of, so seethingly jealous of his passion for her friend? The libretto was as sickly as the very worst romance and yet he made the words sound reasonable when he held Olivia to him.

What eyes on earth can compare with your lustrous black eyes? It is there that my whole being is riveted. Eyes tender in love, fierce in anger, what others on earth can compare with your black ones? Tosca, my adored one, everything about you delights me... My life, my anxious love, I will always say, Floria, I love you!

If she hadn't been with Dominic, whom she knew would guess exactly what was in her mind, Calli would have vacated her seat in favour of a cigarette and a double scotch. Normally, when the likes of Berg and Britten were sent to challenge her musicality, or lack thereof, she'd long for Puccini's accessibility, but tonight his heart-on-sleeve music was more than she could bear. The torture scene to come in Act Two had nothing on what she was suffering and she just wanted the interval to come.

'Yes!' said Olivia triumphantly to herself as she entered the wings and saw Marshall waiting to greet her, his face lit up with admiration.

'Well little lady, you sure as hell showed them. Feels great, don't it?'

'I can't tell you just *how* great,' she smiled, accepting his affectionate hug with immense pride. She was in the wings of one of the greatest opera houses in the world, not just an awed onlooker but a participant in the magic that was weaving its way into the souls of everyone gathered under its roof, Marshall Lincoln Small had his arm around *her* shoulders as he awaited his entry, and Angelo Verasano had just told her in the most romantic way a girl could be told, that he loved her. She needn't pinch herself to make sure it wasn't a dream, because not even in her most delusional of reveries had she come up with anything *this* good.

To prove her point - Cavaradossi having arranged for Angelotti to hide in his villa - Angelo came off stage and sank immediately to his knees in front of her, kissing her hands and praising her till she felt she might burst with emotion. Even the chorus seemed prepared to give her her due and found it in their hearts to bestow a few acknowledging smiles as they gathered for the last scene.

Now the sacristan rushed back onto the stage, almost out of breath with excitement and finding the painter gone, called for the choir to come and hear his good news. From all sides choristers, clerics and novices came rushing in, the less than angelic choir-boys dancing madly around him as he declared that Napoleon Bonaparte had been defeated and that tonight there would be a gala festival in the *Palazzo Farnese*, with Floria Tosca singing a new cantata to celebrate the King's victory. *Doppio soldo... Si festiggi la vittoria!* - Double fees... we'll celebrate the victory! the chorus sang to the amusement of the musicians in the pit below, as the choristers rolled up their music into swords and bounded about the church in mock battle.

Then suddenly the menacing chords that had opened Act One broke into the joyous song and all fell silent, terror-struck as Baron Scarpia appeared, closely followed by his weasel-faced second, Spoletta and his police-agents. Marshall was indeed a fearsome sight, clad in black from head to toe, a floor-length cloak just begging to be lifted with Dracula flair as he swept into the midst of the revellers, sending them fleeing in shame with his condemnation of their unseemly behaviour in this sacred place, before setting the agents to the task of turning the church upside down for evidence of Angelotti's whereabouts. Within moments, all became clear to Scarpia - the Attavanti chapel gate was open, a new key found in its lock and within, an empty food basket and a lady's fan bearing the Attavanti crest was discovered. Not much deduction needed from thence to conclude that Mario Cavaradossi was involved - Cavaradossi being already in Scarpia's bad books for being the lover of the woman he too lusted after.

And here the story took a turn towards its tragic culmination as Floria Tosca came back to tell Mario that thanks to her expected appearance at the victory fiesta, she would not be able to join him at the villa.

As Scarpia taunted Tosca with the Marchesa's fan, using it with the skill of Iago to raise the flames of jealousy, Olivia's mind turned to Guy. Who else could have provided her with so much fuel for this role? Where there was insecurity to find, her thoughts would point to him like a compass finding North. She had guessed that he had been unfaithful long before he had admitted it. How she had cried when she'd seen him with that girl, but how angry had been the denial when she'd challenged him. So angry that she had believed him, so angry that she had cried too for the guilt she felt at having so wrongly accused him, that guilt seeming worse than the suspicion itself. But much later, when he was confident that she loved him enough to forgive him anything, he had confessed his sin, by which time there were no tears left, no recriminations. Just self doubt. Worthlessness.

Where are they? If I could catch these traitors! The villa is the sanctuary for these deceitful love affairs. Oh, my pretty nest defiled with mire! I will surprise them. You shall not have him tonight, I swear it! sang Tosca, raising a threatening hand towards Cavaradossi's painting of the Marchesa before leaving, surreptitiously followed by Spoletta.

Gradually, the stage now began to fill; the choristers filed in carrying lit candles, worshippers filled the pews, soldiers in regalia, priests perfuming the air with incense, the cardinal's procession holding a highly embroidered canopy as he carried the heavy gold crucifix to the altar. Fifty, a hundred, two-hundred extras and members of the chorus took their places, a rich profusion of black, purple and crimson velvet swirling behind Scarpia as the *Te Deum* was sung over the solemn march that rose from the pit along with the chimes of church bells, the dull thud of a bass drum. Many a hair stood on end as Scarpia took the first act to its ominous close, Marshall Lincoln Small's voice somehow crushing all opposition from the huge chorus, forcing its way to the fore, leading towards the tell-tale sounding of those dreadful opening chords once more...

Ah, di quegli occhi vittorï osi veder la fiamma illanguidir con spasimo d'amore! Ah, to see the fire of those proud eyes grow dim in the ecstasy of love! *La doppia preda avrò. L'uno al capestro, l'altra fra le mie braccia* - Twofold will be my prey: one to the gallows, the other in my arms...

* * *

'Someone walk over your grave?' Dominic had quipped, registering Calli's undisguisable shudder as the curtain fell on the first act.

Actually, it was more like she'd just woken up in her coffin, buried alive, thought Calli as Alexander Petrov once more made his way to the podium. She'd abandoned the champagne in favour of something stronger during the interval, but the hoped for dulling of her senses had been elusive. The pain was as keen as ever as Scarpia's apartment at the Farnese Palace was unveiled. The right hand corner was given to Scarpia's monumental desk, an ornate candelabra at its edge illuminating the gold ink-wells, curled quill-pens and sepia documents scattered upon it. Behind the imposing oak chair with its mellow leather upholstery and shiny brass studs, bookcases masked the walls from floor to ceiling. A grand bed jutted diagonally out of the other corner, draped in leopard skin and heavy burgundy silks with gold braid and tassels skirting the floor. To its left a vibrant fire had been set in the vast stone fireplace and to the front of stage there stood a table set for an intimate dinner for two, by a ten-foot high window through which came the gentle sound of a flute playing a gavotte, mingled with moonlight. Sat there, secure in the knowledge that his plans would soon come to fruition, was Baron Scarpia. He poured himself a glass of wine and sang his chilling words - *For the love of her Mario she will submit to my pleasure. The depth of her misery will match the depth of her love. A forcible conquest has keener relish than a willing surrender…*

Calli's every nerve-ending winced. What would Olivia know about it? It was all very well to play the lovesick Tosca of the first act - for Christ's sake, if an opera singer couldn't play the role of an opera singer, who could? But this act took more than that. Maybe she wasn't a natural like Olivia, but Olivia would never be able to play the upcoming scenes with the conviction that the critics had noted in her performances. Olivia didn't have the bones of Tosca in her, thought Calli, ironically comforted as her mind discarded the anxieties of the present in favour of the anguish of the past.

Meanwhile, Spoletta returned from Mario Cavaradossi's villa, having failed to find Angelotti. Only the fact that he has brought Cavaradossi in for questioning, saves him from Scarpia's threat of the gallows for his incompetence.

'Are you ready for this, my love?' asked Angelo of Olivia just before he was led on stage by three agents and a torturer, all of whom had been playing poker backstage and knocking back tequila for the better part of the evening; they hardly seemed capable of standing, let alone virtually beating the life out of a man.

'I feel ready for anything tonight,' she replied with all the breathlessness of a romance fiction heroine. How many times had she smiled to herself at the way Calliope would wax and wane through character after character, apparently blissfully blind to the contradictions with reality, always utterly convinced that she was whoever she acted she was, until the next role worked its magic? And yet now Olivia was so wrapped

133

up in the grand romance of the night that she could not distinguish herself from Tosca, nor Angelo from Mario Cavaradossi.

'Anything?' her hero said significantly.

'What do you have in mind?' whispered Olivia, immediately picturing herself with him later that night, just as she was now, cosseted in black velvet, a fabulous draped purple silk shawl sexily falling off her shoulders and long evening gloves just asking to be peeled off and replaced by sensuously lingering kisses. In her imagined world there was not a moment of self-consciousness, not a sign of the lace-edged beige nylon nightie her mother had given her last Christmas - *It's from M&S, so you can exchange it, if you want.* Though really, how *could* she ask for the receipt?

'Perhaps a late supper in the privacy of my suite at the Savoy?' Angelo suggested impressively. And hopefully - he'd only just reserved said suite in the interval and sincerely hoped that he had not squandered his cash for nothing.

Olivia smiled. It seemed appropriate that she should celebrate her success in the same place that she had so often sought solace. She and Calli had themselves squandered plenty of cash at the Savoy over the years, though only for afternoon tea, and all for the purpose of seeing Vanessa, one of the most feted and most obnoxious singers from their college days reduced to warbling Andrew Lloyd-Webber hits under the chit-chat. Calli had considered it good therapy for Olivia to see that even the most lauded of sopranos could actually be worse off than herself. And, uncharitable though she knew it was, Olivia had to admit that she enjoyed their little excursions. Of course, Calli would always take things ten steps too far by making repeat requests for *Memories*, or even dealing that cruellest of blows, Barry Manilow's *Mandy*.

Olivia was glad of the amusing memories as Angelo left her side and she was faced with the task ahead. To sing with Angelo had been almost easy, his voice a brilliant, shining surface, in which her own could be reflected, enhanced. She had naturally brought Tosca's love and jealousy to the role, but now she would have to do what so many singers could not, she must act. She must utterly convince the audience that she loathed and despised Scarpia, when in fact Marshall Lincoln Small would have stood a fighting chance against Angelo if he'd been a few years younger, so attached had she become to him. That, and her voice must also shine in its own right and convey with true conviction a solo aria which was as well known and as often over-done as Hamlet's *to be, or not to be* soliloquy.

But there was little time to work herself up into a real panic; on-stage Cavaradossi had refused to give Scarpia any information as to the whereabouts of Angelotti and now Floria Tosca was led in and, unaware that as Mario was taken into the next room to give his 'deposition' he was awaited by a torturer, she too claimed that Cavaradossi had been alone at his villa.

Only when Scarpia suggested that the truth could shorten 'a very painful hour' for Cavaradossi, did it dawn on Tosca what was going to happen. Olivia need have had no fears of being convincing, for Angelo was more than that - his agonised cries thrust through the on-stage action and robbed her of all consciousness of reality. Scarpia persevered, Tosca denied, Cavaradossi endured unendurable pain as the orchestra built a sinister momentum beneath that crescendoed and climbed as did Olivia, hitting each higher note with ever more volume and surety than the last, her capacity swallowing up everything that Puccini could throw at it until the hundred or so musicians in the pit had to admit defeat.

She was literally sobbing as she begged to know of Scarpia: *Che v'ho fatto in vita mia?* - What harm have I ever done you? *Son io che così torturate! Sì, mi torturate l'anima!* - It is I whom you are torturing. Yes, it is my soul you are torturing!

This only served to prompt Scarpia to urge on the torture and by the time Cavaradossi was carried in, horribly battered, blood flowing over his ripped shirt, Tosca had betrayed the secret hiding place in the well in the grounds of the villa. Now Scarpia ordered Cavaradossi to be taken off to the jail to await execution at dawn, and out in the audience Katriona was finally truly regretting having brought the children along tonight. She had known the plot in advance but it had somehow never crossed her mind that an opera could expose them so brutally to what she had sought for so long to protect them from. She had failed completely to

136

understand opera's power to grasp, to engulf - it was just singing, wasn't it? So careful to vet the books they read, the TV they watched; she even censored the violence out of Beatrix Potter, and yet now Michael was trembling with fear in her lap and she could hear miserable sniffles coming from the programmes the girls were hidden behind. Aidan, seeming miles from her comforting presence was standing now, little fingers sunk deep into the seat in front, eyes unblinking as he watched the anguished Olivia turn to Scarpia and ask what price he wanted for Mario's freedom.

They call me venal, but I don't sell myself to lovely ladies for mere money! Love of the Diva has long consumed me. But a while ago I saw you as I have never seen you before! Your tears flowed like lava on my senses, and your eyes, which darted hatred at me, made my desire all the fiercer... in that moment I swore you would be mine, responded Scarpia cruelly and advanced towards her.

Così, così, ti voglio! - This is how I want you!

Non toccarmi, demonio; t'odio, t'odio, abbietto, vile! - Don't touch me, you fiend! I loathe you! I hate you, you vile, despicable bully!

Che importa? Spasimi d'ira e spasimi d'amore! - What matter? Passionate in rage, passionate in love.

Her cries for help were terrifying, seizing Guy with an almost irresistible urge to go to her aid, even as he and his colleagues beat out the snare drum march which accompanied the condemned on their journey to the gallows. This evening was not passing as he had expected. Tonight he felt he had the best job in the world, so engaging was the performance. Around him there was not a musician who did not concur - not a smirk, not a glance at a newspaper, not an eyebrow ironically raised as, for once, the egos on stage gave precedence to the music, stripping all vestiges of cynicism away, all sense of the woman on stage being anyone other than a real, living Tosca as she fell to her knees, crushed by her sorrow and sang, oh so quietly:

Vissi d'arte, vissi d'amore, non feci mai male ad anima viva - I have lived for art, I have lived for love, and never harmed a living soul.

It was a joy for Petrov to hold the accompanying strings below her introspection, pure rapture to hear her voice open out like a lily to fill the music with its heady perfume as she looked to God for strength, yet found only words to question her faith.

Always a true believer, I have offered up my prayers at the holy shrines; always a true believer, I have laid flowers on the altar. In my hour of tribulation why, O Lord, why hast Thou repaid me thus? I gave jewels for the Madonna's mantle, and offered my singing to the starry heavens, that they might smile more brightly. In my hour of tribulation why, O Lord, why hast Thou repaid me thus?

Petrov was shaken to the core as he recognised an emotion he was thoroughly unused to, creeping about inside his guts. The sudden arrival of Spoletta with the news that Angelotti had poisoned himself, did nothing to break the mood. Petrov was overwhelmed with remorse at the hell he had put Olivia through in rehearsal. That he had tried to crush this magnificent voice seemed unforgivable. To have had so little regard for the art to which he had dedicated himself for the better part of his life, unbelievable. What had he been thinking? There was no way to make amends, save making sure the orchestra did Olivia's voice justice, and *that* the musicians had clearly already been inspired to do. She had robbed him of all his power and he could only bow his head in deference to her greater talent as Tosca turned her moment of deepest shame and defeat into one of apparent triumph.

Having got Scarpia to sign a letter of safe conduct for Cavaradossi and heard him order Spoletta to stage a mock execution for Mario, just as they had done 'in the case of Palmieri', Tosca took up a knife from the dinner table and plunged it deep into the heart of Scarpia as he came towards her, bent on claiming his reward.

Questo è il bacio di Tosca! - That was Tosca's kiss, she spat out as Scarpia staggered about and called for help. *Ti soffoca il sangue?* - Are you choking on your blood? *Muori, dannato!* - Die you fiend! *Muori! Muori!*

Scarpia gradually gave himself up to his deserved fate and sank to the floor before the trembling Tosca. Finally, she approached his body, prised the letter out of his already stiffening fingers, placed a crucifix upon his bloody chest, lifted two candles from the table to set either side of him and then, crossing herself, ran from the room leaving the final, cautionary chords in the brass and woodwind hanging threateningly in her wake.

* * *

A daunting silence had fallen upon the Opera House during the interval. The canteen lay empty as had, more significantly, both pubs on Floral Street. No one came for the drinks they had ordered in the front of house bars and drawn by the mystical absence of the audience, doormen, bar staff, programme sellers and cloakroom attendants had gathered at the back of the Circle in anticipation as the curtain rose on the final Act.

Out of the quiet came a skeletal fanfare; the lone French horn section playing in unfathomable unison, serving to heighten rather than relieve the palpable tension. High up on the battlements of the *Castel Sant' Angelo* tired soldiers watched out over the city, lulled almost to sleep by the companionable jangle of sheep-bells, their lanterns glowing faintly with the last remnants of candles that had burnt through the night. Framed against the purple, star-filled sky were the distant domes of the *Vatican* and *St. Peter's*, slowly melting away as the pre-dawn light cast its shadow over the scene and a shepherd's lonely lament rose out of nowhere: *For you I heave as many sighs as there are leaves blown by the wind. You spurn me and fill me with despair: my golden flame, you will cause my death...*

With church bells punctuating the sweetly melancholy violin refrain, Cavaradossi was now led onto the battlements and down a small wooden staircase to the casement where he was to remain until the firing squad arrived. With only an hour till his death, he could not think of anything but the woman most dear to him and refused his jailer's offer of a priest in favour of using the time to write her one last love letter.

As he sat there, four cellos and two violas wove together in a heartbreakingly sorrowful prelude to Cavaradossi's famous aria to the glory of Tosca, giving way to a clarinet which seemed to walk, ghostly beneath Angelo's voice as he beautifully evoked the poignancy of the condemned man's thoughts.

E lucevan le stella... e olezzava... la terra... stridea l'uscio dell'orto... e un passo sfiorava la rena - And the stars were shining, the earth smelt sweet, the garden gate creaked and a footstep brushed the sand. *Entrava ella, fragrante, mi cadea fra la braccia* - She entered, fragrant, and fell into my arms.

Then the strings claimed back the doleful tune from the clarinet and followed Cavaradossi to the depths of his despair. *Oh! dolci baci* - Oh soft kisses - Angelo held onto the words until the audience felt themselves desperate for air, and then allowed those words that followed to spill forth like the tears that were splashing down Olivia's face as she listened... *o languide carezze - mentr'io fremente le belle forme disciogliea dai veli!* - tender caresses, while I, all a quiver, unveiled her lovely features! *Svani per sempre il sogno mio d'amore* - Vanished forever is my dream of love. *L'ora è fuggita e muoio disperato! E non ho amato mai tanto la vita!* - That time has fled and I die in despair. Never have I loved life so dearly!

Yet just as that bitter irony was lighted upon, so Tosca came to the encasement, jubilantly thrusting the letter of safe conduct before him and explaining the planned fake execution. Freedom was soon to be theirs and as Angelo sang to her... *from you life derives all its splendour; for me, joy and desire spring from you as heat springs from flame...* Olivia felt herself released from years of slavery to her unhappiness. *United and exultant, our love will spread through the world harmonies of colour*, she sang.

We will spread harmonies of song, he replied, exhilarated at the look in her eyes that told him victory was his, Olivia was in the bag. Both exultant in their individual realisations, they were then left alone by the orchestra, their united voices searching out the furthest reaches of the auditorium until even those seated in the Gods felt as if they had front row seats for one of the greatest moments in the House's history.

Trionfal di nova speme l'anima freme in celestial crescente ardor, Ed in armonico vol già l'anima va all'estasi d'amor - Triumphant with new hope, our souls quiver in increasing heavenly splendour. And in our harmonious flight our souls soar to the ecstasy of love.

Where normally there might have been rapturous applause, tonight there was none. How could there be when all watching felt like voyeurs, eavesdroppers, spying on real people?

L'ora! - it is time, said the jailer and Cavaradossi was taken up the staircase to stand before the assembled firing squad, refusing the blindfold, meeting his executioners with the unyielding bravery and humour of a man destined not to die.

The shots were fired simultaneously, the acrid gun smoke sticking in the throats of the onlookers as it wafted into the stalls.

Tosca smiled as Spoletta went over to Cavaradossi and feigned examining the body for signs of life. As per their agreement, he prevented the sergeant from giving the usual *coup de grâce* with his sabre and then they left Tosca and Cavaradossi alone.

After leaning over the parapet to make sure all the soldiers were gone, Tosca then rushed to Mario's side. *Mario, up now, quickly! Let's go, let's go!* she urged but he did not move. She reached her hand out to touch him and then the horrible truth was revealed. Scarpia had double-crossed her from the grave and her beloved Cavaradossi was dead. Olivia threw herself upon Angelo, pulling his limp body up against her, consumed by Tosca as Spoletta was heard coming back to arrest her, having discovered Scarpia's corpse.

Tosca, you shall pay dearly for his life, he threatened as he dived towards her.

With my own! she countered, pushing him back with all her strength before running to the parapet. It had seemed, even to those who had seen the opera before, that somehow it would be different tonight, that love would surely triumph over evil. All over the theatre, silent pleas for an alternative truth gathered into a collective, horrified gasp as Tosca swiftly climbed the stone steps leading up onto the battlements of the towering fortress.

Tosca turned her eyes upon Cavaradossi one last time and, in that second, Olivia felt that she would indeed kill herself if she were ever to lose Angelo.

Scarpia, we meet before God! she cried and hurled herself into oblivion.

CURTAIN.

chapter eight

ACT TWO

'Fabulous. Fabulous. So, next Tuesday at ten it is. Just let the photographer know we've only got half an hour; Olivia's on a very tight schedule. Fabulous...'

Fabulous! If Olivia heard that word one more time she'd scream. Instead she sighed and leaned her head wearily against the rain-speckled window of their black cab, as Laura arranged yet another photo shoot.

'That was *Classic CD*. They want to do a cover photo of you and Angelo for next month's issue.'

'Don't you think you should find out if Angelo is free before making promises?'

'Are you kidding? Angelo Verasano's people know which side their bread's buttered - he'll be free all right.'

Olivia thought to point out that she and Angelo might actually have planned something in their lives without asking their agents' permission but, no sooner had Laura put it in her Prada handbag, the damn mobile had started to ring again. Were she ever to be stuck in a taxi with Simon Cowell, Olivia was sure that the stench of megalomania could not be thicker in the air. Like all the best dictators, Laura was short. Sickeningly petite really, in a way that made men flock to buy her drinks and offer jackets on cold nights, though they could not be accepted as her unashamedly retro power suits had shoulder pads that could take an eye out at ten paces. Forty or sixty-something? *Au naturel* or hung, drawn and quartered under the plastic surgeon's knife? There was a timelessness about Laura that left everyone guessing. Olivia had never seen her as happy as she was now, bullshitting away, negotiating all manner of media opportunities. By the time she was done, it would be a miracle if she'd left any room in Olivia's insane itinerary for performing.

'Wednesday? Darling, unless it's Saturday you can forget it. Tell your producer that. If you come back with a yes, of course I'll hold,' laughed Laura intimidatingly and placed a hand over the phone as she whispered excitedly to Olivia, 'They want you and Angelo to do the National Lottery draw.'

Olivia's disgusted look was wasted on Laura who was already 'talking money', her dismayed sigh only being noted by the driver who caught her eye in his rear view mirror and gave her a sympathetic smile, and a *pain in the arse, your agent* raise of his eyebrows. Not that he wouldn't ask for her autographed picture at the end of the journey, and add her name to the list of celebrities to tell his tourist passengers about. Olivia returned her tired gaze out to Regent Street.

The traffic was packed solid under a gunmetal sky, their taxi at a standstill just before Piccadilly Circus, behind three double decker buses, one on a tour of historical London, its open top offering no protection to a very sad looking bunch of passengers who were huddled together against the elements beneath incompetent umbrellas bought, no doubt, from some dubious street trader along with the prerequisite *I went to London and all I got you was this stupid T-shirt*, T-shirt.

Hearing that Laura was now engaged in conversation with Sir David Langley's secretary, suggesting that this afternoon would be an ideal time for her to get together with him and discuss a re-negotiation of Olivia's contract, Olivia considered getting out before she had blood on her hands, and walking up to Covent Garden, but the endless envious glances that came her way as she sat there, furious but dry, convinced her to stay put. Pedestrians were stacked ten deep at the crossings, policemen shouting at them through loud hailers to wait for the traffic to stop - a somewhat contradictory direction given the circumstances. The nearby entrance to the Underground was similarly overwhelmed by the relentless crowds. Clearly someone had failed to point out to the hordes of shoppers out there that the Christmas rush was not due for at least another month.

As the taxi next to theirs moved a fraction forward, Olivia now saw her image on the huge screen covering the upper floors of a nearby building - draped languorously on a chaise longue by a roaring fire, apparently at ease in a tight red velvet dress and not the slightest bit pained by the holly entwined in her hair, with a dinner-jacketed Angelo stood behind, his hands reaching down to rest on her bare shoulders. *'Great love duets from the love duo. What are you getting for Christmas?'*

'Bloody hell,' she exhaled at the sight.

'Fabulous isn't it?' sighed Laura.

'I don't know,' said Olivia.

Somehow she'd assumed that when they'd talked about marketing the love duets CD for Christmas, they had meant next year. She had posed for so many photographers over the last few weeks that she'd not surprisingly failed to link the hurriedly organised recording session with the picture that now demanded her attention.

'I don't know,' she repeated, looking back over her shoulder as the taxi finally jolted into life.

On the opening night of Tosca the final curtain had been met by absolute silence. Olivia had been terrified by it, Angelo having to pursue her as she fled backstage in tears, convinced that she had been so swept up in the romance of the opera as to delude herself into thinking she was singing well. Angelo's powers of persuasion had been tested to the full as he worked to get her to trust his judgment, take his hand and claim her applause.

When she'd finally stepped through the parted crimson velvet, Marshall on one side, Angelo on the other, a wall of sound had come at her like a tidal wave. At their feet, the full complement of musicians, whose normal dash to the pub was almost simultaneous with the final downbeat, had pressed forward to the front of the pit, their rhythmic stamping on its hollow floor making the front of stage shudder under her. From all around, flowers were launched onto the stage as the cheering incomprehensibly intensified by the second. And then, just in case she were in any doubt as to whom that applause was addressed, Marshall and Angelo suddenly let go of her hands and stepped back, the audience rising *en masse* with a primeval roar of approval.

No amount of dreaming could have prepared her for that moment nor what had followed, she realised now. In fact, it seemed that she had only just begun to wake out of her shocked stupor, unfortunately to discover that during these virtually comatose weeks yet more unbelievable things had been happening. Just yesterday she'd snapped out of her daze to find herself opposite Gina and John, live on *This Afternoon*. This morning it had been *This Morning*, tomorrow promised *Woman's Hour* on Radio Four.

If she had had time to think it all through, she would have put her foot down and refused to play the game but it seemed that once you were on the merry-go-round you were expected to go round and be merry until you were told to get off. She had signed things - what things she wasn't sure - and that meant she had obligations to fulfil, and not least to the *fabulous* Laura who had, by her own definition, stuck faithfully by Olivia through thick and thin.

This was what she had wanted, wasn't it? Success? Fame? Calliope had always seemed happy enough signing napkins and having her local cafe send round coffee and croissants for the paparazzi who regularly camped on her doorstep - if they're going to stalk you, might as well keep them sweet and make sure they don't put your cellulite on the cover of *Hello*.

That was a laugh - cellulite and Calli were not something you'd ever see on the same page, unless it was in a fashion magazine and Calli's own ripple-free thighs were being compared to those of a less fortunate celeb, with Calli being asked for her gems of wisdom on keeping toned. Strange how they never printed Calli's miracle cure - a pint of coffee, a pack of fags, a bottle of champagne and packet of Homewheat every day.

Yes, Calli seemed happy enough, but just thinking about her had dampened Olivia's own spirits. There was no time to spend with her friend these days. Calli was in town, about to start a season at the Coliseum, just a five-minute walk from the Royal Opera House and yet they hadn't even managed to grab a drink together in weeks. Olivia tried to remind herself of all the times Calli had been too busy touring, rehearsing and doing the media rounds to get together with her. Their friendship had survived nonetheless, so surely it would weather this period of adjustment too. But Olivia had her secret doubts. If she looked back, she had to admit to herself that what Dominic had pointed out time and time again was true - when Calli did have a window open in her schedule, Olivia was expected to drop everything to see her. Now, with life spinning Olivia around in all directions at once, the idea of dropping everything to see Calli was tempting and impossible all at once. How Calli might be reacting to her calls remaining unanswered for days on end, Olivia could only imagine, but she knew from bitter experience, that if Calli felt slighted there was usually hell to pay. In fact, it was more the fear of Calliope's reaction than her schedule that kept Olivia from calling her. She could have called at two in the morning, if she'd wanted to, but the longer she left it, the more difficult became the task of picking up the phone, and Angelo was no help at all.

After their momentous stage debut, the same desire to prolong the addictive high that propelled some to the pub and others to lines of cocaine after a performance, sent Olivia and Angelo to the Savoy. In her intoxicated state he could have been the worst lover ever to prematurely ejaculate and she would have thought him to be to sex what Pavarotti was to *Nessun Dorma*, Einstein to physics, Gandhi to peace. Lucky for her then that once the adrenaline and endorphins had begun to ebb, his reputation in that department, at least, had proved well-deserved. It was a pleasant surprise after her infrequent and always disastrous liaisons since the heady days when she'd lost her virginity to Guy and mistakenly assumed that all men would be as capable, given that they were all endowed with essentially the same paraphernalia.

Tell herself all she might that sex was intended for procreation only, and that to desire it for pleasure was a sin, she could not prevent herself wishing that God had given out imagination and staying power as part of the basic equipment. Once experienced, life without orgasm seemed like strawberries without cream but a return to the guilty nighttime self-explorations of her teen years had not been an adequate solution, the pleasure entirely stolen by the memory of Father Timothy's searching questions as she'd struggled to find something other than that to confess. She'd made up all manner of transgressions but he'd always pressed on, questioning and questioning until he got to hear what he wanted, whether or not she'd given in to temptation that week. Not raped perhaps, but not left unscathed by those Sunday ordeals.

But now, whether it be once, twice or thrice nightly, Olivia was making up for lost time and on top of that, she was in love. Despite all the warnings about his love 'em and leave 'em reputation, Angelo was still there at her side every morning and at every other time of day. To slip into semi-conscious slumber, wake up or just turn her head at a press conference and discover herself caressed by a surreptitious, admiring gaze thrilled her to the core, made her feel as though she had crossed over some dimensional divide to that plane where she'd always suspected another Olivia Tarrent had been living the antithesis of her own existence. Now that she was here, she didn't want to relinquish her right to happiness, so she wasn't going to admit to herself that, between *Tosca*, sex and photocalls, there had been zero opportunity to find out if she and Angelo really had anything more than an opera-induced infatuation between them. Nor was she about to give Calliope the opportunity to harp on, yet again, about the herd of sopranos who had supposedly passed through these green pastures before her, only to find themselves slaughtered and minced up in what Calli colourfully described as Angelo's *abattoir of love*.

For once, Laura was just what the doctor ordered - someone tirelessly devoted to the promotion of the idea that Angelo and Olivia were opera's answer to Astaire and Rogers, Burton and Taylor, Nureyev and Fonteyn, though she might have been a little less keen to draw those comparisons if she'd actually cared to examine the true nature of those relationships. Before the curtain had gone up on their second performance of *Tosca*, Laura had been all over town planting the seeds of speculation about when the wedding bells would sound for the darlings of the opera world.

'Oh look at that. Fabulous!' she said, quickly glancing behind to satisfy herself that the photographers who'd been tailing Olivia since early that morning hadn't been lost as she spied Angelo waiting, with flowers and an umbrella, for his beloved outside the stage door. 'Now that's what I call love!'

As Olivia alighted, there was a lightning-strong flash of cameras, followed by a thunderous barrage of questions, none of which were answered as Angelo ushered Olivia across Floral Street to the offices. He had waited, no fool, outside the stage door specifically so that the taxi would pull up on the wrong side of the street and necessitate this dash with journalists in pursuit. As

Olivia was thinking that yes, fame was what she wanted if it meant being held in Angelo's protective arms like this, so Angelo was thinking that if it meant having this kind of fame, he'd happily stop questioning his sudden desire to stick around the same woman for more than the time it took to seduce her.

Not that he for one moment doubted he was in love with Olivia, for Angelo was always sincerely besotted by his leading ladies - it was that sincerity of emotion that made him so successful - but he was used to things turning sour pretty smartly, all divas being flawed in the end, by virtue of it being as impossible for him to love them as much as they loved themselves, as it was for them to love him as much as he loved himself. Olivia was different. The cues to depart were absent. Her saviour, she treated him as a God would wish to be treated and, if that weren't enough, the press were currently as open in their adoration of him as she was. Always in the lingering shadow of the 'big three' and brought close to vomiting at the very mention of Roberto Alagna, Angelo Verasano felt, in his own way, as liberated from the hinterland as did Olivia.

'So my darling, how was *This Morning?*' he asked, as they sat together in the eye of the storm that was raging between the amassed press officers, agents, publicists, designers, finance directors and men in black from the record company.

'Well, if you're asking was it good for me? Then, you were fantastic as ever,' she responded with a naughty smile before planting a supple kiss on his lips, 'but if you're asking about *This Morning,* then it was just a nightmare. Laura gave them a press pack which, from the questions they asked, must have been lies from beginning to end. I just kept zoning out and wondering who the hell they were talking about. I must have looked a complete fool and I don't suppose it did much for their journalistic credibility either. That, and they made me go over and join in with the chef's slot too - meringue everywhere. Anyway, it can't have gone as badly as I thought; Laura says they want you and me to come in sometime in their Christmas week to do a number from our duets CD. Of course, that might just mean that Laura has decided that that's what they want, but it amounts to the same thing.'

'Yes, Laura is a very persuasive woman,' said Angelo, entirely glad of the fact. His own management had always treated him as a serious artist, booking him in the best venues at the right prices, but it had never felt enough to the man who'd wanted to score a goal for Italy. Since the opportunistic and intransigent Laura had started interfering he was, at last, starting to feel like a hero of the people - there was even a modelling contract in the offing, with *GQ* doing a spread on Italian suits and some lucrative ads for the boorish aftershave he'd worn as a young stud. Angelo couldn't have been happier. The woman was nothing short of a genius and Olivia's reticence towards her was a mystery to him.

'Your shortsightedness is utterly beyond comprehension,' snapped Laura at a quaking publicity officer. 'You're still talking about which poster should go front of house when I've already got Olivia's face on the side of every bus in London. Don't you understand what we've got here? They're what we in the business call a 'phenomenon'. If you get your way it'll be a case of here today and gone tomorrow. It's sink or swim time; we've got a tsunami of popularity sweeping across the nation - even the plebs love'em - we don't want to be feet on the ground, waiting to get washed away, we want to be riding that wave.'

Olivia half expected her to develop an American accent and add the word *baby* on the end.

'So what do you suggest?' came the quivering response.

'Well, looking at the season, I'd say the House should be scrapping that modern fiasco in the spring and going with *Traviata* or *Butterfly*.'

'Good God woman,' blustered Sir David. 'The sets are under construction, the cast was booked a year ago, the conductor engaged, the programmes are going to print next week. Are you insane?'

'No, but you are if you let this opportunity pass you by. I know what kind of shit you're in. There's no mood to give opera houses cash when the government is cutting funds to hospitals and schools. The way I see it, is this: you've got Olivia on a contract that wouldn't have kept Pavarotti in handkerchiefs and I've come here intending to re-negotiate, knowing that she might well develop a nasty throat infection before tonight's performance if you were to cause her emotional stress by undervaluing her worth to the House. Alternatively, Olivia could generously agree to continue working for peanuts, if you would make sure that our little fairy story also continues. Tarrent and Verasano are so important a find that the House feels they must be given priority. Think of the publicity such an unprecedented move would provoke. From the enragement of the modernists to the delight of the plebs, it would sell the Valentine album.'

'What Valentine album?' chorused everyone in the room. Even the men in black seemed in the dark.

'The Valentine album that is the natural follow on from the Christmas love duets and from which a portion of the sales - to be negotiated at a later date - will go to the Opera House future development fund,' smiled Laura, turning snakish eyes towards the clueless Sir David and laughing secretly to herself at the thought of just how much cash she would be twisting out of him by way of compensation for the singers that the House had booked through her for that modern piece of shit they'd been set to stage. (She knew it was a piece of shit because she was acquainted with the composer and, when last she'd seen him, he'd been suffering from an alcoholic writer's block and tearfully using the unfinished score to roll joints.) That unbeknownst to Sir David, most of those singers were already booked elsewhere, made the thrill all the more vibrant.

Meanwhile, eyes rolled back into heads around the room at the pure brilliance of her strategy. Everyone had the sparkle of greed upon them and Olivia, who was still trying to work out how Laura could call the obscene amount of money she was getting her fifteen percent of 'peanuts', was utterly convinced that if the Valentine album became a reality, Laura's cut would leave even the record company feeling well and truly rogered.

'So that's settled then. Fabulous!'

'Absolutely,' came a snide half whisper from within the ranks of severely out of joint noses.

'Very funny Peter. Yes, you sorry bastard, I know who you are,' said Laura, looking down her perfectly aligned, perfect little nose at the press officer who was now huddled in foetal position behind Sir David's robust frame. 'Oh for Christ's sake come out you snivelling wretch, I've got better things to do than have you fired, though don't think you couldn't be replaced in an hour. Fortunately for you, there isn't an hour to waste in getting this show on the road.'

Olivia shifted uncomfortably in her chair. Laura had that terrifying look on her face she got when everything was going her way - an almost constant state of affairs - and if implying that she had the power to hire and fire Opera House staff at will was to be the jumping off point, then Olivia daren't hazard a guess at what despotic plan the woman might be about to lay before them all.

'Look here, I don't think I like the idea of 'getting this show on the road', if you mean to prostitute the House in the process.'

Sir David's last stab at maintaining credibility with his entourage was clearly deemed almost suicidal, every one of his collected staff preferring to avert their eyes rather than chance being suspected of sharing his nostalgia for the old ways. They had all had a good laugh when the English National Opera had resorted to plastering underground stations with sexy photos of singers, directors, stagehands and the like in an attempt to drum up new audiences, but times were yet harder these days. Sir David wasn't about to see his opera house being turned over to lowbrow musical theatre performances all summer long like their troubled rival down the street. Besides, he liked his salary and leather-bound office; he was going to cave without a doubt. Before Laura set about her rebuttal, he was pouring himself a large surrendering scotch.

'Sir David, the House has relied on prostitution for its income from time immemorial. Just about every operatic heroine is a whore, so I hardly think the House should be above using a little of her feminine wiles to get through this financial ice age. Right Peter, I expect tonight's *Evening Standard* to carry rumours of impending wedding bells - pile on the romantic crap about them singing *Tosca* together. That'll be followed up with news of Olivia's engagement to Angelo. Then we'll give it a few days and announce the change in the spring line up. Let's call it 'an engagement gift from the House to the happy couple.' I'll get onto my old friend at *Vogue* and wangle a spread on what the bride'll be wearing. Perhaps we can get that holiday show to film them on their honeymoon? Angelo shows his diva the land of his ancestors, or something like that. There's just no end to where we can take this, if we put our heads together. Let's get suggestions and some good strong coffee on the table and thrash it out now. So, *are* there any suggestions?'

'I suggest you all find yourself another Tosca,' said Olivia with quiet contempt. 'You're despicable. You've humiliated and embarrassed me. I can't believe you think I'll sanction your lies. I mean, for God's sake Laura, do you really think you can force Angelo to marry me just so there'll be a honeymoon to film?'

'Well, of course not. I rather thought he'd do it willingly!'

That was it then, thought Olivia. The end of her romance with Angelo. It would have been nice to continue in this dreamy fantasy world a little longer but when someone else drew the same fictional conclusion to this whimsy, the reality of the situation banished the magic without mercy. This was, after all, Angelo Verasano she was in love with and there was nothing like the suggestion of marriage - even one for publicity purposes only - to send a man like him scurrying.

'Angelo, I hope you'll believe that I had nothing to do with this ridiculous plan,' she said, knowing that it was a wasted effort and already seeing herself in the small hours of tomorrow, alone but for her cat Tosca - a bitter reminder of what might have been - watching *CSI* reruns through a blur of tears, surrounded by takeout boxes and un-ironed laundry.

'But Olivia, this has everything to do with you,' said Angelo, seeing himself walking the vineyards of Tuscany with camera crew in tow, 'Laura has only seen the inevitable. She has guessed my feelings for you as surely as you have not.'

'She has?'

'She has.'

'Oh.'

'Come, my darling. Let us go to our favourite patisserie and leave these people to plot. There is no shame in allowing the Opera House to profit a little from our happiness. Opera has given us each other, let us give something back.'

Laura watched Olivia melt as Angelo turned up the heat, and smiled to see a kindred spirit at work.

'*Yes!*' she hissed with a sportsmanly pump of her arm as the door closed behind the blissful couple.

- chapter nine -

'Fuck you too!'

Dominic winced as he stood outside Calliope's front door, wishing that he hadn't already rung the bell - she didn't sound in any mood to rehearse. The sound of the telephone hitting a wall with considerable force further persuaded him that making a run for it might be the best course of action.

'Dominic!'

Too late.

Seeing her there, mid afternoon, with hair tousled and an embroidered, black silk kimono tied so carelessly about her as to be barely clinging to her naked body, a stranger might have been shocked that Calli had not bothered to get dressed yet. Dominic knew better. This was deliberate, in a sub-conscious sort of fashion. He had coached her through more personality changes than he'd had new haircuts, and was not at all surprised by her sleazy appearance. Calli *à la Salome*. Usually it was all

162

good fun to witness Calli mid-morph but this was something he'd been awaiting with dread, though he was not sure why, save that she didn't really have the voice for the role and would make his life hell until he could make her sound like she did. And it was down to him entirely this time, as faced with the magnitude of the task, Calli had gone back to Dame Cecelia Jones for a lesson, only to be told with brutal honesty that she had absolutely no business attempting *Salome*.

A second glance told him that his sense of foreboding had been well-founded. What he had at first thought was deliberately smudged kohl around her eyes, now looked suspiciously like the result of actual tears cried. This was not going to be any kind of fun.

'Come on in darling. You look like you could do with a drink. You know where it is. Help yourself. I've got to make another phone call and then we can get started,' she drawled lazily.

Calli had already been hitting the bottle, realised Dominic as she slinked off towards her bedroom, leaving him to close the front door. The telephone lay in pieces in the drawing room and as he stooped to gather the bits up, he noticed the shredded remains of the latest *Opera Monthly* in the fireplace. There was nothing for it but to mix himself a stiff martini.

Sitting on the edge of her bed, Calli had to fight hard against the temptation to crumple back into it. But how long would she have to stay put for everything in the world to be as she wanted it? Certainly the last two days hadn't done the trick. And now Dominic had shown up. She couldn't even remember arranging the rehearsal. It was remarkable how a triumph could so quickly feel like a catastrophe. From the moment Olivia had told her about the contract with the Opera House, *Salome's* charms had begun to wither along with their friendship, evidenced by the shattered telephone and the terrible loneliness she was feeling now. It was a loneliness that she had once been well-accustomed to, and to feel herself being swallowed up in its vacuous expanse anew was terrifying, for the only person who could guide her out again was the very person who had abandoned her to it – the pain of it was almost physical.

Olivia was the only person who knew everything there was to know about Calliope and her alter-ego, Caroline Smith and, as it was Caroline Smith who was sitting here right now, she was in desperate need of her friend. That desperation only compounded her isolation. Calliope would never have called more than once, totally confident that Olivia would come running sooner or later, even if Calli had done something thoughtless and her friend had actually found the courage to be angry. But Caroline Smith had left messages and when they weren't returned, she'd left more and now, when *only thanks to a bloody magazine* she'd discovered that her dearest friend had got engaged, she'd gone ahead and called again. Desperate.

She wished that she could have seen this all coming but Calli, for self-preservation's sake, was not given to seeking enlightenment. If she were to reflect upon anything, it would most likely be the sad state of her rivals. For them she had words of wisdom and the number of a psychotherapist she had once slept with - she passed that number on not because she thought a therapist might be helpful, but because she believed that most of her 'friends' were in need of a good screw.

Though she'd blamed this season on her agent, she had in fact bulldozed him into securing *Salome* and *Dialogues des Carmélites*. That her voice was heard more times on *Classic FM* than any of the grand dames of opera was neither here nor there when snooty sods, who couldn't hit a high 'C' if they sat on a red hot poker, felt at liberty to qualify any compliment they might be obliged to pay her after a good performance with a suggestion that, though fantastic for the likes of Puccini, her voice was limited in its scope. How many times had she read in the 'serious' press that she'd never be Joan Sutherland - no *Ride of the Valkyries* for Calliope. To land two roles that didn't belong to her – well, it had been a bit of a game really. After all, every role was achieved with bugger all talent and a thousand coaching sessions, so why not these? No better revenge could she imagine for those pretentious critics, who'd been so busy defining the boundaries of her voice that they had completely failed to notice that she couldn't really sing at all.

Once gained though, *Salome* had served to remind Calli of more than her lack of innate musicality. It was, on the face of it, the perfect opera for a woman as dramatically over the top as Calliope. *Salome* - the story of King Herod's lascivious stepdaughter, after whom he lusts. To rile her stepfather, Salome insists on having the prophet, John the Baptist, brought to her from the jail where Herod has imprisoned him. She then attempts to seduce him. The more he refuses her advances, the harder she tries to tempt him but eventually, after she has demanded a kiss, he curses her. Later that night, Herod asks Salome to dance the dance of the seven veils for him and promises that in return he will grant her any wish. She agrees and after the dance, Herod's pleasure turns to terror as she requests the head of the prophet be brought to her on a platter. When the deed is done, Salome sings to John the Baptist's head of her revengeful and lustful thoughts as if he is still alive, completing the horror by triumphantly kissing his mouth. Fearing that they will all now be struck down by God, Herod immediately has her killed.

Caroline Smith had heard the story on many a cautionary occasion, compared by the nuns as she was, to Salome. From the moment the first signs of womanhood had become apparent, she had been the subject of ridicule and denigration. The very fact that the nuns noticed the defiant fleshing out of her adolescent body was, to them, proof that she was using it to wanton end. Her changing body was a thing to be ashamed of and her refusal to acknowledge this, was something viler still. But no one could have guessed to what extremes of corruption Caroline Smith would succumb. In all the years the school had been guiding young girls towards lives of good grace, none had opened the door to the Devil as flagrantly as had Caroline Smith. Forget all the years of teaching to the very opposing viewpoint, God's powers of forgiveness were not boundless after all. She had tried to seduce a priest and when he'd shunned her, she had fabricated so heinous a tale that she was assured that no amount of contrition on her part would ever save her from the terrors of Hell. God would punish her most dreadfully for having so revolting a mind that she could utter the offensive words that had made up her accusation of Father Timothy. But, just in case He should, in His infinite mercy, choose to offer so unworthy a soul as hers clemency, the nuns had made it their vocation to extort a confession to falsehood out of Caroline. It was never achieved. *Thou shalt not lie.* And she hadn't. Father Timothy had raped her. There was no changing that with beatings.

But was she responsible for that hideous act? Therein lay the heart of her disquiet. Transfiguration had become so much a part of Calli's life that it was difficult to remember the true identity at her core. As she had struggled to conquer *Salome,* rather than taking on the mantle of the role, she found herself being gradually denuded. The part came at her like a paring knife, peeling away until she was raw with pain, reunited with the self-loathing and perversely sluttish Caroline. Guilt pressed down on Caroline's chest like the rocks piled on the tortured heathens of old, but did that mean that still deeper there was someone innocent and blameless, or did it just confirm that she was guilty as charged? Calli needed Olivia to reassure her that the former was the case. She had done it before, enabling Caroline's metempsychosis into Calliope. Yet there was Caroline Smith, glowering menacingly at her every time she looked in the mirror. Dead but not forgotten, a ghost stalking the graveyard where her many personas had been lain to rest. Claiming Calli for her own, Salome offered no prospect of redemption.

And now, to cap it all, Calliope's interfusion with Salome had so disturbed the director, that he was expressing doubts that she would be able to play the timid Sister Blanche in *Dialogues des Carmélites*. Ignorant of her too close for comfort knowledge of the Catholic church, Douglas had decided that she might benefit from a little research. At the last rehearsal, he'd handed her the telephone number of a Carmelite monastery and suggested that she go on a visit. The idea was appalling to Calliope and yet, she could see his point. ENO was well-known for challenging its audiences' expectations with radical, contemporary stagings, but the way Calli was feeling, they might get a more extreme experience for their money than they had bargained for. Of course, so might the Carmelites, if they agreed to allow her through their hallowed gates.

Receiver squeezed between neck and shoulder, Calliope lit a cigarette and contemplated the varnish on her toenails as she listened to the ringing. She'd heard that there was only one nun in the order allowed to speak; perhaps it was her day off. Calli was just about to hang up when an abrasively serene voice surprised her mid-inhale.

'Good afternoon. You have reached the Carmelite Monastery of Little Easton. Sister Margaret speaking. How may I be of service?'

Calli felt herself immediately fill with the desire to unburden herself of a little anger. How dare she sound so peaceful, so happy, so caring? Calli knew that that same voice must just as readily become infused with bitterness when the line to the outside world was disconnected. Some poor novice would probably have a thing or two to say about how peaceful, happy and caring Sister Margaret was in reality.

'Hello, I'm wondering if you could help me,' said Calliope, her voice taking on the deeply reverential tone she had been schooled to use when addressing a Sister. It was hopeless. How many years had it been since her escape? And yet she was as incapable as ever of expressing her inner fury when presented with the impenetrable wall of righteousness that seemed to rise up around every nun. Even as her mind was turning over ways to humble this woman, her lips were betraying her.

'My name is Calliope Syrigos. I'm sure that you won't have heard of me, but I'm an opera singer and I'm about to perform Poulenc's *Dialogues des Carmélites*. Being a Catholic myself, I am very aware of how often the Faith is misrepresented and I feel it to be my duty to make sure that the production is as true to reality as possible. So, I was wondering if it might be possible for me to visit your monastery and perhaps talk to one of the sisters about life in the order.'

'An opera about the Carmelite order, how very interesting. If you don't mind waiting a moment, I'll just go and ask the Mother Abbess if we can help you.'

'Oh, thank you so much.'

Sister Margaret's footsteps echoed as they receded down what Calli imagined to be a very long cloister. Calli could almost see the worn parquet flooring, a rough-kneed novice dutifully polishing it to a dark shine before the nuns dulled her work as they headed in from the gardens for evensong. One thankless task after another for a lifetime, only to be just as dead and unresurrected as every other human being at the end of it. Really, thought Calli, you had to treat them with respect or there'd be no point to their lives - one just couldn't let that happen. It was like watching a dire school orchestra; however bad the intonation, however scratchy the violins, however split all the notes from the trumpets, you'd find yourself applauding like they were the Berlin fucking Philharmonic.

By the time the *tap, tap, tap* of Sister Margaret was heard anew, Calli had had time to paint her nails.

'I'm so sorry I was away so long.'

'That's quite all right,' said Calli, grabbing a pen so as to take down directions to the monastery - Douglas had said it was hidden, deep in some woods, between the *middle of nowhere* and *who the fuck knew where*.

'I've spoken to the Mother Abbess and I'm afraid we're unable to be of assistance. Ours is a hidden life and we don't do the sort of thing you are asking. I'm sorry, my child.'

'Well thank you for asking anyway,' said Calliope without rancour.

170

Dominic's hand shook as another crash sent shock waves of almost seismic proportions through the apartment. There went the original deco, bakelite telephone in the bedroom and probably a good portion of plasterwork with it.

'Bloody Carmelites,' spat out Calli, resting the bottle of vodka from Dominic and flopping sulkily onto a vast sofa. 'Honestly, how the fuck am I supposed to research the role if the bitches won't talk to me?'

'Sorry, you've lost me. Would the 'bitches' you're referring to be nuns by any chance?'

'My word Dominic, surely you're not going to allow a little irreverence towards a few nuns to upset you. Some atheist, you are. Whatever happened to burning us all at the stake?'

'Hey, I never suggested any such thing and you know it.'

'Oh right, that was me!' she laughed hollowly and took a huge swig of vodka. 'I just don't get the point of all this reclusive adoration of God. What's the sense in seeing the light if you're not going to lead other people to it? I mean, you wouldn't want to let them through the door, unless they looked worth corrupting, but at least those Mormon and born again types are doing something with all that belief. *Ours is a hidden life and we don't do the sort of thing you are asking,*' repeated Calli sarcastically, 'You'd think I was asking them to do the can-can, the way she said it.'

'Oo la la, are you bitter and twisted today.'

'Yes, well it's how I fucking feel,' Calli responded with sudden seriousness.

'Been getting a little of your own medicine, I take it,' said Dominic with an eye on the fire grate.

'Maybe,' she replied unwillingly, 'but two wrongs don't make a right, do they?'

'No, but Olivia would have to do quite a lot of wrong to redress the balance, wouldn't she?'

'You know what Dominic, you're not helping. I feel like shit and I can do without the *I told you so* routine. Save it for after we're done rehearsing *Salome,* then you'll have good cause to feel vindicated.'

'Having trouble?'

'I'm thinking of developing nodes on my vocal chords. There's no hope of me pulling this one off. I won't tell you what Douglas had to say - even I blushed.'

'It's not like you to shy away from a challenge.'

'As I said, I feel like shit, ' reiterated Calli and took another slug of vodka.

'*That* is not going to help,' said Dominic, taking back the bottle. 'You get warming up and I'll go and make some coffee. On second thoughts,' he said having seen the evil cat skulking in the hall, 'I'll nip down to that new cafe and pick up some espressos. You might want to get dressed while I'm gone.'

Why he had suggested that she get dressed was a mystery to Dominic. As he lovingly bore the coffee and a couple of crisp biscotti back to her home, he'd had time to be amused at this bizarre request of his. When had a little nudity ever bothered him before? The female form was of only aesthetic value to him, and then for the most part it was not prone to meeting his criteria for what he considered beautiful. Besides, working in theatreland, one got *so* used to all manner of gorgeous, toned, naked bodies parading between showers and dressing rooms that Adonis himself could go unremarked upon. Yet today he felt curiously uncomfortable, reluctant even to go back. In order to give himself adequate time to delve his subconscious for an answer to this anomaly, he was obliged to drink his espresso and double back to the cafe for another. Yet, he could only come to the foregone conclusion that he was not experiencing any sexual attraction to Calliope. But if it was not that, then what was it?

She had not taken the opportunity to clothe herself but she was, at least, singing when he returned. And singing well, at that. He had expected this session to compare unfavourably with an afternoon at the dentist but even halfway down the street he could hear her hitting note after note with all the power one might expect of the greatest dramatic sopranos. More than that, she was actually hitting the right notes. Apparently something had clicked and she was at one with the role.

It was not until they were running through the seduction scene between Salome and John the Baptist that Dominic realised that it was her oneness with the character that was making him so nervous.

How wasted he is! He is like an ivory statue. I'm sure he is chaste as the moon. His flesh must be very cool, cool like ivory. I would like to take a closer look at him, sang Calli, coming to rest one elbow on the piano to the right of the music stand and allowing the other arm to rest gently on Dominic's shoulders as he accompanied. She had done it many a time before when a journalist was around to see; an interested look at the score could only be for show when she could barely read a note. Dominic felt the hairs on the back of his neck stiffen at the apparently innocent gesture.

'What are you looking at?' he laughed, landing on a couple of wrong notes.

'You,' she said. 'I was just wondering if you've ever slept with a woman.'

'Calli, gossiping about my sex life isn't going to get you a good write up from *The Times.*'

'Oh come on Dominic, humour me.'

'You know the answer already,' he reminded her grudgingly. 'At sixteen - a singularly unpleasant experience for the both of us, and one best forgotten. So, can we get back to *Salome?*'

'Yes, I know all about the teenage flailings on the playing field, but have you ever had sex with a *woman?*'

'No, thank God. And now I've met Andrew, I hope I will never be on the market again, full stop.'

'Andrew?'

'The painter I got in to do my bedroom wall.'

'Good God darling, I've never thought you one for a bit of rough.'

'If you must know, he's a graduate of St Martin's and he's painted a *trompe l'œil* moonlit garden for me.'

Calli didn't like his tone. There was a softness to it that got her back up. Dominic's beaus weren't usually kept on the scene long enough to finish breakfast, let alone a mural. Could it be that both Olivia and Dominic had dared to happen upon love?

'So, you bastard, I take it he's just my type as usual! Drop dead gorgeous, I suppose.'

'Not in the classic sense, no, but there's just something very sweet about him.'

Well, that confirmed it. Andrew was not in the least bit gorgeous but Dominic didn't care because he was such a nice guy. Calli was livid.

'We should get started,' she said brusquely. She could not see that she was jealous of people in love generally, and felt it only as an intense possessiveness towards Dominic. With Olivia ebbing away, something had to fill the void. It seemed to be of barely any importance that Dominic was now, and had basically always been, gay. Calli felt rejected and convinced with lightning speed that she was in love with him. She must do something to get him back for herself. She launched into *Salome* with renewed vigour.

Dominic wished he had raised the lid of the piano as Calli lifted herself up and sprawled on her back across its shiny surface, which was so well polished that there were now two Calliopes to face, both of them working themselves free of the silk robe as she slid closer towards him with every syllable.

I am lusting for your body. Your body is white like the lilies of the field... Your body is like the snow on the mountains of Judaea... Neither the roses in the Queen of Arabia's garden, nor the moon as it lies on the breast of the sea... nothing in the world is as white as your body. Let me touch your body, sang Calli with alarming intent.

As he spoke John the Baptist' s refusal to listen to Salome, Dominic's voice cracked a little. He felt a fool to be so filled with fear at the approach of his friend, and yet he could not stop himself shifting back his chair until the keyboard was almost at arms length. Surely this was not happening. He must be misinterpreting the vibes. Calli was drunk, that was all. Any minute now she would burst out laughing, glorying in his ridiculous discomfort.

Calli sensed Dominic withdrawing and flipped angrily onto her front and used Salome's words to express her displeasure.

Your body is hideous. It's like the body of a leper... It is like a whitened sepulchre full of loathsome things. It is horrible, your body is disgusting.

Terrifying though her rendering was, Dominic was glad that Calli had got the message. Glad too soon. Immediately the sigh of relief had escaped his lips,

Salome had snapped Calliope back into seductive mode and her long fingers were suddenly entwined in his hair, leaving him in no doubt that worse was to come as she moved closer, uncaring that her magnificent breasts were now unleashed from her robe and alarmingly reflected in the piano's lush surface.

It is your hair that I am enamoured with. Hair like the clusters of black grapes that hang from the vine-trees of Edom. Your hair is like the great cedars of Lebanon that give their shade to lions and robbers. The long, black nights when the moon is hidden, when the stars are frightened, are not so black as your hair. Nothing in the world is as black as your hair. Let me touch your hair.

'Back daughter of Sodom. Don't touch me,' said Dominic, wishing that he could find it in him to say the prophet's lines in the jocose fashion he would normally have used for Calli's amusement. Unfortunately, he had sounded rather like he meant it.

Your hair is horrible. It's like a knot of black serpents writhing round your neck. No, I don't love your hair, she retorted with distaste, tightening her hold on it nonetheless.

With his discomfort now being both mental and physical, Dominic found himself in the unprecedented position of actually wishing that her dreadful cat would make his customary mid-rehearsal attack. But he was obviously enjoying the spectacle, stretched out as he was along the windowsill, eyeing Dominic with self-satisfied smugness. Surely that cat had seen the opera, knew what was coming up. Dominic knew too and his vision began to blur, but it mattered little as Calli had somehow contrived to be between him and the music, sliding down onto his lap as he struggled valiantly on with the accompaniment, trying to maintain the illusion that this was a normal rehearsal.

It is your mouth that I desire, she continued, seething with sexuality. *It is like a pomegranate cut with an ivory knife. Redder than roses, the pomegranate flowers in the gardens of Tyre are not as red. Your mouth is redder than the feet of those who tread the wine. Redder than the feet of the doves that haunt the temples. Your mouth is like a branch of coral in the twilight of the ocean, like the vermilion of Kings. There is nothing in the world as red as your mouth... Let me kiss your mouth.*

'Never, daughter of Sodom,' replied Dominic, his hands falling away from the keyboard.

I will kiss your mouth, she sang on regardless, her lips hovering threateningly close to his. *Let me kiss your mouth,* she urged, pressing her bare breasts against his chest. *Let me kiss you...*

Salome was nothing if not persistent, thought Dominic in one last moment of humour and sadly futile hope before Calli's voice slid out of song and into a husky spoken whisper, 'Let me kiss you... Dominic.'

'For Christ sake Calli, what's got into you?' burst out Dominic, throwing Calliope aside in his desperation to escape, the lid over the keyboard slamming down as he did so, leaving the sound of the impact vibrating up and down the strings, echoing in the uncomfortable silence that ensued.

'I was rather hoping you might,' smiled Calli, as she sidled up to an astounded Dominic.

'Stop it,' he said, brutally extricating himself from arms that were already creeping like a boa constrictor round his neck. 'What the hell are you playing at?'

'Oh, come on Dominic, we both know it's been on the cards for years.'

'So, I suppose that's why - between the two of us - we've screwed every good looking man in Europe, is it?'

'Well, we couldn't be selfish! But isn't it time we put all that experience to better use?'

'Please tell me you're joking,' he said, putting more distance between them.

Seeing his look of barely, if at all, disguised disgust, Calli became aware of just how bizarre it was to be standing naked before an old friend, and a gay one at that, virtually begging for sex. She turned away from him, rather than let him see the mortification on her face, picked up her robe with deliberate laziness. He must not know how much she wanted to hide her body now, how much she wanted to run away from the scene of her humiliation. She must be Calliope Syrigos or no one at all.

'Good grief, you're easily wound up!'

Calliope's laughter as she put on her robe, did not have the reassuring quality that either Calli or Dominic would have liked. He did not need to know that it was not Calli's but Caroline's laugh he was hearing, to understand that everything was very wrong.

He'd never put his arms around her before; for fear of creasing their clothes, it had always been air kissing between them.

But he did it now.

'I'm sorry,' he said gently. 'Some friend I am.'

It was nice being held.

'What is it that you want Calli? Not me, for sure. Can you tell me what's wrong?'

Calli was surprised at his perspicacity. He was so adept at playing the flighty queen it was easy to forget that there was more to him. She said nothing, for fear of saying everything.

'I guess I'm just not Olivia, am I?'

'I'm not gay, if that's what you're inferring,' Calli laughed weakly.

'Laugh it off if you want, but you need her.'

'Well, that's a busy line right now, but if you'd care to get drunk with me, I'd appreciate it.'

'Will yours be a vodka or a gin martini?'

With the cocktail shaker and Calliope's entire collection of booze placed for convenience on the coffee table between their two sofas, they whiled away the rest of the day.

And when they were very drunk, Calli found herself telling Dominic about who she had once been and what had happened to that girl. Dominic had nothing to say, he'd never managed to out drink Calli and had passed out some time before, but it didn't matter.

When she was done, Calli crawled over to the sofa where he lay and knelt down. 'Thanks for listening,' she whispered, 'You're a good friend.'

Then she laughed quietly to herself and planted a gentle kiss on his beautiful lips.

- chapter ten -

On the night *Salome* opened at the Coliseum, the Royal Ballet was performing at Covent Garden, leaving Olivia and Angelo free to attend the performance.

Olivia was hugely excited at the prospect of seeing her friend after so many weeks of missed messages and cancelled coffees. Calliope had sent her complimentary tickets, as usual, so she was confident that Calli understood it wasn't a lack of commitment to their friendship that had caused her to be so elusive since her debut at the House. And now, with Angelo having stood the test of time (though by scientific standards it was too short a test to provide adequate data for a valid conclusion) she felt confident enough to face Calli's critical eye.

It was reassuring too to hear the applause when she and Angelo went in to take their seats; she couldn't have felt more like royalty had the national anthem itself been played and she was delighted to see that Dominic and Andrew were to be sat next to them. Both rose out of their chairs in mock deference and wouldn't be seated until she was.

'This is wonderful,' she said to Dominic when they were all settled. 'It's just great to be away from Covent Garden for a change. The audience here is brilliant, isn't it? The atmosphere sends shivers up and down my spine. Look, the opera's not even started yet and already I'm covered in goosebumps.'

Dominic looked at her arms. She was right. He had them too, but for a different reason.

'Olivia,' he whispered confidentially, 'have you seen Calli recently?'

'No, it's been too hectic for us to find a moment to ourselves. Why?'

'No reason.'

He had been hoping that Olivia would enquire further. Jesus, she really was self-absorbed at the moment, he thought as Olivia smiled indulgently at Angelo instead. So, he ventured forth once more.

'I've just been a bit worried about her. She just doesn't seem herself.'

'You mean, like she wasn't herself when she was doing *Carmen, Butterfly,* or *Traviata?* Really Dominic, you of all people should be used to Calli by now.'

'No. It's different this time... she tried to seduce me,' he whispered.

Olivia's overzealous laughter made heads all around them turn.

'That's been on the cards for years, Dominic. I can't tell you the number of times she's threatened to pull that one on you. What did you do to deserve it?'

'Nothing. It wasn't like that.'

'What has made you laugh, my darling?' asked Angelo, annoyed to be left out of the conversation.

'Dominic has just got his comeuppance for all the pranks he's played in the past,' said Olivia through yet more laughter and to Dominic's horror started to recount the story to Angelo.

This was not the Olivia Dominic liked.

Andrew took hold of Dominic's hand as the lights went down. 'You did your best.'

* * *

'My darling, you are crying,' remarked Angelo with surprise when the final curtain fell. 'Surely Salome, as you say, 'got her come-up-pance'? No?'

He was on his feet cheering with the rest of the audience before Olivia could beg to differ.

Now that Olivia had seen this, what was she going to do? What could she do? Dominic had tried to warn her but she hadn't heard. Though she may have been blinded by love to what was happening over the past weeks, it was clear to her that tonight she'd been deaf through choice. The performance had rectified that; she was now deaf and blind to everything but the plight of her friend.

All around her there were people screaming their appreciation for the production but only Olivia could understand why Calliope Syrigos was not coming out to receive her reward for suffering the irreparable damage that this role must have inflicted. They could pound the floor and throw flowers all they wanted, Calli wasn't going to let them see that Salome had not departed when the curtain hit the stage.

The papers would be full of insultingly astonished praise for Calli's venture into the musical minefield Richard Strauss had laid. There would certainly be plenty written too of the almost pornographic eroticism that Calli had brought to the dance of the seven veils. Now there were sopranos that an elephant couldn't hide behind, it was no longer necessary to get a dancer to stand in for the scene, but after tonight's offering up of a woman's every last ounce of self-regard, it might well be impossible to find anyone, singer or dancer, to equal the shocking baseness of this evening's performance. At this rate, they might be able to tap into a whole new audience and put a stop to the public unrest over funds going to elitist opera companies. It would have been amusing, had it not been Calliope up there, stripping away all that was good in herself for the entertainment of people infinitely less deserving of respect and love than she was. Olivia felt physically sick with guilt. By every person in her life of whom she had rightly expected love and protection,

Caroline Smith had been let down. And now Calliope Syrigos too had been failed.

'I'm going back stage to find her,' Olivia told Dominic, glad of his appreciative smile which told her that he at least would accept her apology.

* * *

'Calli?'

There was no answer to her knock on Calliope's dressing room door, but it had been a very timid tap.

'Calli,' she repeated, and slipped into the room.

Calli had heard Olivia the first time - every sound, no matter how close to silence, tore like a fighter-jet through her skull. She watched Olivia's approach in the light-ringed mirror over her dressing table. She saw with muted satisfaction the change in Olivia's face when she registered the mess of tears and makeup that adorned her friend's swollen face.

'Why are you here?'

'To see how you are. When you didn't come out for your curtain call I...'

'I think you know bloody well how I am, darling,' interjected Calliope, lighting up a cigarette, despite the NO SMOKING sign.

'It was an amazing performance. I thought they were going to rush the stage when you didn't show,' said Olivia, with cheeriness brought on by cowardice.

'Well, count yourself lucky that you were here for it - I'm not going through that again. My little bitch of an understudy can get the big break she's been praying for; after tonight they'll pan her anyway.'

Olivia laughed self-consciously.

'You think it's amusing do you?'

'Of course not.'

'Want a drink?'

'No, I'll get one at the party.'

'Oh yes, the opening night party. How could I forget that?' said Calliope sarcastically. 'I suppose I'd better go, if only to get trashed at someone else's expense.' She leaned closer in to the mirror. 'What's left isn't a pretty sight, is it?' Calli sucked hard on her cigarette and started to remove the stage makeup.

Olivia knew full well that it wasn't the makeup to which Calli was referring.

'It's funny,' continued Calli, 'I remember years ago, watching a documentary about some girl who took an overdose and everyone thought she was dead. But she wasn't. She was totally aware of everything going on around her, just completely paralysed. If the guy doing the autopsy hadn't seen a tear run down her cheek, he'd have cut her open, alive. Can you imagine that? I was scared shitless after hearing about that. That's why I never tried to do myself in, even when I felt like it. Shouldn't have bothered fighting the urge - I might have been successful. Instead, I now know exactly how that girl felt, only no one noticed the tear on my cheek, did they? Not even you.'

Olivia looked away from Calli's uncompromising, icy stare.

'Enjoy it did you? Seeing me turned inside out?'

'How can you say that?'

'What else did you come for? You've shown fuck all interest in me since you got yourself discovered. How is that little shite, Angelo, by the way? When's the happy day?'

Olivia had to fight not to jump back at Calli with a defence of Angelo.

'That's just publicity. You of all people should know that. You're my closest friend, surely you don't think I'd get engaged without telling you?'

'Whatever. Is lover boy here with you tonight?'

'Yes.'

'You know, if you're going to end up with that sleaze, you might as well have married Guy.'

'Why did you send me tickets, if you didn't want me to come?'

'Don't flatter yourself. I didn't - my agent's got a standard list and you're at the top of it. Where do I fall on yours these days?'

'Please don't,' said Olivia tearfully, 'You know how important you are to me. I'm so sorry I've let you down - really, *really* sorry. Our friendship means everything to me. I love you. I can help you through this. Please forgive me. Let me help.'

Calli felt a certain gratification at the sight of the tears, but that was all. Why should she feel remorse for this when Olivia had everything - success, real talent, love and beauty. All Calli had was the latter and then she knew all too well that most people thought that was only skin deep. No, not even that. No deeper than the makeup on her skin.

'It's not too late, Calli, I understand how you feel now, but...'

Suddenly Calliope shot out of her chair and came at Olivia, 'Understand! *You?*' she yelled, 'Understand how I feel? Darling, you haven't a clue. Frankly, for my sake, I hope you don't, because if you did and still let me go through this alone then there's nothing left of our friendship.'

'That just isn't the case,' insisted Olivia, backing away a little.

'No? Have we *ever* been friends? You've always been jealous of me. Jealous of my looks, my career, my sex life. Admit it!'

Calli was nose to nose with her again.

'Yes, I've been jealous of you, but it's not important. What matters is that we've seen each other through so much. That's what friendship is about. What Father Timothy did to you, what Guy did to me, we survived it together - give me a chance, it really isn't too late for me to help you. Whether I'm jealous of you or vice versa, it just doesn't matter in the long run.'

'*Vice versa?* Me, jealous of *you?* Oh, you'd love that, wouldn't you?' spat Calli, desperate to hurt Olivia. 'The only thing I envy, is your abortion.'

There it was. That word they never used. The 'procedure', the 'terrible business with Guy' but never, never *that* word.

Olivia wilted into the nearest chair. Calli retreated to her dressing table and plugged the bloody, gaping wound of silence by filling her glass with opening night champagne.

'Why would you say such a dreadful thing? How can you say you envy that?'

'*You* terminated that pregnancy, Olivia. Not me. Not Guy. You. Of course I envy you; at least you had a choice.'

'You bitch,' said Olivia softly, 'Does it really make you feel better to punish me with that?'

'It's about time you faced up to the truth.'

'Face up to the truth? That's rich coming from you. You've got so used to hiding behind your roles, you haven't a clue who you are. You're denial personified,' she retorted with building fury.

'Why don't you piss off to the party and save your amateur psychology for someone who gives a shit?'

'I can't believe this. I came here to help! I was feeling so bloody guilty for letting you down. And why? Because I'd actually dared to be happy for a change. Why the hell that didn't make me stop to think about what kind of friend you are, I don't know. Thankfully, you've clarified that for me. I know exactly what kind of person would say what you've said to me. So fine, have it your way, I had a choice. Now why don't you admit that you had one too?'

'Get out. Go on, get the fuck out of here,' exploded Calliope, throwing everything that came to hand at the door as it slammed behind Olivia.

* * *

'Here, drink this,' ordered Dominic, forcibly pushing a large brandy into Olivia's wringing hands. 'You're a white as a sheet. What the hell happened?'

'Oh Dominic, I've said the most terrible thing to Calli.'

'I'm sure she'll forgive you.'

'No, not this. I don't think we can ever be friends again now.'

'Don't be so melodramatic darling. Nothing could be that awful.'

'Oh yes it could,' insisted Olivia, shrugging off the comforting arm Angelo offered.

'Why don't you run it by us and we'll tell you if it was so bad,' suggested Andrew.

'I can't. Not without betraying her trust and I've done enough already.'

'Well knowing Calli, I should think she deserved it,' Dominic smiled reassuringly. 'For you to stand up for yourself, the *prima donna* must have been pretty unforgiveable herself.'

'This isn't funny. I'm worried about what she might do after what I said.'

Her regret at the accusation she'd levied against Calli had been simultaneous with the crunch of the door behind her as she'd walked out on her friend. Her fingers were still on the door handle as the deluge of projectiles hit, just waiting for the thunder to subside before going back in to retract her words. But then the primal sobbing had come. Horrible, inconsolable grief seeming to fill the room until the pressure bowed the door outwards, pushing against Olivia's back as she listened, filling her with the desire to run.

Watching the performance, Olivia had known that Calli was once again questioning whether or not she'd asked to be raped - holding herself responsible for the unforgiveable crimes of a man in a seemingly unassailable position of power. Olivia had known that and still managed to walk right into the trap Calli had set. She had expected Calli to goad her - it was her way of testing the strength of Olivia's conviction that she was not to blame for Father Timothy's crime - but she had not prepared herself for just how far Calli was going to push. That Calli had used that most terrible of all weapons was a frightening measure of how desperate her need for reassurance must be.

It had been a cruel and unfair test. Olivia still felt it, still felt sick to have been reminded. And yet Calli had been right and she had been wrong.

'What am I going to do?' said Olivia with desperation.

'Go to her and say you're sorry, if you feel you have to.'

'I can't.'

'Then wait till she makes her appearance at the party and sort it out - a standing ovation always soothes the savage beast. She'll have forgotten whatever it was after a few drinks and a hundred autographs.'

'There's no way she's going to show up here tonight and even if she'd let me back into her dressing room, this isn't something I can solve with a simple apology. Why can't you understand?'

'Either I'm being told that a mere man like myself can't possibly understand how strong the friendship between you two is, or I'm being told that the same friendship is over within one short argument. What am I supposed to think?' laughed Dominic.

'Damn it, Dominic, I'm serious. After what you say she did at your last rehearsal, I'd expect you to be a little more sensitive - you yourself said you were worried about her.'

It suddenly seemed to sink in that Olivia was suffering from more than the usual post-traumatic stress that so often resulted from a run in with Calli.

'Fine, I'll go backstage, make sure she's all right and I'll persuade her to come to this tedious party,' offered Dominic.

'I don't think you're going to be welcome either, unless there's something you didn't tell me about that rehearsal of yours.'

'You're right,' said Dominic immediately, thinking that tonight, given the state she had left Olivia in, Calli might be more than he could handle. His deep discomfort during the performance should have prevented him from making that rash offer in the first place, he thought, desperately grateful that Olivia had knocked him back. To face Calliope, fighting with the knowledge that had she gone as deeply into Salome's character in rehearsal as she had tonight, she might well have – no, would certainly have - succeeded in seducing him, was a nightmare he could well do without. Tonight he had been shown a side of himself that was disgusting. Not a part of him that found the female form attractive after all, but one that found the debasing of a human being, any human being, a turn on. He didn't want to think about it. Andrew was a good man and Dominic wanted that, and not this other hideousness, to be what he had been looking for through the endless one-night stands. He wanted to forget about tonight and be happy.

'Dominic? Are you all right?' asked Andrew with timely tenderness.

'Yes, I'm fine,' he responded, already halfway to forgetting. Then he noticed one of their number was missing. 'Where's Angelo got to?'

'I've sent him to get Calliope. He managed to get me through the first night of *Tosca*, so there's a chance he can persuade her to come up to the party. It won't solve everything but you're right, the standing ovation she'll get from this lot may dull the pain a little.'

Dominic's inner voice screeched with alarm.

Are you insane? Don't you see how bloody dangerous that woman is now? For Christ's sake, she tried to seduce me of all people! Do you feel so guilty about whatever fool thing it was you said that you have to martyr yourself for Calli's sake?

And then his more tactful self asked, 'Do you think that's wise, Olivia? Calli's never been a great fan of Angelo. It's perhaps not the best time for Angelo to get his first impression of Calli. Animosity between a girl's lover and her best friend can ruin a relationship, you know.'

'Look, why don't I go? It's not too late for me to catch Angelo,' suggested Andrew, already in motion.

'No!' exclaimed Dominic, yanking Andrew back to his side in blind panic – there were limits and if Olivia wanted to be a naive idiot that was her business.

- chapter eleven -

Longstaff & Drew! How many times had she looked in the window longingly, dreaming of a recital worthy of one of their dresses, not to mention a pay cheque equal to the price?

'I'll take it,' Olivia said with huge pleasure, now admiring herself in a deepest blue crushed velvet evening gown, imagining her entrance at the opening night party for *Madam Butterfly* next month. Nothing, not even the fact that the dress was a size or two bigger than she had thought she was now, could take away from her happy state of mind - no matter, she looked great. She didn't even glance at the price before handing it over.

While she waited, she couldn't resist wandering back into the rear of the shop to gently lift a couple of wedding dresses from the bulging racks of tulle, taffeta and beaded silk.

'Perhaps you would like to try that on too?' suggested the sales assistant with a knowing smile as she handed Olivia her very first *Longstaff & Drew* bag, with its perfect pink satin handles. 'You are about to get married, aren't you?'

Olivia blushed, her eyes falling to her ring finger where there was, as yet, no engagement ring. She suspected that that would be changed over Christmas.

'I'm sorry, I didn't mean to speak out of turn. It's just that I've seen your picture in the papers. With two opera houses around the corner, we tend to notice what's happening in the opera world.'

'Oh that's OK. I just can't get used to everyone knowing something that we haven't actually officially announced yet. It is a beautiful dress,' she added, 'But I'm pretty sure it's bad luck to put on a wedding gown before the engagement ring's on the finger. Don't worry, I'll be back in the new year.'

'OH! Well, we won't let the cat out of the bag.'

'Thanks. Merry Christmas,' said Olivia cheerily as she stepped out. For a few minutes she just stood there in front of the window, enjoying seeing the same dress she was carrying displayed before her, savouring the moment before braving the seasonal craziness of Covent Garden. The air had a crispness to it that reminded her of winter in New York. Cold and dry, so that it hurt as she breathed in. New York seemed a lifetime ago now. Going to Mass at Saint Patrick's on Fifth Ave with Calli, window-shopping at Saks and then ice-skating at Rockefeller Center in the twinkling shadow of the massive Christmas tree, repeatedly falling in hopes of having a couple of rich men rescue them from the ice. It worked more often than not. Olivia laughed even now, though to think of Calli was to feel pain. Calli hadn't spoken to her since the opening night of *Salome* and Olivia could think of no way to mend the rift.

Thank heavens then, that all the punters wanted to do this time of year was take their kids to see *The Nutcracker*. Though the Royal Ballet was churning it out night after night, English National Ballet were still able to sell out their shows at the Coliseum, so perhaps now that *Salome* had been laid to rest, Calli would heal enough to see that there was still something of their friendship worth holding onto. As she walked up the street, Olivia cast a regretful look back towards the Coliseum and then picked up speed with the end of the day in mind. Just one more rehearsal for *Butterfly* this afternoon and then she and Angelo would be free to enjoy themselves.

And it was just as well that Olivia had looked back over her shoulder at that moment for had she not, she would have seen Angelo and Calliope whispering and kissing at an intimate little table in the Italian restaurant which she hurried passed.

'Is there something wrong?' asked Calli, moving away a little to look at Angelo's face, which had paled noticeably underneath his perpetual tan. Why the sudden pulsing of his jugular vein under her nibbling lips and the hair at the nape of his neck jumping to attention beneath her searching fingers should have alerted her, she did not know - this reaction was what she had been

199

aiming for - but his reassuring denial did nothing to convince her that all was well.

'Tell me!'

'Olivia just walked by.'

'Did she see us?'

'No, I do not think so.'

'I thought you said she was going for a costume-fitting.'

'That is what she told me.'

'Are you sure she didn't see us? Maybe she lied. Maybe she followed you here.'

'No, no. She had shopping bags.'

'Probably out buying some sexy little outfit to surprise you with,' said Calli jealously and completely disentangled herself from her lover's arms.

'My darling, please don't,' sighed Angelo, taking her hand in his and pressing the softness of it to his cheek. He hated to see her unhappy and yet this vulnerability in one so self-assured was bewitching. That was how it had been when they'd first come together. He had sat through *Salome* in constant fear that he might climax. Decapitation had seemed a minor price to pay if it meant feeling those mouthwatering lips on his. When Olivia had sent him back stage, his mind had been awash with images of what he could do with that sultry body, especially when its owner appeared so uncaring of propriety. By the time he'd arrived at Calliope's dressing

room door, he had already cast aside what thoughts he had of remaining true to Olivia and was convinced that she would not find out if he were to pick the forbidden fruit just this once.

Just once was all he had intended, but on the other side of the door he'd found a woman who was as nefarious as he could have wished for, though only after she'd sought solace from him, crying bitter tears whilst cradled in his strong arms, bathed in kind words. Since success had come her way, Olivia had not needed support and Angelo had missed the attestation of his manful power. With Calli he felt needed to the extreme, whether it be sexually or emotionally, and that spelled love. Not that he didn't love Olivia still - he was nothing, if not thorough and his heart was surprisingly capacious, given how great his love for himself was.

'I need a drink. Waiter! Would you bring me a martini please?' called Calli, reaching for her cigarettes, playing agitatedly with the box. 'Angelo, I don't think I can go on like this much longer. I can't bear to think of you and Olivia together.'

'But my love, it was you who told me that I must continue this charade.'

'I know, but I didn't realise how horrible it was going to feel. Do you *really* love me, Angelo?'

'Do I love you? How can you ask this question? You are right, this cannot go on. I must tell Olivia the truth today. Now!' he responded with utter conviction, brought on by the sight of tears welling in Calli's fabulously feline eyes. He could not think of anything but making her happy at this moment.

'No. No you can't,' she retorted, pressing him back into his chair. 'Not until the end of the season. If we told her the truth now it would be a disaster. Olivia's only just got her career back on track, it wouldn't be fair to take that, as well as you, away from her now. And think what damage it would do to your career if the press were to get a hold of this, not to mention what it would be like performing *Madam Butterfly* with Olivia a total wreck. That's all there is between you and me being free. Only *Butterfly*. Surely our love can sustain us through that.'

Her words were music to Angelo's ears. What magnanimity in the face of her distress. Surely Olivia would not be so generous if she knew the half of what had been going on. How he loved Calliope Syrigos.

And she in turn truly felt herself to be finally, genuinely in love. There had never been a love as deeply felt as theirs. But how could there have been, for what other than the most fathomless of loves could justify her striking this death knell for her once precious friendship? When Angelo had come to her bearing tidings of regret from Olivia, Calli had wanted nothing less than to return Olivia to the quicksand of failure from which she had remarkably escaped. For what she had said and for being fool enough to send Angelo, Olivia deserved to have him fucked to within an inch of his life.

But afterwards, with all the hate dispersed in one explosive moment of revenge, she could see what a dreadful thing it was that she had done. If she did not love Angelo then what Olivia had said to her became true. Olivia became right. Olivia became undeserving of this punishment. There was nothing for it but to believe, believe, believe that she loved Angelo. And yet she could not have Olivia fall apart - she knew well that it was, more than anything, the sight of herself in collapse that had driven Angelo to infidelity in the first place, and Olivia might well have the same power over him if the truth came out.

'Yes,' agreed Angelo, 'Just *Madam Butterfly* and then we will be together for all the world to see. Ah, I am so tired with all these rehearsals. I cannot wait for this evening to come. Oh my darling. I am sorry, I have upset you once more.'

'I wish you didn't have to go. Can't you make some excuse? Spend Christmas with me, Angelo. *Please*,' Calli begged, sorrowfully resting her head on Angelo's shoulder.

'If you will not let me tell Olivia about us, then I have no choice. It was arranged well before you and I found each other. If I do not go she will suspect something. I am sure that she is expecting me to make the formal proposal of marriage while we are there.'

'And what are you going to do?' asked Calli, once again withdrawing contact.

'I don't know,' Angelo lied. Olivia's agent had frogmarched him down to Aspreys just days earlier, where a freelance photographer had miraculously snapped him buying an engagement ring. It did not sit well, to be so obviously manipulated. He had half a mind to give it to Calliope instead, here and now, but she would surely be the first to remind him of his career. An engagement could just as easily be broken as made.

'You're going to go through with it, aren't you?' snapped Calli.

'Of course not, my love, my life.'

'You are! I can hear it in your voice. How can you say you love me and do this? Why don't you just take a knife and cut my heart out now - it couldn't hurt any more,' she sobbed like a true diva, then snatched up her bag and cigarettes before storming out of the cafe.

What a magnificent woman she was, thought Angelo as he picked up the chair she'd sent flying. He did not go after her, he knew it was too late and he had a rehearsal to get to. Besides, was the engagement not proof of just how little Olivia meant to him? After all, it would make hearing about his true love for Calliope all the harder on her. Calli would certainly come around to his way of thinking once he'd explained it with the right amount of Italian charm.

* * *

Once upon a time the Royal Opera House canteen had been a sordid, hot and sticky sort of chamber in the bowels of the building, where ceiling fans turned so slowly that they always appeared to be running down as they pushed through the stagnant, smoke and grease heavy air. There had been no better argument for refurbishing the building and it was now an airy rooftop space, yet still as fearsome and oppressive a place to Olivia as she stood in the queue, her eyes wandering over the crowds of almost invisible ballet dancers stuffing their faces with the one thing that came out of the kitchen that could be deemed edible. Chips. Not only edible, but worthy even of the royal crest that the chefs laboured under. Everyone from footmen to divas scorned the multitude of fantastic eateries in Covent Garden market for the exquisite, golden crispiness of the House chips. Thinking, however, of the dress in her bag and the rehearsal ahead, Olivia resisted temptation, grabbed a cup of vivid orange tea, and looked around for a space to park herself.

It was then that she saw the Mafia, otherwise known as the percussion section, sitting out on the balcony overlooking the old Covent Garden marketplace, despite the cold weather - probably because it was packed with lovely ballet dancers. As usual they were all laughing, and for the most part at Guy. He always had told the best jokes Olivia reflected with a smile as she continued to scan the room for a spare seat. Her smile faded when she realised that Fate had provocatively left the only vacant chair at Guy's table.

If she hovered long enough, surely another table would be bound to open up, but the orchestra could already be heard through the speakers and she could see from the TV monitors, which showed a constant mind-bending view of the stage, that the stagehands had almost readied everything for the *Butterfly* rehearsal.

OK Olivia, she said to herself, *Just pull yourself together and go out there. You've got nothing to be frightened of. For God's sake, just do it!*

'Hello,' she said awkwardly, 'what's the joke?'

For one surreal moment, Guy thought that he'd heard Olivia's voice. Not that he hadn't been hearing it in his head ever since he'd first clapped eyes on her in rehearsal; they were always bound to bump into one another and his imagination had taken him through all possible scenarios. This one was just one more, though neither the *Olivia begs for forgiveness and I laugh in her face* nor the *Olivia begs for forgiveness and we go back to my place* outcome seemed appropriate to this situation. How dare his subconscious give him a dose of reality to contemplate? he thought angrily and decided to snap out of this particular nightmare before his colleagues noticed his absence from the conversation - any less than a joke a minute and they'd know something was wrong. Only then did Guy notice that they too had ceased to talk, suddenly finding the insides of their newspapers quite riveting reading.

'Oh!' said Olivia when faced with the uncomfortable silence. Of course, she concluded, it must be she herself who had caused them so much amusement. Suitably embarrassed, she made to go.

That this was a real dose of reality barely had time to register before Guy reached out an instinctive hand to stop her from fleeing. 'No stay!' he heard himself say with a far friendlier voice than he had prepared for her over the weeks. 'We're not laughing at you. No, *really!*' said Guy.

His firm grip had a dangerous potency which sent an unwelcome shudder through Olivia. She wished she hadn't found the courage to come over in the first place but Frank was already pulling back a chair for her and smiling, warm and welcoming, as he had when she'd been his best buddy's girl - before she'd broken his best buddy's heart, that was.

'What's so funny then?' she asked

'That!' offered Guy with a nod in the direction of an eager-faced woman, chatting with a solitary horn player, who was incongruously as attentive to her every word as he would have been if she'd been a gorgeous young ballerina. 'It's what's her face. You know, that novelist.'

'What's she doing here?'

'Writing a novel about opera apparently. Doing some background research. Scrounging around for some realistic snippets.'

'And what's so hysterical about that?'

'Let's just say she's a little gullible.'

'A little!' laughed Charlie. 'You wouldn't believe the bollocks she's lapped up - if you'll pardon the expression!'

The whole schoolboy lot of them snickered at this, including Olivia, who was glad that nothing had changed.

'And?' coaxed Olivia.

'Well, from the spark in her eyes when I was telling her about our maestro, I wouldn't be surprised if there was a thinly veiled Sasha in the book. Did you know, for instance, that he wears a toupee?' smiled Guy.

'Or that he only got the job because of the strong Masonic influence hereabouts?' said Frank, giving Olivia a limp hand shake and a saucy wink.

'Or that he's impotent?' she joined in, thrilled at the prospect of getting her own back on Petrov.

'But of course, everyone in the know, knows that!' laughed Guy with that laddish look that had made her heart tremble all those years ago.

For a while Olivia felt totally at ease as they concocted more tall tales about life in the Opera House, planning to pass them on to other members of the orchestra, just to add corroborating evidence and credibility to their lies.

And then the mobiles started to beep. Gone were the days of sitting patiently at the back of the pit through hours of music they were not needed for. Nowadays they left a sentry post percussionist to count their endless, silent bars of rest in lonely agony, ready to alert colleagues to an approaching entry. Olivia felt a pang of regret at the sound. It had been fun slotting into a past life. The regret, however, quickly turned to panic when she perceived a silent exchange between Frank and Guy. Bloody Mafia, always looking out for each other. Now they were going to cover for Guy.

Alone suddenly, an edgy quiet sat between them for some time.

'Cigarette?' offered Guy.

'Can you do that here? No thanks – I quit,' remarked Olivia, fearful as she said it, that he would come back at her with the old jibes about her piety.

'Good for you.' Guy even surprised himself. 'I don't seem to be able to crack it.'

'Always at the end of the next tour. Right?'

'Yup - same with the booze.'

More silence, all the more loud for the chattering dancers around them.

'Christ, it's cold out here - can I get you a coffee or something?' asked Guy, juggling in his mind all the words that he needed to say with all the words he ought to say, thinking that he should put some space between them before the former spilled out untempered.

'Yes, that'd be nice,' said Olivia, gratefully.

But he just couldn't move. Kept playing with his cigarettes, looking off across the rooftops, then at his shoes, and then suddenly into her watching eyes.

'I really loved you.'

That had not been what either of them had expected him to say.

Now neither could look at the other.

'You shouldn't have got rid of our baby, Olivia. We could have made it work.'

'Do you really think so?' she said quietly. 'It didn't feel like I had a choice at the time and it doesn't sound like much has changed.'

'So the fact that I still smoke and drink means I'd have made a lousy dad?'

'You know it's not just that.'

'You didn't give me a chance. Maybe if I'd had something to be different for, I'd have changed.'

Olivia wanted to scream at him at the top of her glass-shattering voice and felt furious to have to restrain herself to a sandpaper whisper, 'But you did, Guy. You had me, and you still carried on with other women. I know, I know - it didn't mean a thing. But it did to me. Anyway, if we'd really been meant to be together we'd have got through all that. I wouldn't have wanted to change you in the first place and you'd have forgiven me for going ahead with the... there would have been another time that was right for us, another chance.

Instead you ended it right there and then. You didn't give me a chance either.'

'Not because you had an abortion Olivia.'

Guy took guilty pleasure at seeing Olivia's eyes dart away as he used the forbidden word. *Good.*

'Sure, I'd have liked to have had a chance to be a dad, but I don't think you're going to hell for not wanting to be a mum - that's your crazy guilt trip. But you made the decision without a word to me. That bitch friend of yours, always interfering. Calli was so fucking pleased with herself.'

'No she wasn't. She understood what a horrible thing that was for me. She was the only one there for me. Think back Guy. Be honest with yourself – you were the first to know that I was pregnant. I did the right thing – I told you. And what was your response? What did you do? You disappeared on a bender with your mates, so don't give me all that romantic crap about wanting to be a dad. You left my friend to do what you should have done. Calli has her faults, but she was there for me then, when I needed help. She was there for me.'

Guy had nothing to say to that. He turned his pack of cigarettes over and over on the table, thinking.

'You're right, I'd have made a terrible dad,' he said finally, his eyes still focused on the gold box.

Olivia glanced secretively at him and was shocked to see the tears she thought she would be shedding rolling instead down his cheek.

'If it makes you feel any better,' she said gently, 'a day hasn't gone by when I haven't thought of that child and regretted what I did.'

'Strange, I thought that was exactly what would make me happy, but... now I'm not sure it does.'

'Not sure? Thanks!'

'All right. It doesn't make me happy. OK? You win - I was a shit and now I regret it.'

'So now what?' asked Olivia.

'I guess we just get on with our lives. You've obviously got what you want sussed out, though you might as well have stuck with me if you're going to end up with that arsehole.'

Olivia laughed, 'Funny you should say that; Calli said the same thing.'

'We're just jealous,' remarked Guy dryly.

'You always were,' commented Olivia in an empowering moment of clarity.

'Well, she won in the end.'

'Love's not supposed to be about winning.'

'Maybe not, but I don't think Calli would agree. You should watch her.'

'That's below the belt, Guy, and you're wrong.'

'Possibly, but all's fair, etc., etc.'

'Did she ever come on to you?'

'No.'

'Exactly.'

'But I really did love you.'

'And, by that, I suppose you mean that Angelo doesn't love me.'

Guy looked at Olivia hard. Should he tell her that he'd seen Calli and Angelo tucked away in a secluded corner of the National Gallery a few days earlier? She'd hardly be likely to believe that he was now given to frequenting art galleries on rainy afternoons, and right now she was so magnificently, beautifully indignant at his suggestion that she took his breath away.

'I'm sorry,' he said quietly. 'It's just that I really *do* love you.'

There was no time for a response before Angelo descended upon them, bristling with jealousy, determined to usher Olivia off to the rehearsal as expeditiously as he could.

He had spotted them together the second he'd pressed his face to the round window in the dangerous swing door and had proceeded into the canteen without a care for whom he flattened in the process. All thoughts of Calliope were banished at the sight of Olivia and Guy sat in silent union. The moment his back was turned that *musician* had leapt at his chance to get his slimy hands on Angelo's beloved Olivia. How dare he, when everyone knew that she was soon to become the wife of Angelo Verasano? And vastly more of concern, was the fact that

Olivia was giving him the time of day. Was she? Could she? Did she still love that oaf?

The thought incensed Angelo and it was only pride and the desire not to be cruelly parodied by the bestselling authoress he'd clocked in the far corner, that prevented him from hauling Guy out of his seat to settle their differences - that, and the fact that he was well aware that Guy would more than likely beat the crap out of him if he did so.

Instead, no pause in the rehearsal was not filled with Angelo's questions about Olivia's conversation with Guy. She might have been irritated, had it not been so flattering to have a man like Angelo beside himself with jealousy over her. And through her persistent denial of any lingering sentiment for Guy, she could hear Guy's voice telling her that he still loved her.

Between the two of them, they were doing wonders for her self-esteem.

- chapter twelve -

Calliope had had a miserable Christmas. If not working in foreign lands, she would normally have been welcomed into Olivia's family, decamping with them to their Norfolk cottage, feeling all at once joyful to be included and resentful of the closeness that served to highlight her own lack of a family. That not being an option this year, she and Scarpia had instead curled up on the sofa in front of a string of Disney classics, Bond movies and religious epics, the cat contentedly hooking his claws through the jacquard fabric whilst Calli knocked back martinis and Homewheat biscuits till she felt quite sick.

Calli preferred to think that her nausea was clear evidence of how deep her love for Angelo ran, for it returned again now as she raced her red MG across the interminably flat Norfolk landscape, thinking of Angelo nestled by a fire not far from here. Once again she pictured him asking Olivia's father to go down to the pub in the village so that he could ask for Olivia's hand in marriage, and yet again she saw the entire, jubilant family raising their glasses of barely drinkable wine over dinner to toast the happy couple. The scene was a pine cone and cinnamon scented, log-fired, candle-lit cliché. It was enough to make anyone sick.

A hand-brake turn took the car off the road into the corner of an empty field. Calli rested her head on the steering wheel, between white-knuckled hands, and struggled to find a more comforting image. When, for instance, had there ever been anything warm and glowing about that cottage? It was a dank and poky place, the nearest village being just far enough away to make the walk to the run-down pub, with its biker clientele, an unpleasant thought at any time other than the height of summer. Having arrived late at night, the Yuletide festivities had always been launched with a good family argument, with Katriona's children wrapped in sleeping bags, and shivering nonetheless, as the adults congregated round the prized Aga, all accusing someone else of having forgotten to bring the matches. This year they might finally see the upside to her revolting smoking habit, thought Calli, her mood beginning to lighten as she imagined Angelo chilled to the bone, valiantly wading through a very unItalian Christmas lunch, wishing that he had taken Calli up on her idea to surprise his own family by showing up in Tuscany for midnight Mass on Christmas Eve.

'Right,' said Calli, 'where the fuck am I?'

She gave the SatNav a good thump but both it and her smart phone had clearly passed judgement on her dubious expedition, so she rooted around in the glove compartment for a good old-fashioned and thoroughly unwieldy map.

Though the malevolent thought of ruining the family gathering with a surprise visit had been firmly in Calli's mind as she'd hurtled up the M11, she had in fact made the journey to seek out the Carmelite monastery she'd contacted earlier in the season. Not that *they* had invited her either - her feelings towards the one, were much as to the other of the two possible destinations of the day. She had felt the rejection by the nuns to be wholly unfair, the words *we don't do that sort of thing* seeming tantamount to implying that she might as well be a prostitute as be an opera singer. So, she was here to do her research whether *they* liked it or not.

Satisfied that she was in more or less the right place - a dimly recollected nightmare orienteering field trip in the company of those other much-hated nuns giving her a false sense of security in her map reading skills - she hopped out of the car and struck out across the field towards a wood. The wind was bitter as it slapped her across the face, the land hard beneath her unsuitable boots. Where grass had managed to take a hold in the barren, plough-rutted soil, it was covered in a crisp white frost that would not melt, but crunched like snow underfoot along with empty red bullet shells. The sight of them gave Calli a thrill. Looking over to her car she half expected to see a crazed farmer, with shotgun in hand, coming after her. There was no one, but the eerie silence stood the hair at the base of her neck on end.

The sun was already low on the horizon as she disappeared into the trees. Here, even the wind was quietened and Calli, courageous though she was, turned at every crack of a twig and flight of a bird. The woods were sadly unkempt. Trees had toppled and remained where they had fallen, rotting slowly inside their clothing of velvety moss. It was therefore more by accident than design that Calli happened upon what remained of a path. Decaying railway sleepers sank under her weight into the half frozen black mud of decomposing leaves, taking her deeper and deeper into the darkening woods, until she began to lose her enthusiasm for this escapade. Only when she came upon a gate with an enticing PRIVATE PROPERTY - NO TRESPASSING sign hanging by one nail from an askew post, did her excitement build once more. It was an invitation to climb over, if ever she'd seen one. Henceforth, the ground grew wetter, the sleepers fewer and farther between but she didn't care, her boots were done for anyway and with what strength was left in the sun's rays being absorbed into the tangled branches above, there was little choice but to press on.

It was almost dark when the trees suddenly petered out and there, across a small, grey, unmoving lake stood a sprawling manor house of a jumbled mix of periods, the original Elizabethan timber framed building having been added to by every generation. It was surrounded by fruit trees and there were several walled gardens in which Calli imagined the nuns toiled over vegetables and roses during the summer months.

Faced with her goal, Calliope couldn't move. As dusk imperceptibly transformed itself into a late afternoon night, reality began to dawn and Calliope recognised the bizarre nature of her quest. Had she really come here to spy on a bunch of nuns? Whatever, a confirming glance into the blackness behind told her that it was too late to retrace her steps now. Fearing that the ice on the lake might crack and swallow her without trace if she tried to cross it, she followed its circumference, accompanied by the dull toll of a bell, calling the nuns to *vespers* in the Victorian chapel.

When she reached the chapel, Calli realised that there was no way to get into it from outside the house. It appeared though, that there might be an entrance on the other side of the building. It had never struck her that it might be acceptable to just drive straight up to the front of the monastery. But of course, hidden though their lives were, they couldn't function without some access for tradesmen and the like. Now, it seemed a far preferable option than sneaking up to the windows to have a peek at their private lives. Suddenly, with memories of just such occasions rearing up at her out of the past, Calli didn't want to get caught here. What had seemed like an amusing game, now seemed like a terrible invasion. A part of her was furious to feel all the indoctrination show itself to be so effective. Why should she respect these women, just because they chose to hide here and pray for those in a world whose trials they knew nothing of? And yet, seeing shadowy forms moving through the dimly lit rooms of the house towards the chapel, Calli felt ashamed of herself for having come to the place. There was nothing for it but to scale the high wall that was designed to keep prying strangers out of the grounds. Luckily for Calliope, it was not designed to prevent the escape of inmates and so she achieved her aim in no time at all, by way of an aged wisteria.

On the other side she discovered that there was indeed a front entrance to the monastery, with a car park and a door with 'reception' written over it, but clearly she could not have got in; there was an entry phone beside it for identifying visitors. There was, however, a public entrance to the chapel, through which a couple of people had just disappeared, apparently having failed to notice her ungainly descent from the wall. She was glad there had been a flower bed to break the fall rather than concrete to break her ankles. For a moment she hesitated. She had not been in a church in many years. St. Patrick's in New York was it since she'd been kicked out of convent school and that didn't really count, as Catholics and atheists alike went in there; it was just one of the things you did on Fifth Avenue. Still, this was only *vespers* and it was also likely to be the nearest she'd get to the Carmelites.

The chapel was grand for all its modest size. It was entirely candlelit tonight, but there was a series of small round stained-glass windows that must shed a beautiful, kaleidoscope light when the sun hit them. Beneath each one, a station of the cross was intricately carved into the wall. The vaulted ceiling was painted a rich, pavonine blue, the shimmering gold bosses reflecting the flickering candle light like stars. At the altar, the eye was irresistibly drawn to the lustrous, ornate cross, its surface so deeply burnished that it seemed almost on fire. To its left there were three steps up to a huge arch, with massive oak doors opened to reveal a nun slowly heaving upon the bell rope, her sisters filing past her one by one into the unseen chapel where they worshipped.

Calliope dipped and crossed herself before she knew what she was doing. It felt as if there should be a congregation turning to look disparagingly at her, whispering *hypocrite* as she took a seat, but except for a man sat in the front row of chairs, she was alone. He was praying. Calli could not.

When the bell stopped it was replaced by music. Music which surprised Calliope. Bach's concerto for oboe and violin, accompanied by an organ, swirled gracefully around the chapel. At first she thought it was recorded and wondered what the world was coming to if even Carmelite monasteries piped in *Classic FM* elevator music, but then one, tiny mistake belied that assumption and gradually her ear recognised that the organ pipes to the right of the altar were live with music - played perhaps by the other person she'd seen entering the chapel - and more startlingly, the interweaving lines of the oboe and violin were coming from within the hidden side chapel. If it was not opera, Calli was not usually interested, but now she found her eyes closing so that she could better focus on the exquisitely lyrical playing. That those musicians were performing where none could see them, and perhaps without knowing that there was even anyone in the main chapel to hear them, gave the music a divine purity for Calli. The elegance of the two instruments in loving conversation seemed of unsurpassable beauty until the *vespers* prayers were sung.

A lone voice, so lovely it could have been Olivia's, would pierce the waiting silence with innocent simplicity, turning the high modal phrases like a mirror to the sun so that the radiance of the music illuminated the heart, warmed the soul. Under different circumstances Calli knew that she would have laughed to hear the awkward answering phrases as they were sung by the remaining sisters. As evidenced by the many out of tune notes, they were not universally musically gifted, but in their singing there was none of the blind to reality conceit of the amateur choruses Calli so despised. Rather, there was an alchemic joy in the sounding of those words that brought tears to her eyes.

As the spoken prayers were said in gentle tones, Calli could do nothing but jealously try to imagine what it would be like to be that nun; to have faith enough to want no more recognition for her talent than to sing in the house of God. But she could not imagine what it was to be that girl, for not only did she feel the lack of religious faith in her life but also faith in herself. An audience applauding was confirmation of a kind she could not do without.

Had she ever had faith in herself? wondered Calli as that enviably celestial voice claimed once more the attention from all else that glittered in the place. What was it that Olivia had said? *You've got so used to hiding behind your roles, you haven't a clue who you are.* She'd been right and yet it was not strictly fair because Calli felt that there never had been a person there to start with. She'd been an only child, despite her parent's devout Catholicism and Calli had always felt that they hadn't even been pleased to have the one child. It was as if they truly believed that the act of conceiving her had been a sin, that she was the embodiment of sin and a constant reminder of their weakness. If she were told that they had had sex only the once, Calli would have believed it. Perhaps all that pent up sin was the fuel for their terrifying anger towards her. Though had her father been angry? In actual fact she could remember very little of her relationship with him. It was her mother's vitriolic attacks, so unpredictably sparked, that stuck in the mind - the afternoon when no more than five years old, she'd danced around the house in her pink leotard, the moment of panic when she'd started to bleed for the first time, the day of her confirmation when she'd proudly worn her miniature wedding gown and said that she wanted to marry daddy not God. All had ended in violence. She was glad her parents wanted nothing to do with her.

She had been aware of it since she'd walked through the door. The confessional box was behind her, to the left. If she kept her eyes to the altar, its dark doors evaded her peripheral vision but the supreme effort entailed in blotting it out, made it all the more present. Horrifying though the feelings that *Salome* had provoked were, like the sundry other emotions she took on board for roles, Calli had successfully filed them away once the performances were over, helped by the heady romance with Angelo. And because they were so easily dispensed with, Calli had thought of them as just an unfortunate glitch in an otherwise happy existence. All that was in the past, nothing to do with her as she was now. She was a survivor. But, if it was all behind her, why was Father Timothy's voice now so distinct in her ear that he could be standing next to her, asking her to step into the confessional? The dulcet lines of *vespers* were no match for him and nor was she.

Sober and alone - this was a combination she'd been avoiding at all costs for years and yet only now, when there was neither audience, be they friends, lovers or patrons of the opera for her to play to, nor a bottle of vodka to hand, did she recognise it. The truth was making itself heard and it was terrifying. More than any physical harm that he had wrought, it was Father Timothy's voicing of his thoughts in that threatening twilight that had done the real damage. Vile thoughts that had both held her up to ungodly worship and deconstructed all that was blameless in her. His voice was always with her. Always. A discordant counterpoint, never entirely drowned out by the exuberant salsa tune she'd made of her life. Calli bowed her head, closed her eyes and clasped her hands over her ears. His voice was louder still. Only tears provided relief.

The prayers were long over before Calliope realised it. When she uncurled, the man in the front was gone and she thought she was alone. There was, however, another present. Sitting at the top of the stairs to the side chapel, tantalisingly balanced between their two worlds, was a nun. Calli felt a surge of anger at finding herself observed. Was life so tedious in their haven that she made entertaining viewing? *Ours is a hidden life and we don't do the sort of thing you are asking.* No, but give'em half a chance and they'll treat you like a sideshow, thought Calli bitterly. What would that nun do, she wondered, if she were to brazenly walk up those steps and into the monastery? Just as they had accomplished musicians in their ranks, did they leave a black-belted karate champion to guard against intruders between services?

Calli got up and walked down the right hand side of the chapel very slowly, pausing at each of the stations of the cross to examine the details of the carving, aware now that the nun was almost certainly waiting for her to leave so that she could come into the chapel to snuff out the candles. In a world where Calli had suddenly found herself totally without control, there was something reassuring about this warped little game she was playing. At the front she paused as if considering running the gauntlet, chancing being struck down by a bolt of lightning as she passed the altar. Thinking of the constriction she had felt as a teenager, faced with disbelief and false judgement wherever she had turned, she acknowledged a certain pleasure at the thought of this woman, so representative of her banishment from the Faith, finding herself powerless to expel Calli from the chapel. A silent life, a hidden life, not a *please get the hell out so I can go back to my prayers* life.

Calli looked the nun in the eye, expecting her gaze to be averted, and when it was not, she expected to meet a look of defiance to reflect her own challenging stare, but instead she found a disturbing air of dignity and pity broadcast by the watery blue eyes of this beautiful old woman. Calli was embarrassed to have cast blame here and could not accept the benign smile that came in response to her visible contrition. She turned and walked swiftly to the back of the chapel but found herself unable to leave, paralysed in the face of the confessional box she would have to pass by. Again she turned, thinking to retrace her steps, but the nun was still there. She turned again and then again and again until tears of sheer panic began to fall, and then again and again until she was sobbing, and then again, again, *again* until she was on her knees rocking, shaking, choking, suffocating.

If she had not felt the fabric of the sister's habit against her face, she later felt sure she would have just carried on crying forever. As it was, she looked up through her tears into the old woman's face and could do no more than quietly repeat over and over, 'He raped me. My priest raped me.'

There was little doubt that she was about to be cast out of the chapel. It was the way these things were dealt with. Though barely able to feel her legs, Calli attempted to rise. 'Don't worry,' she said, 'I'm going.'

The sister's hand around hers, strong through years of weeding in the vegetable garden and kneading bread in the kitchen, shocked her into silence.

There were no words spoken by the sister, nor did there need to be. Calli allowed herself to be hoisted into a chair and when her surprise at finding the nun taking the seat next to her had subsided, she began to speak without fear. For several hours she sat there in the candlelight with her silent companion, feeling her hand squeezed with comforting understanding wherever she anticipated that it would be dropped with disbelieving disgust. She had not expected her Faith ever again to find a place in her heart, and yet here today she had discovered that just as Father Timothy's voice was always with her, so was her God. In her darkest hour He had sent her someone who was not only prepared to give up her whole life to His glory, but also prepared to risk getting in trouble herself, in order to rescue a stranger.

And yet, to be received with inexorable compassion was both ecstasy and agony, for nothing could make her grieve more than to have herself brought with every reassuring pressure from the sister's hand, back to the moment at the Sainsbury's check out when finally someone had shown themselves to be on her side. Until now, Olivia was the only person who had both known the truth and accepted the truth.

Olivia.

Betrayed.

She told the sister about that too.

By the time the bell began to toll for Evening Mass, there was such illuminating joy at Calli's core that she felt none of the iciness in the wind as she left the chapel and walked into the dark night. For all the sins she had confessed to the sister, she could not find it in herself to admit how she had come to be at the chapel that afternoon, and so there was no choice but to walk the far greater distance than she had come cross country, along the winding lanes, back to her abandoned car.

That her feet hurt, her frozen fingers felt as if they would snap off, and the MG, not thrilled to have been left so long in the cruel wastes of Norfolk, needed an hour of coaxing into action, did nothing to dampen Calliope's inner glow.

As she headed back to London, Calli was smiling. She knew what she had to do and for the first time ever, what she knew she had to do and what it was right to do, were one and the same.

- chapter thirteen -

'Are you all right, Calli?' asked the stage manager, seeing her turn green as the orchestra struck the spiky opening chords of *Dialogues des Carmélites*, and fearing that opening night was about to be wrecked before it had begun. Members of the company had been dropping like flies since the latest super-flu hit London.

'I think I'm going to throw up.'

'Shall I call for the understudy?' he asked, praying that the answer would be a firm negative - Calli had astounded the director with her reformation and transformation since the much heralded *Salome* and there were potential sponsors in the audience who would sign away their heirs' inheritance to the impoverished company without a second thought, if the performance came even close to the dress rehearsal.

'No!' gasped Calliope, swallowing the bile in her throat at the suggestion. 'I'm not going to let those bloody critics have their predictions come true. I'll be absolutely fine.'

'Well, I'll leave this here, just in case,' he said, gingerly placing a sand-filled fire bucket next to her before running off to avert the next disaster.

On stage, the scene - a library in a grand chateau - was set, the curtain raised. Calli looked on from the wings and rued the day she'd set her mind to have this role. The thought of the unforgiving array of journalists, at the ready to destroy her career, made her wretch into the bucket as the Marquis meanwhile discussed his fragile daughter Blanche with his son, Le Chevalier.

- *Blanche is just too sensitive and intense. A happy marriage is all she needs. All pretty girls have a right to be nervous...*

- *Mark my words; more than fear endangers my sister's health, perhaps even her life. It is not fear alone that causes her sorrow, but something deeper in her soul. Fear destroys her from within, even as the unseen worm eats away at a fruit.*

And wasn't that the truth? thought Calli wryly as she sipped some water before going on stage. Who was she kidding? Why lay the blame for her nervous state on tonight's performance, when she knew all too well that it was really for fear of her rendezvous with Angelo after the performance? Tonight would be the end of it, if she only had the courage to do the right thing.

But, take her cue from her character right now and she would be undone, for Blanche de La Force was as pathetic a creature as Calliope could have imagined. Of all the asinine operatic plot devices, and just about all were laughably absurd, this one had to be the lamest.

Virtually fainting with fatigue from attending Mass, Blanche described her all-consuming fear during the rough carriage ride home and then begged to retire to bed, only to scream in terror after glimpsing the manservant's shadow on the wall as he lit the candles for the night, and then return to her father to announce her consequent decision to become a nun!

And yet what made Calli want to laugh out loud also spoke to her tortured conscience, resonated through her and gave the audience reason to suspend disbelief.

Alas! sang the Marquis. *One should mistrust all decisions taken in a moment of fervour. One should not renounce the world out of spite.*

I neither hate the world nor despise it, responded Blanche, *I am quite unable to bear the strain... if my nerves were only spared, you might see what I could accomplish.*

My beloved child, if this is so, only your conscience can decide whether this attempt is more than your strength can endure, retorted the Marquis with irony, causing his daughter to throw herself at his feet.

Oh father, pity my grief and let me hope that I shall find some cure for the dreadful torment that makes my life so unhappy. If I could not believe that our Lord is guiding my life and fate, I would die of shame at your feet.

Now Calli rose and, with the rest of the scene fading into black, a spotlight followed her slow walk to the front of stage as, shaking, she sang with chilling gravity. *I give my life to Him. I abandon all. I renounce it all. So that He may restore me to grace.*

As she stood looking into the expanse of darkness that hid an audience transfixed, it struck Calli that she might learn something if she were to follow Blanche's lead. At the end of tonight's performance she was to break off her relationship with Angelo but it did not seem enough to make amends for all the wrongs she had done over the years. When she had left the Carmelite monastery she had felt that giving up Angelo was adequate, but now it seemed too easy. As she had predicted, the news of his engagement to Olivia had been announced in the new year and in the flurry of activity since, there had been no opportunity for them to meet. Calli had been furious when she'd heard the news and felt still more annoyed to realise that even if she had not decided to do the right thing, she would have dumped the bastard anyway. It somehow took the righteousness out of what would have been a magnanimous act.

What then could she do? Tell Olivia what she had done? What was to be gained by breaking her friend's heart? There was some hope that Angelo himself would not do it; he hadn't ever offered to marry any of his other leading ladies, so perhaps he really did love Olivia. Perhaps he was planning to ditch Calli tonight. Wouldn't that be an unfair twist of fate? she thought miserably. But maybe God wanted more from her.

She was not unaware that this performance was a watershed in her career. From the very first notes she had brought to life this evening she had sounded as she had always wished she could. Throughout the rehearsals she had seen the surprise in the eyes of her fellow singers, felt the excitement building as the first night approached. The Coliseum was buzzing with it now. *Carmélites* was going to be a hit. *Channel Four* and the *BBC* would be fighting for the rights to film it and rake in the international royalties. Calli was going to get the credibility she had envied Olivia for and in gaining it she would, to some degree, be robbing Olivia yet again.

It was not Angelo that she should be walking away from tonight, but her success. To end her career now and join the sisters behind the high walls of the convent would be the supreme sacrifice, the truest proof of friendship, the ultimate act of worship.

While her imagination ran romantic riot, stage crew dressed in footman's garb had been busy around her, taking away the Marquis' chair, revolving the bookcases to reveal contrastingly plain wooden shelves and pushing them to the rear of the stage to flank the vast oak doors that had dropped in from above as the windows lifted into the gods. Now a red metal grille, the full height and width of the stage, descended. Representative of the double grille that was supposed to separate the nuns from their infrequent visitors should they need to speak, it cast its shadow over Blanche as she sat awaiting the Mother Superior, like bars in a prison. And as Blanche prepared to justify her urge to become a nun to the Mother Superior, so Calli watched the entrance of Dame Cecelia Jones with trepidation. The ripple of applause that spread through the audience at the sight of the famous diva served only to heighten her anxiety. Before giving up singing, more than anything else she wanted the approval of this woman. She wanted to prove that she was worthy of such a great teacher.

The Mother Superior was so old and ill that she could barely walk and had to be supported to her chair by two sisters. She was nonetheless an imposing, uncompromising woman, not willing to let Blanche fool herself with a romanticised image of life in the monastery. The fiction did little to curtail the flight of fantasy on which Calli had embarked. This was no more than a practice run for the real thing - the challenge now to make the audience believe this unlikely story and willingly embrace the Mother Superior's acceptance of such a doubtful character to the Order. With that sincerity she would later gain acceptance herself, thought Calli as she spoke with the Mother Superior

What is it that draws you to the Carmelites? asked the Mother Superior.

The quest for a life that is heroic.

Or a certain manner of living which you believe quite wrongly would make it easier to be heroic - would put it in the palm of your hand? the Mother Superior challenged brutally.

Calli lowered her eyes to her wringing hands and answered humbly.

Reverend Mother, I can promise you I have never harboured such desires.

The most dangerous of our desires are those we call illusions.

In that case I had certainly better be deprived of them, rejoined Calli resolutely.

Difficult trials await you, my daughter.

What matter, if God has granted me the strength to face them?

It is not your strength but your weakness that God wants to test in you.

Blanche and Calliope broke down in tears at the harshly addressed words.

Go in peace my child, offered the Mother Superior gravely.

The brass section of the orchestra now accompanied the change of scene to the convent workrooms, the music reminiscent of a sci-fi sound track as the horns and trumpets fanfared through the darkness. Meanwhile, aided by a dresser - though with her nails bravely clipped short for the role, buttons and hooks no longer presented the problems they once had - Calli was in the wings making the quick change into her novice's habit.

'Suits you darling!'

Calli turned in alarm at the familiar, aspish voice. Sure enough, Olivia's agent was there at her side.

'What the hell are you doing here?' whispered Calli, with no less venom, even as her panicked eyes darted to the stage and saw what she had expected. Evidently, even the understudy must now be sick as a dog and ready to come to the rescue at the last moment and take over the role of Blanche's fellow novice, Constance de Saint Denis, was Olivia. For fuck's sake, God had some sense of humour - for an instant Calli thought to call in her own understudy, but the lights were already beginning their ascent, so with Laura's amused chuckle still niggling at her, she joined the other nuns as they went about checking through the recently arrived provisions and folding laundry.

Faced with Olivia, Calli's guilt over everything she had said and done made it impossible for her to look at her friend and besides, she was at a total loss as to know how she should 'be' now. Olivia knew well how intractable Calli usually was, and must assume therefore that things between them were as they had been on the opening night of *Salome*. Her decision to end the relationship with Angelo was irrelevant; Olivia could never know about this redeeming act of friendship, as its worth would then be obliterated. Would seeing contrition so soon in Calliope's eyes lead Olivia to suspect her of hiding some other sin? If so, it would not be the first time she would have been correct, though it had never before been Olivia's man Calli had gone after. With her mind so much confused, Calli was grateful that it was Constance who opened the scene.

For her part, Olivia's eyes too averted themselves from her friend as she sang sweetly of the memory of her brother's wedding when she had danced with all her heart. Her voice was bright and joyous, though her heart felt heavy with regret at the memory of the last time she had seen Calli. She could still hear her sobbing and desperately wanted to find a way to heal the rift between them, but Calli was not one to forgive easily.

The tension built by the two sopranos as they refused to look at one another, even as they sang together, was something to be marvelled at by the critics the next day. A stroke of genius that the director was more than happy to take credit for.

Meanwhile the pain of confrontation was very real to his stars.

The Mother Superior was dying and they were discussing it.

If I could save the life of our dear Mother, I would gladly surrender my poor life, such as it is, sang Olivia, feeling that the ill-health of the Mother Superior was a metaphor for their ailing friendship, and that the ensuing discussion on mortality was laden with meaning for them both, the two of them having come so close in the past to forgetting the value of life, that only their friendship had prevented tragedy.

But have you never feared death? asked Blanche, clearly terrified at the very word.

Maybe yes, long ago when I did not know what it was.

And now?

I no longer know what I think of death. I try to do whatever I am told and I always find it delightful. Can I be blamed if the service of the Lord gives me so much joy?

As Olivia hit the culminating magnificent high 'C', Calliope was haunted momentarily by the jealousy of old. Brought back somewhat to her senses, there was a flash of anger in her voice as she continued on, *Are you not afraid that God will grow tired of so much good humour?*

Forgive me Sister Blanche, responded Olivia finally daring to raise her eyes to Calli's, *I cannot help thinking that you came here to do me some harm.*

Silence.

Very well, sang Calliope, *You are not mistaken. In fact... I envied you ...*

You envied me? This is the strangest thing I have ever heard. You envied me when I fully deserved to be punished for having spoken so thoughtlessly... Oh Sister Blanche, will you help me atone for being so foolish? Let us pray together and offer our poor little lives for the life of our beloved Mother.

There was a great warmth in Olivia's voice that seemed to reach out for Calliope, offering unexpected forgiveness. But Olivia had always forgiven in the past, so why be surprised now?

Because this time was different, but Olivia would never know and all could be well, thought the deluded Calli, still wed to the idea that she would be ready at the close of the performance to sacrifice everything for the sake of friendship. Her eyes therefore returned the smile of reconciliation, thus enabling them to complete the scene in character rather than in person, though as usual there was little to distinguish the two.

How very childish, chided Blanche.

No, Sister Blanche. I think it is such a lovely inspiration. The thought came to me out of nowhere - I have always wished that I would die young.

And what have I to do with this foolishness?

The very first time I looked at your face, I knew my wish had been granted.

What wish? demanded Blanche, violently, recoiling at the inevitable.

I knew that God would do me the honour not to let me grow old and that we would die together. Where and how, I assure you I do not know.

Are you not ashamed of believing that your life could ever redeem the life of someone else? Stop! cried the terrified Blanche, turning away from Constance.

I would not hurt you for the world, Constance then said, Olivia's voice lifting to a gorgeous ethereal high before the orchestra crashed in and the lights went out as Blanche spun back to look Constance in the eye.

As the stage was now set for the Mother Superior's deathbed scene, Olivia and Calliope stood awkwardly for a while in the wings. The scope for expressing the grander sentiments of life seemed far greater in the musical rather than the spoken word. On stage there was a freedom to feel every emotion to its infinite reaches. Off stage, in the wings, it was all whispering inhibition.

'I'm sorry,' said Calliope eventually.

Astounded that Calli had, for the first time ever, apologised first, Olivia flung her arms around Calliope and squeezed tightly.

Almost immediately, Calli broke away, her hand over her mouth as she dove towards the fire bucket, only just making it before she threw up.

'Sorry about that,' she smiled weakly when she was done, 'I've got that flu that's going around.'

'Well I hope you're not pregnant, Sister Blanche,' joked Olivia, already wondering how long she should wait before asking Calliope to be her bridesmaid, hearing Calli's rejoining laugh with deep gratitude. She had been terrified to come here tonight, sure that at the very least Calli would explode and give the press something juicy to write about - which was exactly why the now bitterly disappointed Laura had pressed Olivia into stepping in so late in the day. But, Laura's disappointment was Olivia's victory.

Meanwhile, the story continued on stage with the harrowing death of the Mother Superior. Dame Cecelia was in her element, Olivia and Calliope in awe, as she portrayed a woman tortured, both physically and spiritually, contorted by agonising pain and doubting her belief just when she should have been comforted to know that she was going to the arms of her maker.

I am alone. Alone and helpless, without the slightest consolation... God has become a shadow. Alas, I have been thinking of death each day of my life and now it is of no help at all, she despairingly told a nun, who could only be disturbed by this sudden lack of religious fortitude.

Then Blanche knocked at the door and was bid come and kneel at the Mother Superior's bedside.

My daughter, you are the last who came to us and for that reason you are the closest to my heart, sang Dame Cecelia. *Dearest child, no matter what happens you must not surrender your simplicity. Remain always so sweet and pliant in the hands of God. The Saints did not always resist temptation. They did not rebel against their nature. Rebellion is always the work of the devil. Above all, never despise yourself. God has taken your honour into His keeping and it is safer by far in His hands than in your own. Goodbye, my dearest child.*

Kneeling, with head bowed, as Dame Cecelia sang with a tenderness that could easily have convinced Calliope that she actually thought of Calli as the Mother Superior thought of Blanche, Calliope was cognisant that here was an opportunity to be completely carried away by her earlier dreams of becoming a nun, and yet suddenly the idea was receding with dizzying rapidity, replaced by only one thought. A question that she would never have thought to ask in her current incarnation, had Olivia not been here tonight.

When exactly had her last period been?

As Mother Marie struggled to deal with Mother Superior's worsening condition, the patient writhing in her bed, begging for drugs and ranting in her delirium about seeing the Convent Chapel empty and desecrated, the altar rendered in two, straw and blood on the ground, the Order forsaken by God, abandoned by God, Calliope was still asking herself that question.

Despair clings to my skin like a mask that chokes me, cried Dame Cecelia, her voice devoid of its great beauty, carving through the flesh with its serrated edge as she wrenched off, one by one, the pieces of her vestment, until the revelation of her hair that had been long and lustrous just hours earlier but had now been cropped aggressively short in a mad moment of method acting, caused a shocked gasp from the audience as she called out for God's forgivness.

There was no difficulty for Calli in finding the tears for Blanche, who was sobbing for the loss of the Mother Superior as the curtain came down on Act One.

* * *

The sight of a nun running along St. Martin's Lane with her skirts hiked up over her knees and dodging traffic in the Charing Cross Road before disappearing into Soho, cheered even those dejectedly searching the streets for entertainment, having failed to secure theatre tickets. But wider still were the eyes of the sales assistant at the all-night chemist in Soho, when the same nun tipped her lipstick, hairspray and cigarettes out of her handbag onto the counter in her search for the twenty pound note lurking beneath. Until tonight, working in this area, she'd been secure in the knowledge that she had seen just about everything, but she was still aghast, mouth open like a goldfish after a toaster has fallen into its tank, long after the nun sprinted out, habit swirling, the words *keep the change* barely out of her lips.

'Shit!' cursed Calliope, realising when she got back to the Coliseum that she was already due on stage. In thinking she could get to Soho and back in a twenty minute interval, she had neglected to allow for the difficulty of running in this ridiculous get up. The stage manager, who had been forced to hold the second curtain for her, hurled abuse at her as she legged it past him.

'Where the hell have you been? Some of us would like to get to the party before bloody midnight,' hissed Dame Cecelia, sending a wave of expensive perfume over Calli and Olivia as she flopped back into her open casket, just seconds before the curtain rose on the chapel, lit only by the six candles that flanked the Mother Superior's coffin. At its foot, Blanche and Constance knelt in prayer. From the heaving of her shoulders it appeared to the audience that Blanche was still in tears as she guarded the corpse, but having been apprised of her state over the phone on his podium, the conductor held things up just long enough for Calli to catch her breath.

'You OK?' whispered Olivia. 'Where did you get to?'

'Just ran out for some Lemsip.'

'Couldn't the company doctor fix you up?'

'God, I must be ill; I didn't even think of that!'

243

'Will you just get on with it girls?' hissed the Dame from her coffin.

Lazarum resuscitasti a monumento fœtidum, sang Olivia, overjoyed to hear the diva's rebuking tone, harkening as it did back to the days at the Royal Academy of Music when she and Calli were inseparable partners in crime.

Tu eis, Domine, dona requiem et locum indulgentiæ, Calli responded, hopes of retaining her friendship with Olivia ebbing silently away beneath the beautiful Latin as she thought of the next interval with a mournful heart.

Quiventurus es judicare vivos et mortuos, et sæculum per ignem, continued Olivia.

Tu eis, Domine, dona requiem... Calli almost sighed.

Et locum indulgentiæ. Amen, they intoned together, the opposing moods of their voices mingling to poignantly express the dichotomy of feelings that death must always evoke in the faithful.

They had never previously had the opportunity to sing on the professional stage together and, but for life's bitter and twisted turns, this might have been a night to look back on from old age with immense pride, after a lifelong friendship, thought Calli as they took the stage for the next scene. Carrying armfuls of flowers for the grave of the Mother Superior, Blanche and Constance sat down together on a bench.

Who would have thought that she would have had such difficulty in dying. One could say that in giving her such a death, the good Lord had made a mistake, like being given the wrong coat at the cloakroom. Yes, I think her death belonged to someone else. Too small for her, so very small that the sleeves barely covered her elbows...

What do you mean? asked Blanche.

It means that another, when it comes time for him to die, will be surprised that he finds it so easy. We do not die for ourselves alone, but for each other.

Now that would solve everything! Calli thought to herself and would dearly have liked to have the energy to indulge the thought with the attention she'd given to so many other fancies, but it took all her concentration to keep up her smile for Olivia's benefit and keep the churning stomach acid where it was.

With nothing more in her mind than getting away from Olivia and back to her dressing room, she knew well that the performance was unlikely to be the *tour de force* she had first thought it would be. And yet, if she could have stepped outside herself and seen how readily the fear of what awaited gave life to her character, she would have laughed at herself for ever believing that she could walk away from the insatiable, addictive kind of success that every critic's pen was handing her as the opera snuck quietly up upon the audience, ready to surprise them at its conclusion with an act of love so tragic, so pure that it outstripped anything Puccini could dish out.

By the close of the second act, the French Revolution had begun with a vengeance and Blanche was

245

completely terrified by Sister Marie's suggestion that the nuns should take the vow of martyrdom.

* * *

Blue.

Unquestionably, undeniably, unbearably blue.

It had been hard to hit the mark whilst hoisting up her habit, but clearly she had.

Pregnant.

It didn't seem possible, nor should have it been, but the pill had been the last thing on Salome's mind, let alone Blanche's.

Calli sat there for the rest of the interval, spellbound by the little line that stood between her and doing the right thing.

It was no less present in her mind as she stood with the other nuns in the devastated chapel when the curtains opened upon the Third Act. Olivia's words of concern as they took their places had to be blocked from her mind if Calli weren't to run screaming off the stage like a madwoman. She hated Olivia for the ease with which she had jumped to forgive. How could Calli then do differently than go through with her initial plan to ditch Angelo? But if she did, then there could be no baby for Angelo to claim as his and thereby screw up Calli's grand gesture towards sisterhood.

Abortion?

Just the thought of it was surprisingly abhorrent now that it was her own womb harbouring life, and there was surely a difference between a woman making that choice when she was in her twenties, versus Calli's current position - closer to forty than she'd admit even to herself. If not now, when? Was she really supposed to wait for that mystical Mr. Perfect to come along? If she looked deeply enough she would have to admit that Salome and Blanche could not be held entirely responsible for this accident. Always convinced that no one would ever love her enough to commit, for years she had been inviting just such a mishap in countless moments of forgetful abandonment to passion, perhaps never quite able to shake her upbringing - not ever able to fully take control of her own reproductive capability. When it could result in just such a situation as this, neglecting to use contraception on the odd occasion was, in a sense, as good as never bothering. But to so confidently advise Olivia that it was the only right choice and then not be prepared to do the same? What kind of person would she be, if she did that?

Cornered by her friend, just as Blanche was now as the nuns went one by one behind a screen, each to tell the chaplain in secret whether they agreed to take the martyr's oath. Any dissenter and all could go free, without guilt or regret. When the chaplain came out he announced that there had indeed been one against, and Sister Mathilde could immediately be heard inferring to her neighbour that it had been Blanche.

Not so, said Constance, claiming that it was actually she who had done so, but that she was now ready to take the vow.

Cornered by a friend.

Blanche began to weep, but stepped up to take the vow with Constance, nonetheless. However, as the other nuns came forward to do likewise, Blanche fled.

It was in her father's ruined home that Blanche sought refuge, thinking that this would be the last place the angry rebels would expect to find her. But, Mother Marie was hot on her heels, ready to bring her back to her sisters. It was a painful scene for Calliope; sharing in the character's guilt and shame.

Why are you crying? asked Mother Marie.

I cry because you are so kind. But I feel ashamed of my tears. I was born in fear and I have lived in fear. All the world despises fear, so it is only right that I too should be despised. I have had this feeling since I was a child. The only person who could have kept me from saying this was my father...

To be despised, my daughter, responded Mother Marie, *is not the real tragedy, but only to despise oneself.*

* * *

As the curtain went up on the final act, a deep throbbing bass line walked under a slowly repeated low note in the clarinet, punctuated by a sombre beat on the timpani before the French horns marched over the top like a Roman legion gathering, as they progressed the chilling funeral theme, the rest of the brass section and

248

then the strings into a terrifying, advancing mass. All was black, save the cardinal-red scaffold centre stage, around which was gathered a restless crowd all clothed in cream, visually linking the revolutionaries' upcoming act of injustice to that of the aristocracy in the first act.

With the music continually building layer upon layer of tense harmonies and the snare drum rattling into life, the nuns got down from the carts that had brought them to *Le Place de la Revolution* and one by one mounted the scaffold. Having been forbidden to wear their habits any longer, the nuns were now clad in black rags, crimson scarves wrapped symbolically about their heads as they stood united in their fate, eyes front. Beneath, the chaplain who had taken their vow brought them absolution, furtively making the sign of the cross before disappearing into the crowd.

Suddenly the music seemed to entirely cut out, until the ear adjusted and recognised the omnipresent bass line and above it the perpetual theme now voiced by gentle, low flutes. It was now, with only their faces lit that the nuns began, to the same theme, to sing the *Salve Regina*, waiting for the guillotine to descend. In other productions there would be warning for the audience as each nun walked to her fate, but here there was no opportunity afforded for anything other than trembling anticipation. Every departure jarred the spine, made eyes instinctively slam shut.

Salve Regina mater misericordæ, vita dulcedo et spes nostra, salve at spes nostra salve...

The sound of the guillotine falling was simultaneous with one of the nuns stepping suddenly back into the surrounding darkness as the others continued unflinchingly.

Salve Regina mater misericordæ, vita dulcedo...

Again the guillotine swooped, another face disappeared.

...et spes nostra, salve at spes nostra salve. Salve Regina mater misericordæ, vita dulcedo et...

Again it fell, another voice silenced.

...spes nostra, salve at spes nostra salve. Ad te clamamus...

That the now dreaded sound came at seemingly unpredictable moments in the text made the heart leap even when it need not.

...exsules filii. Hevæ ad te suspi...

The voices ceased one by one.

...ramus gementes et flentes. Ad te suspiramus gem...

Calli could barely breathe for the bitterness rising at every relentlessly judgemental snap of the blade.

...entes et flentes in hac lacrimarum valle...

Still the blackness swallowed back the courageous faces.

...Ergo, advocata nostra, illos tuos miseri...

The heavenly line of their voices was sliced apart, yet fought on unerring, with Olivia always sailing gracefully, joyfully over the others.

...cordes oculos ad nos converte. Et Jes...

Still the audience flinched in their seats.

...um benedictum fructum ven...

Now only three voices struggled on.

...tris tui, nobis post hoc exsilium osten...

Now they were shrunk to a duet.

...de. O clemens, o pia, o dulcis Virgo Maria, o dulcis, Virgo Ma...

Now Constance was alone,

...ria. O clemens, sang Olivia, her voice rising, like the sun, through the pervading gloom in the Coliseum to a magical high 'A' as Constance caught sight of her friend Blanche, making her way through the crowd to take up her vow. Then she smiled, radiant with understanding and continued to the last.

...O pia, o dulcis Virgo Ma....

It was easy for Blanche, thought Calli as she stepped up to the scaffold, God had given the Mother Superior a horrible death so that she could face the guillotine with fortitude. In a gesture of friendship and sisterhood, Blanche was doing the right thing. But as she began to sing, Calli could not face her real choice with such certainty. She desperately wanted to have the guts to do the right thing, but how could she, when whichever she chose - to have this child, or to end this child - she would be doing the wrong thing?

Deo Patri sit gloria

Et filio qui a mortuis

Surrexit ac Paraclito

In saeculorum saecula

In saeculorum…

CURTAIN.

chapter fourteen

ACT THREE

Luckily she had the money for the private clinic.

She'd heard so many horror stories about N.H.S. terminations. She did not know if they were true or not, but she wasn't about to find out for herself. The thought of having to go through with this, in a maternity ward, surrounded by women with babies, was sickening. She could imagine the disapproving stares when they discovered what she had done. Not one of these imagined women had ever in their lives done such a thing - they were all gloriously content with their little bundles of life and beyond that there were even some amongst them who were in the same position as herself and had chosen to make right their mistakes by nurturing them to term. And how dreadful would it feel to be faced with a woman who had just lost a much planned and yearned for child? Or, indeed, for that poor soul to have to face her? It didn't bear thinking about.

And yet it did not seem right that the anonymous building she was stood before could be where it would all end. She unfolded the appointment letter just to make sure she'd got the right address, just to see in black and white that she really had decided to go ahead. She was surprised how easy it was to go up the few steps and announce herself through the intercom. A double-fronted Georgian house on a quiet, tree-lined street in west London. Save a small brass plaque sticking up from a shady bed of hostas with a couple of doctors' names on it, there was no evidence that this house was any different from the rest. Not even the right-to-life brigade were up early enough to harass her. When she'd been studying in the States, these places were constantly in the news, besieged as they were by fundamentalist Christians who sometimes went so far as to firebomb the clinics or even shoot dead the doctors in them. She'd expected to have to run the gauntlet this morning, to fight for her right to choose. Part of her felt aggrieved that no one cared enough about what she was doing to try and stop her, felt guilty that this was all going to be so easy now that she'd made up her mind.

The counsellor was lovely. Made it clear that they were not in the business of encouraging women to make this choice unless it was absolutely what was best for them, and without a doubt what they wanted. Again she felt guilty. She was being given the opportunity to walk away but she couldn't. The decision was made and it was the right one.

It was the right one.

Maybe so, but she had to punish herself anyway. She had told herself that it was because she had a rehearsal tonight which couldn't be missed, that she was going to take the option of having the procedure done under local anasthetic. She had told herself that but it was the excuse, not the reason.

The room itself reminded her of a dentist's office. Small and sterile, the walls applewhite with a few well-chosen prints hung where the patient could best gain from their relaxing images. Along one side there were cupboards, from which the attending nurse had lifted a crisp white gown for her to wear. To the other there was a long countertop into which was sunk a stainless steel sink. As she sat waiting on the high black table, she wished that the tap were at least dripping, so that she would have something to focus on other than the morning sickness that was, for the last time, beginning to well. Instead she rocked back and forth, watching her reflection distort on the mirror-bright surface of the autoclave next to the sink, but always aware of the tray of medical equipment that lay in front of it, covered with a white sheet of paper. Everything was so white.

'Good morning,' said the doctor, her voice full of compassion and understanding, 'How are you feeling? You look a little pale.'

Who wouldn't with all this white light bouncing off the walls? she thought as she watched the ghostly nurse checking the tray.

'Sick, but otherwise OK,' she lied with an overdone smile.

'You've spoken with the counsellor?'

The doctor knew, all right, but she wasn't going to let that deter her.

'Yes.'

The doctor looked through her notes. 'So, let's see. No gynaecological problems previously, no abnormal cervical smears, regular cycle, this is your first termination and you're just nine weeks, by the date of your last period. Good, that all points to very little chance of complications.'

'Meaning?'

'That should you, at any time in the future, want to have a child, there should be no problem,' said the doctor, unsuccessfully trying not to let her reservations colour her voice. 'On that note, let me reiterate what I'm sure you've already been told; it's very important that you do come back for the follow-up appointment, just to make sure that everything is as it should be. Right then, if you'd like to lay back and place your ankles in these rests. Fine. Now I have to place the speculum, just like we do for a smear test. I know it's hard, but try and relax. OK? Now I'm going to introduce an anesthetic and a muscle relaxant which will dilate the cervix. I'll just let you have a moment to yourself while that takes effect.'

But the nurse didn't leave. Instead she took a chair and perched herself at the head of the table.

'Do you want to talk?' the nurse asked gently.

'Not really,' she replied and turned her head away from the woman so that she wouldn't see the tears trickling down her face. 'It's just the wrong man and the wrong time,' she then added and closed her eyes.

The nurse took her hand when the doctor returned and she did not refuse the comfort, though she also could not prevent herself taking it away by way of asking the doctor if she could see whatever there was to see when it was all done.

'Whatever you feel is right,' the doctor replied evenly; it wasn't the first time she'd had the request.

It really was like the dentist, she thought as the doctor commenced her work with what sounded like the suction tube the dental assistants always shoved into the back of your throat when the dentist was drilling.

'There must be a mistake,' said the doctor suddenly, even as the nurse gasped and dropped her hand with disgust.

'What do you mean?' she asked, propping herself up to see the doctor recoiling, her hand letting the instrument crash to the floor as if it had been red hot, dark drops dripping slowly from her blood-soaked white coat.

'You said you were only nine weeks,' accused the doctor, backing still further up against the wall and starting to scream.

'But I am,' she said, tearing the flesh off her heels in her attempts to fight free of the stirrups, desperately clawing herself into an upright position so that she could look to where the horrified, tearful gaze of the doctor was riveted.

And then she too was screaming as she saw not the tiny, unidentifiable mass of tissue she'd been expecting, but a baby at term, torn limb from limb and yet still crying up at her *mummy, mummy, mummy...*

'Are you OK?' screeched Maggie, the wardrobe mistress, bursting through the dressing room door after hearing a terrified scream.

For a second Olivia did not know were she was. She could still hear that tiny broken voice... *mummy, mummy...* and she looked to the floor expecting to see the horrible image that was still blinding her, confirmed in bloody reality... *mummy...*

'I'm fine... really...' she murmured, shaking her head, desperately trying to rid herself of the horror within, 'Please just go, I'm all right.'

'Suit yourself,' Maggie snapped, muttering *like hell you are* as she shut the door behind her.

'Oh God, how am I going to get through this?' sobbed Olivia, turning to the mirror and seeing the deathly white face of Butterfly, the geisha girl, staring back at her with rivulets of black forming as tears splashed onto the dressing table.

It hadn't been like that at all. Not so easy and not so terrifying either. She had not been alone. Calli had gone to the clinic with her, both the first time, when she'd chickened out, and the second time when they'd had to face a group of life-saving nutters outside the clinic, all of them men and all on their knees praying. Reminding her of all that she had been told about the church's view on what she was intending to do, the image of them praying would have been a more effective deterrent than any of the graphic photographs of aborted babies that the campaigners so often handed out in the shopping centre, had Calli not been there to curse them and remind Olivia of just how hypocritical it all was. Calli had been holding her hand when she went to sleep and there with the man-sized tissues when she woke up.

How was it, that a friend who could be so supportive and loving, could now do what Calli had done? The pair of them, Calliope and Angelo, coming to her to tell her, amidst claims that they hadn't meant it to happen and that they both loved her still, that they had been having an affair, that Calli was pregnant and that they were planning to get married. It still seemed impossible - as terrifyingly real and unreal as the nightmare she'd just had. But the engagement ring, barely past the point where it felt obvious and uncomfortable on her finger, was absent; thrown in the face of that bastard.

She noticed that he hadn't come running when she screamed, despite his dressing room being just next door. He was probably preening himself for the performance, too busy thinking about what was best for himself to hear her distress, let alone the distant whisper of his conscience. What conscience? If the affair with Calli were not indication enough of its demise, his positively enthusiastic welcome of the publicity department's intervention when Olivia had resigned, provided the conclusive evidence.

Let the press and public in on how operatic life was behind the scenes? Never. She was supposed to go on as if nothing had changed, maintain status quo until *Madam Butterfly* was over. Hadn't she lost enough, without losing her career as well? Laura was the smoothest of the persuaders. The publicity department merely waved her cast-iron contract under her nose and waxed lyrical about the treasured reputation of the Royal Opera House.

In the end, she was so numbed she didn't care - Angelo and Calli had done such a thorough job of humiliating her, it was impossible to walk away from this with any dignity. What difference if she sang on till the end of the season? At least this way she could be out of the country when the news finally broke - Laura had booked her up for months to come and what had once loomed ahead as a cruel separation from her fiancé, now looked like a welcome release. Otherwise, she could well imagine that Laura & co. would be expecting her to complete her degradation by dutifully smiling for *Hello* and resist the temptation to tread on the trailing skirts of the designer wedding dress as she followed Calliope down the aisle as old maid of honour. After all, who else could Calli turn to for a bridesmaid, having already slept with all her other friends' partners?

Why had she thought that understanding Calliope's envious motives for destroying every relationship she was faced with would somehow protect her from suffering the same fate?

Looking back, Calli's cautions about Angelo's character sounded more and more like warnings about her own weakness. How many times had Calli finished telling her how easily led astray men like Angelo were, with the phrase, *and I should know*. They deserved each other, thought Olivia angrily as she struggled to her feet under the weight of Butterfly's lavish bridal kimono. They'd be lucky if they even lasted a year. The thought seemed to make it all that much more hurtful. She really loved Angelo, she really loved Calliope, and she knew that had they truly been right for each other, she would have found it somewhere in her heart to see past her own pain and give them her blessing, but to have her heart broken for a love less intense than the jealousy and cupidity that inspired it, was too much to forgive.

The dense, aggressive fugal music hardened Olivia's nerve as she stood in the wings to watch the beginning of Act One. For once Laura had a point. Calli had taken her fiancé, Angelo had taken her friend, but neither must be allowed to rob her of her voice. That they thought she would allow her career to be destroyed all over again was implicit in their concern that it should not. It truly was repugnant that Angelo obviously imagined losing him could be as signifcant to her as the loss of her own child. And, as for Calli, if it were not for the thought of the poor child she was carrying, Olivia could relish the image of Calli looking enviously at her photo on *Opera Monthly,* once the novelty of her latest, greatest role had worn off and she'd realised that her career was just where she'd told Olivia hers would be if she had a baby to look after.

The opening scene was at first reassuring to Olivia - Angelo, in the guise of Lieutenant Pinkerton, conversed with Sharpless, the American Consul to Nagasaki outside the little house he had just leased on a hillside overlooking Nagasaki Bay. Though the characters were doing no more than discussing the merits of the sliding paper walls in his new home, and then meeting his servants, the music was so endowed with romanticism that they could have been singing a love duet. So then, when later scenes called for her to sing of love, Olivia felt that she could give them, in her mind, no more substance than paper screens. And, though it hurt the musician in her to think, for now, of this glorious music as one-dimensional, overblown pulp, she drew strength from concluding that there was no music more appropriate for the philandering, deceitful Angelo than a Puccini melodrama.

How apt, she thought as Pinkerton began to sing about the nature of adventurers like himself and his feelings towards the Japanese woman he was about to take as his wife.

La vita ei non appaga se non fa suo tesor i fiori d'ogni plaga... d'ogni bella gli amor... Il suo talento fa in ogni dove - He's not satisfied with life unless he can get the greatest enjoyment out of each place he visits... and win the heart of every pretty girl... he does what he pleases wherever he goes.

...qual farfalletta svolazza e posa con tal grazietta silenziosa che di rincorrerla furor m'assale, se pure infrangerne dovessi l'ale - she flutters like a butterfly and settles with

such silent grace that I am seized by a wild desire to pursue her even though I should crush her wings in doing so.

'Arsehole,' muttered Olivia as Sharpless attempted to prick at Pinkerton's non-existent conscience.

Sarebbe gran peccato le lievi ali strappar e desolar forse un credulo cuor - It would be a huge sin to tear those delicate wings and break a trusting heart, he sang to no useful end.

Pinkerton had no shame and happily drank a toast to the real American wife he would one day take. It was beyond Olivia that Angelo had the balls to go ahead with the role. It was he who should have resigned, thought Olivia as she went on stage to meet him in the most ironic of scenes. With all Butterfly's friends and family looking on, some with deep reservations, others thinking he was the most handsome man they'd ever seen, she was married to Pinkerton by the High Commissioner.

Olivia was surprised at the ease with which she was able to keep her calm through what she had anticipated being an impossible trial. And, lulled into a false sense of security, she went on without fear through the sad ruination of the wedding party when Butterfly's family denounced her after discovering that she had abandoned the faith of her ancestors in favour of Christianity.

But then Butterfly had to step behind a rice paper wall and helped by her servant, shed her wedding dress in favour of a gossamer white robe as Pinkerton watched, his desire inflamed by the sight of her shadowy form preparing for him. And suddenly it was just the two of them on stage. The wedding night, and all this time Angelo had been feeling aggrieved at the unnerving absence of love or pain in Olivia's eyes as larger, blacker, and more beautiful than ever, they steadfastly returned his every search for some sign that she was bothered, with nothingness. To think that the distress he had felt upon having to give up his beloved Olivia was wasted, seemed too much punishment for his mistake.

He already knew it was a huge mistake. Of the two, it was Olivia that he would have wanted to take home to his mother. But it was Calli who was carrying his child and he could not shake the good Catholic in him, nor pretend that he was not enamoured with the idea of having finally sired a child - he had been secretly concerned for some time about his fertility, given his extraordinary list of lovers and not a baby to show for it. So, it was with Calliope that he would return to his Tuscan village, with TV crew and paparazzi in tow to give up his 'most eligible bachelor' status, but it was Olivia that he was most desperately in love with at this moment, and he gave Pinkerton his all to get the desired confirmation of his enduring place in Olivia's heart.

She fought him hard, but she might as well not have bothered. She ignored stage direction and refused to be held in his arms, he left his mark and came after her, every ounce the predator Pinkerton, attacking her with her own weapons, standing so close behind her as he sang that the notes vibrated every cell in her body.

Ma intanto finor non m'hai detto, ancor non m'hai detto che m'ami - But you still have not told me, you still have not said that you love me. *Le sa quella Dea le parole che appagan gli ardenti desir?* - Does this goddess know the words that can satisfy such burning desire?

Le sa - she knows them, answered Olivia. *Forse dirle non vuole per tema d'averne a morir* - Perhaps she does not want to say them for fear she might die of it.

Stolta paura, l'amor non uccide ma dà vita, a sorride per gioie celestiali come ora fa nei tuoi lunghi occhi ovali - Foolish fear, love does not kill, but gives life and smiles with heavenly joy, as it smiles in your almond eyes now.

His voice closed around her, caressed her, ran up and down her spine, kissed her until her heart was racing, her body yearning to feel his arms enveloping her as foolish, trusting Butterfly caved to Pinkerton's will. *Adesso voi siete per me l'occhio del firmamento* - Now, to me, you are the centre of the universe.

Olivia saw the happiness in Angelo's eyes, and though she hated herself for it, could only feel hope to see that he still wanted her to love him. In complete submission, Butterfly now sank to her knees before Pinkerton.

Vogliatemi bene, un bene piccolino, un bene da bambino, quale a me si conviene. Vogliatemi bene - Love me, just a little, with the love of a baby, the love that is my due. Love me.

Dammi ch'io baci le tue mani care. Mia Butterfly - Give me your lovely hands so that I may kiss them. My Butterfly.

No, she couldn't let him, thought Olivia swiftly turning and rising rather than actually feel his flesh against hers.

Dicon ch'oltre mare se cade in man dell'uom, ogni farfalla da uno spillo è trafitta ed in tavola infitta - They say that in other countries if a man catches a butterfly he puts a pin through it and fastens it to a board.

Angelo was not above doing the same to Olivia. As he sang he put his hand to the back of her neck and forced her round, so that she was pinned to his chest.

Perchè non fugga più. Lo t'ho ghermita. Ti serro palpitante. Sei mia - So that it won't fly away. I have caught you. I hold you as you tremble. You are mine!

It was all so easy.

Sì, per la vita - Yes, for the rest of my life, she responded as if she meant it, and surrendered to the music's consummate passion, living only for the moment as she and Angelo sang together, for what might be the last time.

Dolce notte. Quante stele. Non le vidi mai sì belle - Lovely night. All those stars. I've never seen them so beautiful. *Trema, brilla, ogni favilla col baglior d'una pupilla* - Each little spark trembles and shines with the brightness of an eye. *Oh, quanti occhi fissi, attenti d'ogni parte a riguardar pei firmamente, via pei lidi, via pel mare* - Oh, so many steady eyes, watching, looking from every corner, from the heavens, over the shore and across the sea. *Dolce notte. Tutto estatico d'amor, ride il ciel* - Sweet night. Full of love, the sky smiles down.

Olivia's voice was jubilant in the knowledge that this was something Calli had never had with him, and could never have; that unmatchable, ethereal mixing of two souls as two voices combined.

Vieni, vieni! Vien sei mia! - Come then, come! Come, you are mine! sang Angelo as Olivia's voice wound around his, singing of love and stars.

Banish all distress from your heart! urged Pinkerton, leading Butterfly towards the house and the ill-fated marriage bed.

Olivia resisted to the last, never wanting it to end as Pinkerton swept Butterfly up into his arms.

Ti serro palpitante - I hold you as you tremble. Ah! Vien, sei mia! - Ah, come, you are mine! he claimed triumphantly and carried her into the house as the curtain fell.

* * *

She had not wanted it to end, but the moment her feet touched the stage Olivia was aware of Calliope standing in the wings, and then without a word, Angelo had left her side, called to heel with not even a second's hesitation. There was no place for the ethereal here in the real world. Olivia's had been a hollow victory and she could not bring much life to Butterfly's earnest belief that

Pinkerton had not sailed away forever after their brief time together, but that he would *return when the robins nest*. Poor Butterfly would not hear of remarrying, though the matchmaker said that desertion was grounds for divorce; that did not apply in her country - America. And then when Sharpless came to her with a letter from Pinkerton that clearly indicated he had no intention of coming back, it took some time before she could be made to understand its meaning and even then, she could not accept the truth and insisted that once Pinkerton knew of the son he had sired, he would return.

And so, when the canons sounded the return of Pinkerton's ship to harbour, Butterfly was overjoyed and convinced that she had been right all along. As the second act came to its conclusion, Butterfly sat waiting, dressed in her wedding dress, the house scattered with flower petals.

By the time Pinkerton arrived, Butterfly had finally gained release from her all night vigil in the comforting arms of sleep. Olivia was glad that she could lie there, eyes tightly closed against Angelo as Pinkerton saw the tragedy of what he had done. She wished she were deaf too. She did not want to hear the conviction in his voice as he sang, *Oh l'amara fragranza di questi fior, velenosa al cor mi va* - Oh the bitter fragrance of these flowers spreads in my heart like poison... *Mi struggo dal rimorso* - I am overcome with remorse.

Deaf to advice, deaf to doubt, scorned, obstinately she waited for you and kept her heart for you! charged Sharpless angrily.

Yes, all at once I see my mistake, and I feel that I shall never be free from this torment. No, I shall never be free! Farewell flowery refuge of joy and love. I shall be tortured forever by the sight of her sweet face.

Olivia hoped so, and yet knew that Calli was not far off, making sure that he would not get carried away in his usual fashion by the power of the music. Olivia understood how complete Butterfly's destruction was when she was finally told by her servant that Pinkerton had indeed come, but with an American wife. And not only was she supposed to relinquish all hope of being reunited with Pinkerton, but also give up her son to the couple.

Quella donna mi fa tanta paura - That woman fills me with so much fear. *Ah! è sua moglie. Tutto è morto per me. Tutto è finito* - Ah, she is his wife. Everything is dead for me. It's all over. *Voglion prendermi tutto* - they want to take everything from me.

In essence it seemed to Olivia that Calliope had indeed taken the child that should have been hers. Suddenly she felt very tired. She felt for Butterfly as she closed out the cheery spring day and sent her servant, Suzuki, away. Then she went to her chest of drawers took her father's ceremonial sword from its lacquered sheath, kissed its blade and read in a grave voice the words etched along its edge - *He dies with honour who can no longer live with honour.* She held the sword to her throat, but just then Suzuki having suspected what her mistress intended to do, pushed Butterfly's son into the room.

269

Seeing him, she dropped the sword and ran to the tiny child, embracing him and kissing him with suffocating intensity.

Olivia could barely sing for the tears that fought to be free as Butterfly bade farewell to her child - *My dearest, dearest love, flowers of lilies and roses. May you never know that for you, for your innocent eyes, Butterfly died! Amore addio! addio piccolo amor!* - My love farewell. Farewell my little love.

With that she sat the child down and put an American flag along with a small doll into his hands, persuading him to play with them as she tenderly blindfolded him. Then she took up the sword once more and went behind a paper screen.

Now Olivia raised the sword, her arms stretched above her head so that the tip of the sword appeared to the audience, as they watched her silhouette with dread, to be resting at the base of her neck before being suddenly plunged diagonally down through her torso.

Butterfly, Butterfly, Butterfly! cried Pinkerton, rushing in and dragging her lifeless body into his arms as he sank, repentant to his knees.

Olivia did not take Angelo's hand as they walked forwards to a wall of sound from an audience sodden with tears. And though the curtain pulled back time and time again, acquiescing to the crowd's stamping demand, Olivia was not there beyond the first bow.

'But my darling, you must take your applause. You were magnificent tonight,' Angelo had the audacity to say as he tried to convince her not to make him go out alone and face a crowd desperate only to see Olivia.

'No, *darling*, I don't have to do anything now. Make the most of it *darling*, you won't be singing with me again. *Ever*,' she snapped at Angelo with the last ounce of pride in her, before running from the stage rather than give him the bonus of seeing her cry yet again.

As she ran she heard Calli call her name, full of pity and concern. What was it with those two, that they couldn't feel content with breaking her heart, but had also to self-indulgently feel bad about it and call upon her to make them feel OK by accepting their consolation? Olivia wished she'd taken a leaf out of Calliope's book, becoming the role and adding one more mortal sin to her collection by killing herself on stage. It would have been a fitting punishment for them all. Angelo forever guilt ridden, Calli forever outdone, Olivia forever damned. Olivia almost managed a smile at the idea as she grabbed her things from her dressing room and legged it down the hall, ducking into a ladies room in hopes of evading anyone who might come in search of forgiveness or an explanation for her insult to the audience and sponsors.

She could hardly bear to look at her reflection in the mirror as she removed Butterfly's white makeup, only to find a still paler face beneath. And she cried when she caught sight of herself in the full length mirror to her left. Why the producer had allowed the costume designer to put her in this diaphanous, farce of a kimono she could not imagine, nor how she had come to agree to go on stage wearing it, in front of thousands of people. It showed every contour of her body, every roll of fat, and made a mockery of Pinkerton's comments that Butterfly was the perfect name for so slender and elegant a girl. Perhaps it was the director's way, at the expense of Olivia's self-esteem, of further emphasising the duplicity and insincerity of Pinkerton.

She was just struggling, though the struggle was only in her mind, into a pair of jeans when a very beautiful, extremely skinny ballet dancer waltzed in, almost literally. Hardly surprising she was walking on air, thought Olivia jealously, recognising the girl as one half of the married dancing partnership who were known about the place as 'Mills & Boon', thanks to their sickeningly romantic story. To think that she and Angelo had been compared to those two only a few weeks earlier, when their engagement had been announced. Envy was not adequate to describe what the embittered Olivia felt towards that sylph-like creature as she turned back to the mirror and attempted to steady her hand enough to apply some blusher to her nonexistent cheekbones - anything to kill the time until the cast had gone to the party and the fans had given up their stagedoor vigil.

As she did so, it was impossible not to overhear the sound of vomiting coming from the cubicle behind, and though saddened for the girl and ashamed of herself, it was also impossible not to feel cheered by the realisation that even this gorgeous girl had problems.

When the girl came out, she stood at the next basin, splashing her face with water, then took a toothbrush out of her bag.

Covering her tracks, thought Olivia - a real pro. Olivia put her hand on the dancer's shoulder before she could start cleaning her teeth. The girl jumped a little.

'Sorry, I didn't mean to startle you,' ventured Olivia, 'but I couldn't help but hear you being sick. Are you OK?'

'Oh! I'm sorry, I came in here thinking I'd be alone at this time of night. I did try to mask the sound but...'

'I know you did,' sighed Olivia, 'but that's not the point. Hiding it doesn't make it go away. Believe me, I understand your pain. I know what it's like, and I know there's lot of pressure on you all, but they shouldn't expect you to be this way, it's not right and you can get over this. You can beat it if you get some help now, before it's too late. Please, *please* get some help.'

For a moment the girl looked confused, and then her face brightened and she laughed a little.

'Oh, that's so sweet of you. I really appreciate your concern, but there's no need. It's not what you think. I'm pregnant!' she beamed and rushed out to the tall, dark, handsome man waiting in the corridor.

Olivia could hear them giggling together as they left, happiness receding with them. Olivia turned off the light so that no one would think to come in, and listened as everyone left for the night, waited until none would hear the silence in the echoing backstage labyrinth broken by the sound of her wretching the acrid sorrow out of her guts.

- chapter fifteen -

'See someone you know?' asked Frank, looking back over his shoulder as he and Guy went into the Lamb and Flag pub.

'Maybe. What are you drinking?' said Guy, his eyes narrowed with thought as he leant against the bar, watching the door, half expecting, half hoping that Olivia would come through it. Perhaps it hadn't been her after all, just another woman with long blonde hair. But they were about to start rehearsals for *La Bohème,* with Olivia billed as Mimi, so she must be back in town. Or had he got so used to seeing her face peering at him from the poster ads that were plastered everywhere, that it was burned onto his retina?

'Mine's a scotch.'

'Large scotch and a pint of Greene King,' Guy said with an ever-endearing wink at the girl behind the bar. She blushed, but Guy didn't notice; the wink had been more out of habit than interest.

'So who'd you think you saw?'

'No-one special.'

'So that'd be Olivia then?'

'Smart-arse.'

'Fool.'

'Why do you say that?'

'Because that one's no good for you. Never was and nothing's changed.'

'You mean, I haven't. I know what you're thinking Frank; it's me who's no good for her. That's what you're really saying. You always did have a crush on Olivia.'

'Bollocks, I did!'

'Come on Frank, admit it, if you'd been twenty years younger, you'd have given me a run for my money.'

'Fucking sidestep all you like – I don't fancy her, it's just that I like her. For Christ's sake, you can't be within twenty feet of a woman without giving her the once over, just in case. Olivia's a nice person and she deserves to find someone who'll make her happy.'

'Like that bastard Angelo did?

'Well, if you want to put it like that.'

'I do, Frank, I do.'

'So what are you thinking? Going to ride in on your white charger and save her?'

'Maybe.'

'Better get going then. That *was* her just now!' laughed Frank and shook his head in amusement as Guy sprinted out of the pub into the autumn rain.

'Oh, it's you,' Olivia commented with a joyless smile, when Guy finally caught up. He'd been calling her name all the way but it had been near impossible to make his voice heard over the surprisingly large number of people braving the wet Covent Garden streets.

At first he didn't know what to say. He was shocked when she turned to him. Really shocked. He'd seen so many photos of her in so many places, looking more gorgeous than ever, that he'd assumed the makeup artist had done an award winning makeover to get Olivia to look the part of the consumptive Mimi for the *La Bohème* posters. But now he saw that the truth was just the reverse, for the woman before him was pale and thin, with dark rings around her dull, sunken eyes.

'You're soaked. Here, take my jacket,' he offered eventually, noting that she neither declined nor thanked him as he draped it over her shoulders. 'Why don't we go for a coffee? Get you warmed up and dry,' he suggested, again getting no affirmative response but also finding no resistance as he put his arm around her and guided her through the hordes to a favourite haunt of his, Cafe Paradiso, having sensed her unwillingness to go in the direction of the patisserie he had originally thought to take her to.

'So, how've you been?' he asked, simultaneously kicking himself for asking such a stupid question.

Olivia looked at him, could not think of an adequate answer, and shrugged her shoulders instead. It was astonishing to her that she was even here with Guy. The last thing she recollected of that morning was the huge fight she had with Laura. With past experience to learn from, she knew she shouldn't have been surprised that between Laura and the Royal Opera House there could be no other outcome for a season than the worst possible one she could imagine. But, that their first thought upon losing the tenor booked for *La Bohème* was to call upon Angelo's services still stunned Olivia.

'Can I order you something to eat?' asked Guy when the silence got too much for him.

'Sure.'

Guy felt a pain across his chest as he sat and watched Olivia work her way through a plate of antipasti as if she hadn't eaten in a week. Perhaps she hadn't. The thought intensified the pain, along with the anger and jealousy within. That Angelo had done this to his precious Olivia was unforgivable, that it had been Angelo and not he that had had so devastating an effect on Olivia was still harder to take. If she'd known what Guy was thinking, Olivia would have laughed at the irony of his misconception. Instead, she ate her lasagna and salad in continued silence, whilst Guy switched from coffee to wine and waited for some sign that Olivia was bothered, one way or another, by the fact that it was him sitting opposite. It was hard not to stare at her gaunt features, and eventually he did so unabashed as she didn't seem to care, or even notice. Only when she had polished off a helping of tiramisu did she speak.

'Which way to the ladies' room?'

Well, it was a start, thought Guy not really expecting to get any more out of her when she came back. If she came back. He seemed to be sitting there alone for an awfully long time and even began to wonder if Olivia had managed to climb out of some window out back rather than find herself with no food with which to occupy her mouth in lieu of talking. He jumped when she sat down again.

'Are you all right?' he asked, 'You were gone a long time.'

'Yes, I'm fine,' she responded with such good cheer that he had to do a double take to reassure himself that the right woman had joined him. 'I just wanted to freshen up and put on some makeup. You should have told me what a fright I looked.'

Guy was uncomfortable at the sudden lift in her spirits, suspicious even, but she had put on makeup and her hair had been brushed. However, she still did not look like the Olivia he knew.

'So how are you?' she asked with a disarmingly sweet and cheerful smile.

'Pretty good. Been busy touring all summer. London Symphony Orchestra, mainly. Taiwan, Hong Kong, Singapore, Sydney.'

'I suppose you and your mates behaved like a rugby team as per usual. I bet you've been banned from every hotel *en route*.'

'No, not at all - we're getting too old and mature for all that,' he laughed, pleased to see a genuine smile at the not-strictly-true claim. 'So what about you?'

Olivia looked down into her cappuccino, 'Oh, I've been out of the country ever since... since last season. Laura had me going all over the place. Italy, France, America. I was even in Sydney this summer.'

'It's a shame we weren't there at the same time. We could have had some fun - like old times.'

Guy regretted the suggestion immediately, but Olivia was full of surprises and merely quipped, somewhat suggestively, 'I thought you were too old and mature for all that!'

It was strange not to feel reassured by Olivia's mood, or the more healthy looking face, but Guy could not shake what he had first seen from his mind and this face was, after all, only makeup.

'Listen Olivia, I know you say you're fine and maybe you don't want to hear it from me, of all people, but I just have to tell you that I've been really worried about you. I can't tell you how angry I was when I heard the news about Angelo and Calliope. And now I've seen you, I could kill that pair. I don't care what you say, you're not all right. You look like shit and no amount of makeup is going to hide it.'

'Well, thanks Guy, you've made me feel so much better,' Olivia said wanly.

'I'm sorry, I didn't mean to have it come out like that. I just get so riled up when I think of what they've done. But, I know I don't have a right to comment. I should just shut the fuck up.'

'What would you like me to say? That you didn't make me feel as bad as Angelo has? Am I supposed to admit that *you* weren't so dreadful after all? Well, I can't. I've been here before, you just didn't get to see the mess. You broke me. Not just my heart. *All* of me, right down to my soul. And now, just when I thought I had a chance of being whole again...' she answered, her voice hoarse with emotion, but then she spied a smile deep within his eyes and stopped short.

'You think this is amusing?' she asked coldly. 'I can see you're smirking in there, you bastard.'

'No!' Guy insisted, feeling guilty, 'It's just that - well, I know this is wrong - but I can't help being pleased to know that I meant as much to you as Angelo.'

Olivia slapped him immediately and hard.

'I deserved that,' Guy admitted with a resigned sigh.

'Yes you did. And more. You're an arsehole. You know that, right? But...'

'But?'

'It still makes me smile to hear you say that.'

'Because I'm getting my just deserts?'

'Because it means that you still love me.'

Guy leaned across the table and kissed her gently.

'I do,' he said.

The waiters nudged each other and laughed with courteous restraint as Guy and Olivia retreated into silence and mulled over what had been said and done.

'Look, I've got a rehearsal this afternoon,' said Guy eventually.

'And I've got to go to Wardrobe for a fitting - taking my costume in for a change!'

'You've always been beautiful.'

Olivia smiled at the compliment, but knew very well by the calls she had got lately from photographers wanting her to do fashion shoots, that thinner did indeed mean more beautiful.

'Anyway,' Guy persisted, staggered by how nervous he was of being rejected, 'perhaps when we're both done, you could come over to my place for dinner? Nothing more, I promise. Just dinner, a bottle of wine and a chance to talk - what do you think?'

Olivia thought that there was no such thing as just dinner, a bottle of wine and the chance to talk when you were with Guy, but she didn't say it, because *La Bohème* was not now as terrifying a prospect as it had been when she'd left Laura's office.

'OK,' she said finally, 'but I'll bring the wine,' and then added with a jaunty smile, 'So, does that mean you'll act on your instincts and kill Angelo for me this season? Laura told me earlier today that they're trying to get him in for *Bohème*.'

'Christ, they'll do anything for a sell out.'

'Apparently.'

'And are they getting his bitch wife in to play Musetta, for good measure?'

'If they could, I'm sure they would, but Dominic won't coach her, so she's finished as a singer. Besides, I hear she's rather overweight these days and won't leave the house.'

'Huh, I never thought I'd hear you talk about Calli like that.'

'And I never thought you'd be proved right about her.'

'I'm sorry I was.'

'So am I,' said Olivia thinking for a moment of her friend and trying, given that there was a glimmer of hope in Guy's invitation, to find a spark of forgiveness for her. But it was useless - she could only imagine, with satisfaction, the pure terror the bitch would feel when rehearsals for *Bohème* began.

'You've what?!' cried Calliope, enraged and horrified by Angelo's announcement that Roberto Alagna had had to pull out of *La Bohéme* and that he'd just been booked to take over.

'Come now, my darling, what is the problem?'

'You know bloody well what the problem is. You *promised* me. You promised you'd never sing with her again.'

'And I will not, my darling. Is it not obvious that as soon as Olivia hears that I am to sing Rodolfo she will resign?'

'And what if she doesn't? What will you do then?' she asked, hoping desperately that Angelo would say the words she wanted to hear.

'Calliope, why must you fret about things that will not happen?' he said in his most coaxing of voices, his hands taking hold of her upper arms to pull her in for a consolatory kiss.

Calli was having none of his charm today. The feel of his fingers sinking into the extra flesh she still had, where once there were well sculpted biceps, made her skin crawl. She'd never felt so unsexy as she did now and she twisted angrily away.

'Answer me, damn it,' she snapped, glaring out onto the tiny, drizzle-drenched October garden, darkened still further by the high walls that marked its boundaries. The solitary, imprisoned tree was almost bare, surrounded by piles of mouldering leaves and terra-cotta pots filled with the twiggy remainders of who knew what. This little piece of Chelsea used to be her ideal garden and, even for this, she had needed a gardener but now the sight of it made her hanker after the hundred foot lawns and parallel borders filled with marigolds that she'd grown up with in North London. That made her *really* angry.

Nothing was as she had imagined it would be when she'd decided to keep the baby, and Angelo with it. Even the nuptials, covered by every fashion, lifestyle, food, and music magazine *en vogue*, amounted to less than the fairytale wedding she had hoped for. The dress, the hair, the flowers, the caterers, the venue; all just what she had envisioned and what *Bazaar* would be presenting as next year's in look, but when it came time to walk down the aisle she wished she'd gone for a registry office espousal rather than live with the absence of a father to walk with her. Dominic had always said that he would do the honours in the unlikely event that she got hitched, but unsurprisingly he had been appalled by what Calli had done, so he wasn't prepared to coach her anymore, let alone give her away.

And then there was Olivia.

Over the years they had planned their respective weddings so many times together that they had even decided what they would sing at each other's weddings and alighted upon these choices as coded messages by which to announce any engagement. She should have been calling Olivia and saying, it's time you were dusting off *Now That I've Found You* and Olivia should have been singing it as they signed the register. Only when she was doing just that, did Calli realise that on some level, laughable though it was, she had hoped and maybe even believed that Olivia would forgive this treacherous act.

'Calliope, if Olivia sings, what does this matter? I love you.'

'Angelo, I may be married to you but I'm not fucking stupid - you love whomever your character's in love with.'

'Well then, if you believe this, why don't you start singing again and we can sing always together?' demanded Angelo, also aggravated by the view out the window. It made him desperate to go home to Italy. He hated these grey, damp skies and right now he hated Calliope, or at least the woman he imagined aliens must have beamed down in her place. The siren he had married was certainly not there to throw him to the floor and writhe atop him until he felt like he was coming through every pore on his body. No, this woman hadn't brushed her hair in days, she'd cut her long nails the first time they got stuck to the super glue tabs on disposable nappies and she was still wearing elasticated waists and baggy shirts. And, worse still, since she'd stopped singing, she was lost for a character other than that of an inconsolably guilty Catholic.

'How can I sing when Dominic won't coach me?' she demanded, stomping over to the coffee table and snatching up that month's *Classic FM* magazine to brandish at him, 'I'm not Olivia. I can't do it without him,' she screamed tearfully and sank onto a sofa, dropping the magazine with its cover-shot of a now very thin and lovely looking Olivia, in favour of Angelo's packet of cigarettes. Her hands shook so much she could barely get a cigarette out and when she did, she let out a visceral roar of frustration and threw it, and the box, into the fireplace.

'If it makes you feel this bad, surely one will not hurt?'

'You know damn well that one *will* hurt. And what the fuck are they doing here anyway? You said you'd give up if the doctor told you to.'

'And I will. I promise.'

'Would that be a promise like the one you made when I was pregnant, or like the one you made when he was born? You know, they said there was just as much chance that it could have been *your* fault as there was of it being mine,' she said without conviction, her head bowing as she remembered the day of the ultrasound, when the woman had looked at the screen and her chirpy, annoying little voice had changed suddenly. It was not so serious really, only part of a leg missing, from just above the knee. With prosthetics as good as they were these days, it would barely impinge on his life - far easier for a child to adapt from birth than to face such a loss later - he'd be an Olympian yet.

Not serious to the professionals who'd broken far worse news to others before them, but to Calliope it was as serious as it could get - it was God's retribution for what she had done, and it was her fault for all the smoking and drinking she had done early in her pregnancy. The child, for the mother's sins, would have to face years of being picked on at school - Calli knew, because she had been one of those kids who defended themselves by turning everyone's attention to what set another child apart. Poor fatty-goody-two-shoes Olivia. There was so much to feel guilty about.

And then she'd given birth two months early and they'd taken her son from her and put him in an incubator where machines had done everything for him that she should have. Clearly God had seen the error of his ways, seen that Calli had failed every test. There had been many, many minutes in every hour of every day, of every month that she had sat watching her tiny baby struggle to survive, for Calliope to think about her life. She missed Olivia during that time, felt intensely the absence of the support that her friend would have offered when Angelo was so pathetically useless in a crisis, and yet she knew that to try and salvage the friendship was both selfish and doomed to failure. The only way forward was to do the best for her child.

'Calliope, why must you blame yourself, or me? The doctor only said that to stop you feeling so responsible, so guilty. He said that these things sometimes happen for no reason at all.'

'Or because the parents smoke and drink and don't give a shit about anyone but themselves.'

'Do you say now that I don't care about my son? I love Luciano. I love him more than anything.'

'Then get us a house the hell out of all this pollution and give up smoking like the doctor told you to. If only so that you don't blow the place up,' she begged, looking to the bottle of oxygen that stood in the corner, ready in case Luciano's still immature lungs had difficulty coping.

'You are right. I will do it for Luciano,' sighed Angelo, purely for a quiet life, for in reality he was not sure that he did love his son.

For Angelo too, nothing had turned out the way he had imagined it would. Luciano was going to be neither a singer nor a footballer, and he had turned Calliope into the middle-class, suburban mum at her core. At the wedding he had been proud, by virtue of the envy in the eyes of his brothers, not to have brought home the kind of girl his mother had picked out for them, but they would not be so covetous of his wife if they could see her now, and by contrast his mother would be quite satisfied by the change motherhood had brought about. The child needed round the clock supervision and Calli was determined to be the one to stay up all night watching in case he stopped breathing, flying into a rage should Angelo suggest they bring in a nanny to help take the strain.

Angelo felt betrayed by the pair of them, and Calli wasn't doing herself any favours by waving a picture of

Olivia in his face. It served only to heighten his interest in performing *La Bohème*.

Olivia had never looked as fantastic as she did in that picture; her svelte new figure was even more alluring than the voluptuous one of old. Compared with Calli's deflated stomach, with its alternating wrinkles and stretch marks, Olivia's would be as smooth and white as new snow. And there would be a sex drive instead of tired yawns to greet him in bed. Nor would Olivia be wanting to move out of this stupendous Pimlico address. Calli had been quite happy to swan off to Italy for her extravagant wedding but now, though the air for her precious son would clearly be a thousand times better in Tuscany, his wife was adamant that she must stay in England, that she would be lonely in Italy. Lonely in Italy! What a nerve the woman had, when she'd not one friend to her name here.

'And what about *Bohème?*' asked Calli.

'If you want to stay at home with Luciano and have your house in the countryside, then I must work, I must sing *Bohème,* and that is that.'

'Oh come on, this place is worth a bloody fortune and there's more work to be had than what the Royal Opera is handing you.'

'But my darling, it is you that does not trust me to go away to foreign companies. It is you who wants me to secure work in London.'

'You know that has nothing to do with my not trusting you and everything to do with the fact that you should be here, being a father to Luciano,' Calli retorted, knowing very well that she was lying.

'So, if you can trust me, then there is no need to worry yourself about *La Bohème,* is there?'

'Bastard!'

Angelo felt a pang of regret as he watched his defeated, vulnerable wife moving silently about the place trying to bring some order to what had once been perfection, tears rolling slowly down her cheeks. Regret for his, rather than her sake, but he believed that his motives for trying to make her happier, bring her back to her former glory, were selfless. He went to her and took the sticky Chinese takeaway cartons out of her hands and tossed them back where she'd collected them from.

'My darling. Let us not argue,' he urged, wrapping her tenderly in his arms. 'You are my wife and you having nothing to fear. It is only that you have lost all your confidence since Luciano was born. It is not good for you to be closed up all the time. You have to get out more, *be* in the world a little. Please let me arrange for a nanny to come.'

'No. How many times do I have to say it? No!' she replied wearily and tried to pull away.

'Well, then, a least a cleaner,' suggested Angelo with a poignant glance about the room. He felt her relax a little in his embrace and felt sure that it would only be a matter of time before he could persuade her to his way of thinking. Heartened by the image of Calliope returned to herself, he sank his hands deep into her hair and kissed her persuasively. She softened still further.

Then the monitor burst forth with the familiar, tooth-shattering wail.

As she lifted Luciano out of his cot, Calli heard the front door slam and was glad. These moments just after Angelo's dramatic exits were when she felt most happy; they brought her security, for there was no need to feel jealous and possessive over a man for whom she felt so little that she was actually pleased when he walked out.

And yet, the relief was short-lived, for within half an hour she would be pacing the floor, fearing that he wouldn't come back, wondering with whom he was spending the time and knowing that she would not be able to stay at home with her son or pay for all his needs, present and future, if Angelo were to leave her. And when she imagined what she would do, if he did abandon her, it was at the check out in Sainsbury's that she saw herself, because there were no friends left in the opera world, no chance of even getting help from Dame Cecelia to find a replacement for Dominic. Everyone was, quite rightly, on Olivia's side.

Calli breathed in the warm snugly scent of baby as Luciano nuzzled into her neck, his tiny hands, with minuscule razors for nails, reaching up to paw at her face, get tangled in her hair and tug on her earlobes. If she could look in on her life now, Calli wondered, would

Olivia feel envious or would she see that she had had a lucky escape from Angelo?

But Calli already knew the answer and closed her eyes, praying that Olivia would instead find someone worthy of her love, praying that she would yet have the opportunity to feel this unfathomable bond, praying that she would find pity enough in her heart to turn down Angelo's advances and leave Calli with at least this life, however unsatisfactory it was.

- chapter sixteen -

'You should get a doctor to take a look at you,' suggested Guy when Olivia gave in yet again to a coughing fit as they escaped the congested Underground.

'Maybe, but there's not been any time. Do you want to stop for a drink?'

'Don't change the subject, and no I don't, the last thing you need before a dress rehearsal is to sit in a pub.'

'Stop fussing, I'll be fine,' Olivia insisted, though her voice was croaky and again the effort of talking made her cough.

'Oh sure, you're fine. Listen to yourself. You make Mimi's tuberculosis sound like a tickle in the throat the way you're carrying on. For all you know, you could have TB.'

'Oh don't be ridiculous,' laughed Olivia, unconvincingly blasé.

'I'm not. Haven't you heard, it's on the rise? With all the travelling you've been doing, you could easily have picked it up. They were talking about it last week on the radio - just one person had it on a plane and thanks to the air-conditioning, another eight had it by the time they got off the flight. It's the truth, Olivia.'

'OK, OK, I'll go to a doctor,' she agreed and gratefully enjoyed feeling his arm tighten around her, drawing her close, warming her, making her feel secure as they went down Floral Street to the stage door, behind which was hidden her version of hell.

Walking into the canteen, even with Guy at her side, Olivia was halted in her tracks by a chill blast as she saw Angelo, Calliope and son. The child was screaming and neither parent looked happy, but Olivia still backed up through the swing doors before they had a chance to see her.

'I'm sorry. I just can't face them,' she said to Guy.

'It's OK, my love' he said as reassuringly as he could, despite feeling pissed off to discover that his own reappearance in her life had not wiped out the hurt of the recent past.

Still, perhaps it was to be expected given that this was the first time Olivia had seen the bastard - she'd only given in to performing opposite Angelo when they'd conceded to let her rehearse with his understudy up until the dress rehearsal. How that bitch Calliope had raised the nerve to show up today, Guy could not imagine. Of course, had he examined his own motivations at all, he'd have known that he and Calli had much in common when it came to fearing that Olivia and Angelo were still in love and would fall into each other's arms at the first aria. But, instead, Guy chose to take heart in the thought that it was seeing her treacherous friend that had actually sent Olivia running to her dressing room an hour early.

In her dressing room, Olivia repeatedly put on and removed her costume, frantically swaying between going ahead with the rehearsal and jettisoning her career. Every time she did so, she also stopped to count how many sets of hooks and eyes she passed over before she reached the row that was the right fit. Surely it should have been the last lot the seamstress had added? She felt sure that she must have put on significant amounts of weight, totally blanking from her memory that they had added, along with much concerned criticism, several extra rows just in case she lost even more weight.

'Olivia?'

'Come in,' she replied, quickly brushing away the tears, glad that Guy had knocked first.

'I brought you some sandwiches - it's a long afternoon to get through on an empty stomach,' he told her, thinking that she would disappear in that costume, with its crinoline, heavy taffeta skirts and bustle. 'Here,' he said when she made no move to take the package, 'you take this and eat, I'll get these hooks for you.'

'I'm not hungry.'

'I don't care, you need to eat,' he responded stubbornly, feeling the ridges of her spine against his fingertips as he hooked up the back of her dress. When he was done he sat and watched her eat, then he handed her a bar of chocolate, for good measure.

'Guy, I'm not supposed to eat right before I sing. I'll throw up at the first high note I hit.'

'There's ages yet before you have to do anything, especially with that arsehole Petrov on the podium. We'll be lucky to get through the overture without stopping.'

'Satisfied?' she asked wearily, throwing the empty wrapper in the waste bin.

'Don't sound so pissed off with me, Olivia. I love you and I'm trying to look after you.'

'I'm sorry. It's not your fault. Everything just seems so out of control. Why am I here, having to sing with that bastard? What's wrong with me? I should have said no, and kept to it.'

'Of course you should, but then Laura shouldn't have put you in this position in the first place - she's supposed to be looking after your best interests. After this season, I think you should find someone else to represent you. You're a star now, it won't be a case of having to beg to be heard, you'll be fighting them off once word gets out.'

'I'll do it,' she agreed, though her tone of voice did not shout resolve.

'Christ, I'd better get going,' said Guy as he heard the call for beginners. 'You'll be all right,' he assured her, 'and remember - you don't have to go on if you don't want to. The worst they can do is fire you, and no matter what they might try and convince you, no other company is going to give a shit if you ditch this season. They all know what that arsehole did, they know Laura's a bitch, and no-one will blame you. The work will come in search of you right after the agents do. OK?'

'OK,' smiled Olivia.

The door closed and her smile fell away.

Why did Guy have to be so supportive and caring? It made everything so much harder to bear. Before, she'd managed to convince herself that Calli had been right about him, but now she was confronted with a man who had grown and matured, who might, if she'd given him the chance, have been the right man for her, the right father for her child. She had never felt as guilty for having terminated her pregnancy as she did now, when she was hoping that she and Guy would still manage to end up together. And yet, the sight of Calliope with Angelo had sent her into an uncontrollable convulsion of grief that must surely have hurt Guy terribly. If he could not trust that she loved him alone, it was hardly possible, nor reasonable to expect that Guy would be willing to do the same for her. He would find someone else, just as he had before. She looked in the mirror and saw someone who would have difficulty keeping him, though it was not the person that made Guy wonder if he was up to the challenge of being in

Olivia's life. She grabbed the waste bin and looked with guilt at the wrappers, disgusted with herself.

Outside, Guy had his ear to the door, uncaring of inviting Petrov's wrath by his tardiness as he listened, his face desolate, his mind racing.

Angelo was sure that his heart had stopped when Rudolfo opened the door to Mimi and he gained first sight of his darling Olivia. He could hardly believe that it was her. This was not the woman of whom Calliope had been so afraid. She was so thin, so frail, so grey. Not a woman to inspire a second look, let alone passion or love, unless those emotions were locked in a heart from long ago, waiting to swell in the vacuum that passed for Angelo's integrity, upon the recognition of what had become of her. That his wife had only just stomped out the back of the auditorium with their screaming baby, that Guy had only an hour earlier told him that he was reunited with Olivia and that Angelo should keep away or face disembowelment, that he had been in this state on many an occasion, with many a leading lady, did not deter Angelo from being immediately overwhelmed with regret and love yet again. He stopped singing.

'My darling, my love,' he sighed, reaching out his hands to her.

'Don't do this, Angelo,' retorted Olivia with a trembling voice, clasping her hands behind her back, and then continued with what was left of the strength she'd gained from Guy's reassurance. 'We're here to sing. If you're not going to do that, then let's get the understudy now.'

Angelo hung his head remorsefully and began to weep. As the orchestra stumbled to a surprised halt, Olivia ran to the front of the stage, also in tears.

'How am I supposed to perform, when he's behaving like this?' she asked Alexander Petrov between sobs. 'Do something, or I'll have to go.'

Petrov cast down his baton with such force that it shattered, pieces flying all over the pit, some fragments even finding their way through the 'f' holes in the cello belonging to the disgruntled principal cellist.

'This is unacceptable. Unbelievable. I cannot work like this,' Petrov screamed with fearsome volume, a vein throbbing furiously at his temple, 'Let me look around,' he sneered, turning in a complete circle before leering up at the stage once more, 'Yes, I am in the Royal Opera House. But are we performing *La Bohème?*'

He put one hand up to his ear and then held the other batonless one up for all to inspect.

'No! No we are not, because my *'stars'* think that we are here only as a backdrop for their pathetic little love story. Well, I will not stand for this unprofessional behaviour. Madam, if you cannot perform with Senor Verasano, then please, please, *please*, make me a happy man and get off the stage now. As for you *Senor* Verasano, if you must seduce her, then do it at the Savoy, not on my stage! And, Mr. MacLaren,' he said, turning his attention to Guy, who was being held back by the timpanist, 'if you wish to fight me, then remember that I spent ten years working on the Siberian pipeline and if I can survive that, then you are nothing to me. Now, from the top,' he said and whipped the orchestra into action as quickly as possible, so that Guy would have a forest of moving violin bows to thrash his way through, should he rightly think that Sasha would topple before the first punch landed.

Olivia was not about to do anything to make Alexander Petrov happy, and Angelo Verasano was not about to do anything to alert Calli, who had finally subdued their son and just sneaked back in, to the turmoil the sight of Olivia had stirred up. And so, the rehearsal continued with barely repressed passions only fuelled by the opera itself. There could not have been a better plot to encourage Angelo towards trying to reconcile with his 'true love' - the bohemians, Mimi and Rodolfo fall deeply in love, but after his jealousy causes many arguments, they separate. By the time they are reunited, Mimi is on the verge of death with tuberculosis. Together, they sing of past happiness and regret for what has been foolishly lost and then, tragically, she dies.

If the opera libretto did not clinch the heart of Angelo, then Olivia's deteriorating condition as the afternoon wore on, did. By the time they reached the penultimate act, she could barely sing. Petrov was livid and made endless snipes about her crying over Angelo, refusing to cut her some slack, demanding that she plough on and commanding that she do so in full voice, regardless of how rasping that voice now sounded, or how much she coughed when she was done. When Mimi started crying because she and Rodolfo were to separate, Guy immediately heard that it was for real and, mouthing the words *FUCK YOU* very clearly at Petrov, left the pit.

By the time he got on stage, the orchestra had stopped anyway. Olivia had collapsed, sobbing, clutching a bloodstained handkerchief.

'For Christ's sake, someone call a doctor,' shouted Guy, pushing away Angelo as he lifted Olivia into his arms and carried her off stage, happy to deliberately knock Calliope aside, she having rushed to the wings as soon as her friend began to crumple.

* * *

The ceiling of the throat specialist's office on Harley Street was quite incredible thought Olivia, looking up at its intricate plaster moulding and Georgian brass chandelier. Meanwhile, the doctor peered into her throat, probing with instruments apparently specifically designed to make anyone less in control of their vocal apparatus than a singer, gag.

'A friend of mine suggested that I might have TB. Do you think that's a possibility?' she said as David Sutherland sat silent and grave-faced writing notes behind a grand mahogany desk.

She looked around the room, tried to admire the collection of Chinese blue porcelain that adorned the bookcases either side of the marble fireplace, leaving the doctor's medical textbooks to find their place on the floor, but her eyes were quickly drawn back to the man scribbling away. She liked the look of him. He was about forty, well built but thin, the rowing rather than rugby playing variety of doctor. And there was a mark on his neck, which told her that he played the violin in his spare time. His hair was longer than she would have expected for a doctor with this address, and his face was beautifully lined, from hours on the water at the helm of his small yacht at Bosham, she imagined, or perhaps he liked to ski. She liked his eyes too; hazel with long dark lashes but they were not happy eyes, there was anguish in them as he perused what he had written. Maybe he too was nursing a broken heart, though it was hard to imagine a woman ditching this not quite handsome, but totally enchanting man. Then she remembered that Angelo had been both handsome *and* enchanting, so even David Sutherland could be a bastard.

When he looked up at her, she decided that he was handsome after all and then considered the possibility that the sadness in his eyes was perhaps because there was bad news for her. Certainly he had found something, one didn't write a page of illegible scribble for nothing, nor come round to the front of a desk and perch close to the patient as he was now, unless there was something to tell that might require the handkerchief in his jacket pocket to be passed to her, or a sensitive, good-bedside-mannerly hand to be placed on her shoulder. Nodes on her vocal chords? Or, thinking of the blood she'd been coughing up, throat cancer?

'How long have you been coughing up blood?' he asked after a daunting silence, in which he was clearly trying to find the best way to tell her the bad news.

'For a couple of months, off and on,' she admitted, seeing no point in hiding it from him as she had from Guy, 'but it's got a lot worse now.'

Again there was a difficult pause during which he drew breath to speak a couple of times and then let the opportunities pass.

'Why don't you just come out and say whatever it is you've got to tell me,' Olivia said impatiently. 'You're going to have to do it eventually - there are other patients waiting.'

He smiled at her comment, but still his eyes refused to see any humour in the matter at hand.

'OK, Ms. Tarrent.'

'Olivia,' she interrupted, suddenly wishing to hold off the pronouncement, even if only for a few seconds.

'OK, Olivia.'

He took a deep breath and looked her in the eye.

'How long have you been bulimic?'

Olivia said nothing.

Bulimic.

It was a shock to hear that word. Just as there were many euphemisms in her vocabulary for abortion, so this was a word that had never been voiced either by her, or the only other person who knew, Calliope. In fact its impact was all the more intense because in the end there was no denying the abortion, it had happened, but no-one (and only one person appeared ever to have noticed at all) had ever suggested that her 'problem', her 'weak stomach', her 'anxiety attacks', were bulimia.

She could remember well the first time she had done it. She and Guy had been out for dinner. A wonderful, candlelit meal in a sexy Spanish tapas bar, dark and warm with lots of Rioja and a flamenco guitarist to fan desire. That they'd had an evening to themselves, the percussion Mafiosi mates having finally been sent off by their Godfather to make up some jokes of their own to laugh at, was memorable in itself. There had been a great sense of build up all night, expectation on both sides of the table. Olivia had not ever been as happy since. *Do you love me?* Guy had said as they peeled grapes from the cheese platter, dipped them in their wine and fed them, laughing, to each other. *Of course, with all my heart,* she had replied. *And you know that I love you?* he had asked nervously. She had smiled at that stupid question and kissed him. *Then I have something that I have to tell you.* In her fluttering heart she had felt that he was about to propose.

Olivia, I've been unfaithful.

When she had first met him, Guy had made her see that her image of herself, left over from the adolescent miseries of school bullying, was false. He had made her believe that fatty-goody-two-shoes did not and had possibly never existed, that age had ripened her into something as beautiful and enticing as a Mediterranean peach. But, in his choice for sex-on-the-side, Guy could not have chosen better had he actually set out with intent to undermine Olivia's confidence in herself. Olivia knew the girl. She was a barmaid at Guy's local. Not talented, even to the point of being unable to give the right change and not beautiful, even to the point of being the reverse. Therefore, there was surely hardly a woman on the planet that he must not find preferable to Olivia, that she was not inferior to. And it was too late to say that she didn't love him. She felt powerless.

The first time had been that night. The first time had been her body, without influence from her conscious mind, voiding itself of everything that was pleasant about the evening, everything that had made her believe he loved her more than anyone else in the world. At least that was what she had told herself, being so disgusted by what she had done. But after a while she didn't need to repulse herself by sticking her fingers into her throat, she could spontaneously bring back what she had eaten before her stomach had even had a chance to get to work. Back then it had not been a continuous affliction. There had been stretches of happiness and belief that Guy had told the truth when he'd said it had been a meaningless fling and that she was the one for him. But within those happy times, she was slimming and shopping and preening herself, just to make sure that she was attractive enough to keep his interest. And then, out of the blue, she would catch a flirtatious eye being cast towards another woman and Olivia would all at once feel that everything she'd been doing was pointless. Then she would binge. Then she would purge.

Only after she had aborted their child had it all got truly out of hand. She had betrayed Guy and she had betrayed everything she had been taught to believe in. Neither Guy, nor God would forgive her. Unbearable, her guilt and grief were channeled into an obsession with her weight - if only she had been thinner, then Guy would have been reliable. She could have had it all – love, children and a career. It had not been the cigarettes she'd smoked, or the alcohol she'd drunk, that had left her incapable of singing her debut performance at Glyndebourne. She had been telling herself that lie for years but in reality, she had done to herself then what she had done to herself now. She could have had it all but now she had nothing.

She looked at David Sutherland and saw that there was no use denying it.

'Years. How did you know?'

'Because I'm a throat specialist.'

Olivia actually laughed, but then she was coughing again.

'I have to sing *La Bohème* tomorrow night. Is there anything you can do?'

'You shouldn't be talking, let alone singing. The acid in your vomit has eaten away at the lining of your oesophagus. There are serious lesions and as you've become aware, they're bleeding.'

'But is there anything you can do?'

'I don't think you realise how serious this is Olivia. How often have you been purging?'

'Not very.'

'Lying isn't going to help.'

'Every meal.'

'And?'

'And in between.'

'I thought so. In fact, if you said you hadn't been eating at all, I'd believe you.'

'You'd be right to, sometimes.'

'Well, then let me speak plainly. If you keep this up, not only will you not perform tomorrow night but, if you live, you will never sing again.'

Olivia thought he was being a little melodramatic; she had, after all, been down this road before and still managed to end up singing at the Royal Opera House.

'But is there anything you can do?'

'God, you're stubborn. Why is this performance so important?'

'It's going to be my last.'

'Then I wish I had a ticket. Unfortunately I was abroad at a conference when they went on sale.'

'I'll get you one, if you can patch me up. You can sit next to my sister and nephew, if you like - she'll do plenty of agreeing with you.'

'I wasn't serious. That could hardly be called ethical.'

'But you must treat me, or I'll have to find someone who will, and then I'll perform anyway. Wouldn't you rather I did it against your advice, than against that of another doctor? At least this way, you get a night out at the opera.'

David Sutherland had never, in all his years of practice, felt so saddened by a case. When the door closed he went to the bay window and stood watching for Olivia Tarrent to leave the building, then continued to gaze after her as she went down the road and turned at the corner towards Marylebone High Street. It was hard to believe that this was the same woman as the vibrant, gorgeous creature whom he had had the privilege to see making her Covent Garden debut only just over a year earlier.

Minutes later her voice filled his office as he put on his treasured copy of her love duets CD. Minutes after that he silenced it, because there was no escaping Angelo Verasano's presence. David knew that the man could not be held responsible for her condition, she had told him this had been going on for years but, a keen opera fan, David had been following her fortunes in the press since that very first time he'd heard her sing, and clearly it must be Angelo Verasano's unforgivably public humiliation of Olivia Tarrent that had sparked her to such totally self-destructive extremes. What a tragic waste of talent.

Fuming, David searched his Tarrent collection for something without that heinous tenor along for the ride, but there was none. How, if just the CDs made him this furious, was he going to sit through *La Bohème* tomorrow night? And yet, he could not think of missing it, for he believed Olivia when she said it would be her last performance - no matter *how* powerful, antibiotics and sprays weren't going to save her voice, or her life if she continued as she was. He wished that he could do more for her.

'Hello, this is David Sutherland,' he said, when the florist who usually decked out his office picked up the telephone. 'I'd like to place an order to be delivered to the Royal Opera House, Covent Garden, tomorrow night. Three dozen, deep red... actually, no *yellow* roses. Olivia Tarrent. The message?' he broke off and thought for a moment about medical ethics and just how desperate a condition Olivia Tarrent was in.

Then he happily threw caution to the wind.

chapter seventeen

'Hi, you must be David Sutherland,' said Katriona and held out her hand to him as she sat down, amused by the fact that Olivia had failed to mention that her throat specialist was drop dead gorgeous.

'That makes you Olivia's sister,' he said warmly.

'Yes, Katriona. And this is my son Aidan.'

'You're very young to be out this late.'

'Well, Aidan is Olivia's biggest fan.'

'And I thought that I was!' he laughed, drawing an interested look from Katriona.

'Tell me,' she said, 'How is Olivia? Is she very ill?'

'I'm afraid I can't answer that - patient confidentiality.'

'Oh. I'm sorry.'

'Well, I can tell you. She's not good at all,' interrupted Dominic who'd just come from backstage and was still shaken by the state his friend was in. 'We have to persuade her to take some time off.'

'Mummy, will you read the programme to me?' asked Aidan, who needed to know the story if they were going to sing in that foreign language again, and also wanted to stop his mother talking with her most worried of voices about Auntie Olivia being ill.

'In a minute, darling. I've tried Dominic, but she won't listen to me. Perhaps you could have a go at the party later, when she doesn't have first night nerves to worry about.'

'I can have a go, but then she'll be on that adrenaline high that makes you think you could go right ahead and give a repeat performance as an encore. And anyway, I just got her riled up by telling her not to go on tonight. I'm not sure she'll be talking to me for a while.'

David Sutherland kept his eyes locked into the programme, concentrating hard so as not to leap in and tell them that Olivia would be lucky to make it through to the end of the opera let alone have a choice but to take time off. He was relieved when the lights dimmed and Alexander Petrov made an appearance, silencing his companions.

It was Christmas Eve, 1830. A bleak garret in Montmartre, Paris. To the left in the foreground there was a lifeless, potbellied stove with a rickety old dining table and chairs beside it. To the right was a single iron bedstead with a small writing desk nearby. Wooden stairs led up the middle of the room to a platform which hid, to the right, the entrance to this draughty attic. There, with moonlight pouring in through the massive skylights, there was another desk and a huge canvas. It was here that the two bohemians who had the misfortune to call this shabby abode home, were striving to work, despite the winter being more in evidence within than without. Cursing his painting was the artist Marcello, sitting at the desk and, staring jealously out onto the smoking chimneys across Paris, was Rodolfo.

Despite his lack of respect for Angelo Verasano the man, David Sutherland could not help but chuckle along with the rest of the audience at the humorous performance of the singer, as Rodolfo and Marcello complained about the bitter cold and intense hunger they were suffering for their art, eventually in their desperation alighting upon the idea of burning the manuscript of Rodolfo's play - the oil paints on the canvas being likely to cause too much of a stench.

Act One went into the wood-burning stove and the two critics commented that the writing 'sparkled'. Then, in came the philosopher Colline, tossing his books on the table in disgust because he'd been unable to hock them at the pawnbroker. He joined his friends in their critique of the play as Act Two went up in flames with a crackle that was surely a steamy love scene. Finally, Rodolfo threw in Act Three, but alas it was all ashes before they could get warmth from it.

Gia à scricciola, increspasi, muor - It's crinkling and crackling and withering away already. *Che vano, che fragile dramma* - What a feeble play. *Abbasso, abbasso l'autor!* - Down with the author! they proclaimed.

Just then, all were saved from a miserable Christmas by the timely arrival of the violinist Schaunard, accompanied by two errand boys bearing fire wood, food and most importantly wine. As they enthusiastically went about setting the table for dinner, barely interested to hear how he came by all this and the gold coins which he lay before them, Schaunard told them anyway of how an English Lord had rather bizarrely requested him to play for his pet parrot until it died. Having played for three days, Schaunard had grown tired of his work and given the bird 'parsley'. *Lorito opened his beak, and like Socrates, he died!* laughed Schaunard, drawing his violin bow comically across his neck. Now, he insisted, they should not eat at home on Christmas Eve but save the food for harder times and go out to the Latin Quarter in search of fun.

In the wings, Olivia was waiting for her entry with calm resignation. She had always enjoyed this witty opening scene and the antics of the quartet of philanderers still raised a smile as their landlord came in search of rent and left empty-handed when they feigned shock at having seen him with a young redhead, who was certainly not his wife. As Rodolfo's friends now left him to finish a magazine article, each singer gave Olivia an encouraging hug on their way back to their dressing rooms. Their intention was good, but every embrace seemed not to give, but to sap her strength, as one by one they brought her closer to the moment when Mimi would knock on Rodolfo's door, telling him that her candle had gone out and wondering if he could light it – it was just all too miserably ironic.

On stage Rodolfo sat at the table to write, but could not settle to work and similarly Angelo was agitated. He had not seen Olivia since yesterday and was nervous about how she would be when he opened the door. He found himself hoping that she would not have improved since the rehearsal, that it was not a throat specialist that she needed attention from, but he himself. When the knock came at the door he was not disappointed.

There had always been something laughable about seeing a buxom soprano stagger up the stairs and wilt, with hand across her brow, into the chair by Rodolfo's writing desk, faint from the long climb up to the garret, but Olivia had everyone well and truly convinced that she was having difficulty making it up the stairs. Rodolfo was supposed to help her to the chair, but the thought of him laying a hand on her was too much to deal with so Olivia dragged herself a bit further before giving up and sinking to the ground at the top of the central staircase.

Ad ora come faccio? - And now what do I do? asked Rodolfo rather appropriately, fetching a glass of water, so as to sprinkle some of its contents on her forehead. *How ill she looks,* he then sang, though it came out more spoken to himself than sung to the audience. He moved to put his arm about her, but on cue Mimi came to and

Olivia was on her feet singing, *Ora permetta che accenda il lume* - Now let me light my candle.

Tanta fretta? - Are you in such a hurry?

Sì! answered Mimi, with none of the shy reluctance she was supposed to have in her voice. This Mimi meant it and mused that it would be a very short opera if she were to leave as she wished right now. But, Mimi had accidentally left her key in Rodolfo's apartment and when she came back, he not only concealed its whereabouts but also blew out his own candle when he saw that hers had been extinguished by the interminable, wintery draught.

Looking around for the key in the dark, Mimi and Rodolfo's hands accidentally touched, but Angelo almost had to press on without actually fulfilling the plot, so determined was Olivia not to make contact with him. During rehearsal she had succeeded, but the current effort was in vain and as soon as his hand closed around hers she knew why her urge to evade this moment had been so consuming.

Che gelida manina, se la lasci riscaldar - Your tiny hand is frozen, let me warm it for you, sang Angelo, his voice tender, brimming with passion as he embarked on one of opera's greatest arias.

But her hand was not frozen. At his touch, an orgasmic white light shot from her fingertips to her innermost reaches, making her swoon like the worst kind of romantic heroine, illuminating her with memories of their brief time together, every divine note that passed his beseeching lips, simultaneously breaking and mending her heart. This was an opera. It was not real life. *Shit. How many times do I have to learn the lesson?* she asked herself as her pulse, uncaring of good sense, raced to hear Puccini's music rendered so perfectly in her honour.

In the audience, many a hand came up instinctively to shield eyes from the flash that pulsed through the House as they watched the notorious pair spontaneously combust.

There was brief respite when Rodolfo's friends called up to him from the street below, to hurry him along to the cafe Momus, but on hearing that there was a woman with him, they knew to make themselves scarce.

Alone with Mimi, Rodolfo now pulled out the stops. There was no room for reality in *La Bohème*, thought Olivia, trying to convince herself that this alternative world, where love was only at first sight, had no parallel in her life. She strove desperately to protect herself from being sucked into Angelo's game of manipulation but - who was she kidding? - it had taken no longer for her to fall under his spell, than it had for Mimi and Rodolfo to become totally smitten.

...o dolce viso di mite circonfuso alba lunar, in te ravviso il sogno ch'io vorrei sempre sognar! - Oh sweet face, bathed in the light of the rising moon, in you I see my dreams, the dreams I'd like to dream forever! he uttered with his hands cupping her face, his fingers caressing the fragile, alabaster skin.

317

Looking into his eyes, Olivia felt her doubts drowning in an overwhelming swell of emotion.

Oh, how sweetly his flattery caresses my heart. Love alone command me! she admitted to herself as Angelo simulanteously declared *Fremon già nell'anima... le dolcezze estreme* - Already my soul's alive with passion. *Nel bacio freme amor* - Love trembles in a kiss. *Sei mia* - You are mine...

No, please don't! said Mimi as Rodolfo attempted to kiss her and Olivia clung for dear life to her sanity and self-control. *La Bohème* was just too damn romantic; she'd have to be stone to the core to be unmoved by a man singing to her like that, but that was what she had to be as Rodolfo and Mimi left for the cafe, arm in arm, he singing *Say you love me,* and she nuzzling closer to him, responding *Lo t'amo - I love you...*

Dominic, Katriona and David all shook their heads in dismay as the two voices were then heard fading into the distance, exquisitely united in the final *a cappella* notes of Act One.

Amor! Amor! Amor!

* * *

Not made of stone on any level, Olivia was frantically grateful to find Guy waiting for her as she and Angelo came off stage, whilst Angelo, consumed with his

318

character's passions, was furious to have the momentum of his seduction stalled.

Guy was frightened by the way Olivia looked at him now; desperate for salvation. He wished that he had it in him to give her what she needed, but the last few weeks had shown him his limitations. When he had first seen her, he'd fooled himself into believing the blame for her condition lay with Angelo. But then there had been the many long nights since, when she had felt so slight in his arms as he made love to her that he felt almost like he was holding a child and, repulsed, had lost the drive to shag, instead holding her without demand through the fitful hours of difficult passage into the disturbed slumber that revealed the true roots of her angst.

Then he had tried to put right his past errors, to be there for her, look after her. Yet every effort seemed to proportionally speed her disintegration and as the body dissolved before his very eyes, so the person he'd never stopped loving, despite the denying stream of flirtations, trysts and screws since their original parting, also dissolved away.

Now that he saw the panic in her eyes and saw clearly that she was still in love with Angelo, Guy felt a weight lift from his shoulders. Since standing at her dressing room door the previous day, he had been fighting the urge to act in self-preservation, but now the battle was lost.

'Olivia,' he said in a manner that she recognised with pain.

'You're not coming, are you?' she stated rather than asked, referring to the opening night bash which she was terrified of having to attend alone.

'No. Look it's the A.P.P. today, you know I'd come with you otherwise, but I just can't miss the A.P.P. You understand, don't you?'

The Annual Percussionists' Piss-up. Olivia remembered it well. The day in the year when percussionists gather from all around - even from overseas - to crawl from morning till night and from night until morning from pub, to club, to pub, to strip joint, to pub, to tandoori house, to pub, to casino, to pub, until every liver is enlarged and every kidney in shut down. Of course, Guy and his section would have to race to some rallying point, as soon as the curtain went down. To miss it would be sacrilege - she couldn't possibly expect him to give up the A.P.P. Not that it wasn't clear to Olivia that Guy had been doing the rounds all day with the rest of the Mafia, whilst she attempted to get back enough voice for this one performance - his speech was gently slurred, his nose a bit red, his breath tainted with scotch, his dinner jacket reeking of smoke and beer.

'Yes, I understand,' she said, and did, all too well as he disappeared into the mass of chorus and extras who were already gathering for Act Two.

Stage left was alive with them all when the curtain lifted. Here, in front of the quaint little Latin Quarter shops, street vendors were jostled by the crowds out for the evening. A young girl with a box of satin ribbons suspended around her neck, the eccentric old Parpignol wearing a top hat bedecked with bells, tassels and flowers setting up his kaleidoscopic stand of toys, a cheerfully rotund gent hawked steaming hot roasted chestnuts, dried fruits and candies all ready to be taken away in paper cones, another selling trinkets, another songbirds, another flowers. Their voices piled in upon each other with gloriously symphonic complexity, the genuine laughter of the many rascally children in their midst penetrating the music and bringing a truly Christmassy spirit to the scene.

Out of this confusion, Mimi and Rodolfo eventually emerged, she delighted to have been bought a charming pink bonnet by her new-found lover. Briefly there was a hint of trouble for the future when Rodolfo saw Mimi watching some young students and grew immediately suspicious and jealous, but with love still exploding into bloom, it was nothing but a compliment to Mimi and soon they were happily entering the café that took up the right half of the stage. To its fore were a couple of tables near a bar, where waiters cleaned glasses and iced champagne. Further back a sweaty, overworked chef was to be seen through a hatch into his steamed up kitchen, and above there was a balcony where a noisy group was playing billiards. From a cold room with a lifeless candle for company, to an expensive café surrounded by the most convivial of company - Mimi was happy, Olivia the contrary, having to struggle to relay Mimi's joy as Rodolfo introduced her to his friends and bade her join them in their extravagant feast.

This is Mimi. Her arrival completes the fine company, for I am the poet, and she the poetry. From my mind burst songs, from her fingers burst flowers, from our exultant souls bursts love!

Rodolfo's friends yawned in jest at his romanticism. Olivia shyly averted Mimi's eyes from Rodolfo as he sang and could not have been more relieved to finally be lead to the bohemians' table where she could sit and rest for all that remained of the act. It was one of the opera's greatest attributes, that it did not place the burden of the entire plot upon the shoulders of the one couple. Here then was another love story that was to play under the tragedy of Mimi and Rodolfo's affair, bringing humour now and hope later.

Olivia could have been in a real restaurant, as she sat at the table sipping from her glass of water and finding comfort in the act of smoothing away non-existent creases in the fine white linen tablecloth as she watched the action and tried her best to blank out the ever-present Angelo to her left, though he determined to make it a near impossible task by putting his arm lovingly around her shoulders and whispering at her in Italian, pressing her to allow him a few moments alone with her during the interval.

Front of house, there were few in the audience who did not wonder what the favoured couple of last year's gossip columns were talking about as Rodolfo's friend Marcello tried to ignore the arrival at the next table of his former lover Musetta. It was like watching the end of the ten o'clock news and seeing the readers chatting away as the lights dimmed, and none were more frustrated than Dominic, Katriona and David. It was a great credit to the fantastic acting of the soprano playing Musetta, that she managed to grab the attention back for herself, just as Musetta who was vastly dissatisfied with the sugar daddy she was dining with, threw herself into attracting Marcello. Once again, Aidan was discovering that the Royal Opera House was a wondrously liberating place, as Musetta educated him in the art of seduction by means other than a great aria. Before long, she was complaining that her shoe was hurting her toes and both scandalising her benefactor and torturing Marcello as she sat upon her table, lifting her skirts for the patrons and waiters to take a look at her foot, not to mention everything else up to her garter.

Calliope would have made a great Musetta, thought Olivia without malice as she watched the shameless Musetta send her lover off to the cobbler with her shoe and fall happily into Marcello's eager embrace, almost before the door closed behind the old man. Then, with the chorus singing in the streets as a platoon of soldiers marched through, preceded by a drum-major, Marcello and Colline carried Musetta out of the cafe with Mimi, Rodolfo and Schaunard following. As the curtain fell, Musetta's benefactor returned to find himself saddled with the bill for the bohemians' dinner.

* * *

Angelo did not go back to his dressing room, but stood in the shadows watching Olivia shivering and coughing as she waited in the wings for the stage crew to transform the scene. He dared not go to her; his entreaties during the last act had clearly had a bad effect upon her and there was no doubt in his mind that his best chance to express his feelings at their most persuasive would be through the music of the next act. Upset her any more right now, and it was certain that she would be in no state to go on. Vexed at that thought, he just had to give in and approach Olivia, though only to offer her a chair, snatched from one of the crew as it was hauled off stage.

Olivia's heart squeezed at the gesture, all the more perhaps because he then walked away without seeking gratitude. She wished that Guy had waited until the end of the performance, but then timing was of the essence when it came to the A.P.P. She closed her eyes and attempted to meditate, hoping that she would be able to relax enough to control the spasms that were simultaneously clenching her throat, lungs and stomach so that it felt as if she would be turned inside out by the force of her entire being trying to escape the confines of its flimsy cage.

'Are you going to be able to go on?'

Olivia didn't open her eyes, the voice of her agent was unmistakable, as was the familiar *tap, tap, tap,* of Laura's stilettos against the boards.

'The show must go on. Isn't that right, Laura?' she responded in a very quiet, controlled voice, treating the untimely conversation as an exercise in breath control, only to end up coughing again.

'You *stupid* bitch, look what you've done to yourself. I thought we were done with this nonsense, Olivia. I cannot, simply can *not* believe you're going to fuck up everything that I've worked for all over again. I dare say we can make this bulimia thing work for *Hello* - it is, after alcoholism, the disorder to have if you're rich and famous - but you're not going to be bloody rich and famous for long if you can't sing.'

Astonished, Olivia looked up into the face of the fuming gorgon.

'Oh, you don't *honestly* think I believed all that rubbish about smoking and drinking when you screwed up that Glyndebourne date, do you? Really Olivia, you are *too* precious. Well *darling*, this time I'm done with you. If you want to go back to scraping a living from amateur gigs, fine, but I'm not doing the searching for you. Pull yourself together or I'm finished with you. Do you understand me?'

'Yes, Laura, I understand you,' Olivia said, and then went on with the show.

It was very early one bitterly cold, snowy February morning that Mimi came to an inn just by one of the city gates. Here Marcello and Musetta were enjoying living life at the innkeeper's expense, he having been employed to decorate the facade of the tavern whilst Musetta was teaching singing to the patrons. Fearful of being seen by Rodolfo, Mimi hovered outside until a passing trader could be persuaded to go in and ask Marcello to come and speak with her.

When he did, it was to hear her sorry tale of Rodolfo's insane jealousy that was provoked by the slightest thing - a step, a word, a necklace, a flower.

Quando s'è come voi non si vive in compagnia - Two people like you shouldn't live together, sang Marcello.

Dite bene; lasciarci conviene. Aiutateci, aiutateci voi; noi s'è provato... più volte, ma invano - You're right; we must part. Help us, oh do help us; we have tried but always in vain.

Just then, Marcello saw through the tavern window that Rodolfo was on his way out, and begged Mimi to go home, not realising as he and Rodolfo began to speak of Mimi, that she had instead concealed herself nearby. At first, Rodolfo was determined to stick to his assertion that his jealousy over Mimi was justified and was the true cause of his desire to separate from her. Marcello only had to express his doubt at the sincerity of Rodolfo's accusations for the lovelorn writer to give up the charade. It was to be perhaps Angelo Verasano's finest hour. He set out to slash apart Olivia's resistance with Puccini the gleaming sword in his grasp, deliriously convinced of his own artlessness. Sometimes having to hold onto his friend for strength, at other moments needing to close his eyes against the reality that the words mirrored, he sang for all he was worth till sobs clogged his throat.

Invan, nascondo la mia vera tortura. Amo Mimì sovra ogni cosa al mondo, io l'amo, ma ho paura - In vain I hide my real torment. I love Mimi more than anything in the world. I love her, but I am frightened. *Mimì i è tanto malata! Ogni dì più declina. La povera piccina è condannata* - Mimi is so very ill. Every day she grows weaker. The poor little thing is dying.

What does he mean? Mimi asked herself, but Olivia felt the approaching words with more fear than if she had seen the grim reaper approaching across the stage.

Una terribil tosse l'esil petto le scuote, già le smunte gote di sangue ha rosse - A terrible cough shakes her feeble frame, her pale cheeks are flushed. *Essa canta e sorride, e il rimorso m'assale. Me cagion del fatale mal che l'uccide* - She sings and smiles and remorse assails me. I am the cause of this illness that is killing her.

Though Olivia had heard them sung a thousand times before, the words now seemed to have been written for her alone. Angelo couldn't have been more convincing of his acceptance of responsibility, nor his undying love for her, had he actually meant it. Olivia could not have been more broken by what she heard than had she actually believed she were going to die at the end of Act Four.

She might as well, she thought, for if she did not she was condemned to love this man forever and worse still to know that he loved her more than anything else in the world, yet could never be free. He was married to Calliope now and with a child to bind them together forever, there could be no hope.

No hope.

Olivia went to Angelo and held her hand up to his cheek.

Good-bye, farewell, and no hard feelings.

Angelo looked to her eyes to have it confirmed that these were just words on the surface of very different emotions, and saw with equal disappointment and fury that she was not yet conquered.

Dunque è proprio finita! Addio, sogni d'amor - So, it's all over. Farewell dreams of love, he sang, a tear beginning its slow descent. *Addio sognante vita. Addio baci ch'io da vero poeta rimavo con carezza* - Farewell life of dreams. Farewell kisses that like a true poet I have rhymed with caresses, he sang less with the beseeching nostalgia of Rodolfo, than his own petulant disbelief.

He had no intention of giving up and then took Olivia in his arms, holding her tight so that she could feel their voices coalesce as they united: *Soli d'inverno è cosa da morire!* - To be alone in winter is like dying.

He had squeezed the tear from his eye with quite admirable timing. Nothing could have made Olivia understand Mimi and Rodolfo's reluctance to accept the reality of their tragedy more than the sensation of it combining with her own tears as Mimi and Rodolfo put off their parting until spring.

With Musetta and Marcello coming out of the tavern bickering over her flirtatious behaviour, Rodolfo and Mimi sang of springtime when they would at least have the sun for a companion, the contrasting melodies mingling and enriching each other as the act built to its close with Marcello and Musetta separating as Rodolfo and Mimi reunited.

Angelo was sure that he had won the day as Olivia sang, *Sempre tua per la vita* - Always yours, for life.

But though Olivia meant it, she saw that life for her could be very short.

Vorrei che eterno durasse il verno - I'd like winter to last forever. *Ci lascerem alla stagion dei fior* - We'll part when the flowers bloom again, she sang, knowing that in Act Four it would already be spring.

The moment the curtain was down, Angelo sank to his knees in front of Olivia.

'My darling. Now you know,' he whispered, 'and I thank God that you feel the same. It has been dreadful to be parted from you. I have been so unhappy. I am like Rodolfo; '*Gia un'altra volta credetti morto il mio cor, ma di quegli occhi allo splendore esso è risorto.*' Once I believed my heart was dead, but at the splendour of those eyes it revived. And now, my Olivia, my love, my soul, we can be together.'

Olivia's eyes registered none of the tumultuous joy he had envisaged. They looked down upon him with no emotion he had the humanity to interpret.

'Olivia?'

The silence was disturbing, he was beginning to feel the eyes of the stage crew upon him as they tried to prepare for Act Four. Soon they would be making snide and obscene remarks to move the couple off the stage, or worse still landing scenery on top of them - Angelo knew full well that they called him Mussolini behind his back and would be more than happy if he were *accidentally* flattened like a cartoon character.

'My darling, why do you say nothing? Do you not understand? I will leave Calliope. My darling, we can be together.'

'Si, Angelo, I understand,' she replied and walked away, tears flowing once more as she coughed violently and saw that so too was the blood.

Meanwhile, Katriona was wiping away her own tears and passing tissues across David Sutherland to Dominic.

'This opera gets me every time,' he explained with embarrassment.

'Me too,' sniffed Katriona.

'Mummy, is Auntie Olivia going to be OK?' asked Aidan with genuine concern.

'Of course she is, silly. It's just a story.'

'But Rodolfo said she's going to die.'

'Well, yes, that is what happens. Mimi has tuberculosis, you see, and in the next act she comes back to Rodolfo, very ill. He and his friends send for the doctor but unfortunately Mimi dies before he can get there. It's really sad, but it is just the character, not Olivia.'

'Oh,' said Aidan, not in the least reassured.

David Sutherland was also having trouble accepting Katriona's belief that her sister was fine. He could not imagine by what miracle it was that Olivia had been able to sing up until this point, but he was convinced that as sure as a pact with Satan would result in the loss of a soul, so this performance would result in the permanent loss of a voice. Only for the sake of the little boy to his right did he hold back his own tears.

'Olivia's going to be all right,' he then remarked. 'After all,' he smiled, 'I'm her doctor and I don't have far to go if she's in trouble, do I now?'

He realised it was a mistake to promise the impossible. Children had a way of knowing when an adult was lying to them and now he had conceded to Aidan that Olivia might actually need a doctor. Aidan looked him in the eye and David Sutherland felt ashamed and guilty - it had been a selfish comment for his own benefit, for his own peace of mind, as the lights dimmed once more.

* * *

And so the stage was set for heartrending tragedy; restored to the artists' garret of the first act; everything coming full circle.

'Mummy, that lady's got no clothes on!' exclaimed Aidan, causing the surrounding audience to giggle despite themselves as the curtain lifted to reveal a model posing nude for a distracted Marcello as Rodolfo feigned writing at his desk. The pair tried to appear as if they didn't care as they talked of their former lovers, Musetta and Mimi, who had both now found wealthy new benefactors. Yet, each saw through the other's denial to the broken heart within. It was senseless to keep up the facade and soon the model was dismissed and the lovelorn romantics gave way to nostalgia for their true loves.

Se pingere mi piace o cieli, o terre, o inverni, o primavere, egli mi traccia due pupille nere e una bocca procace, e n'esce di Musetta il viso ancor... If I try to paint the sky or earth, winter or spring, I draw instead two dark eyes and provocative lips and there again is Musetta's face, lamented Marcello sitting defeated at the top of the stairs as Rodolfo went over to his bed and took, from under a pillow, the bonnet which he had given to Mimi, holding it to his chest and singing, *Vien sul mio cor, sul mio cor morto, ah vien sul mio cor, poichè è morto amor -* Come to my heart, to my broken heart, oh come to my heart, for love is dead.

332

Feeling that those words should have been hers, Olivia's eyes watched Angelo whilst her mind took her back to the night in Il Dolce Momente when they had first sung together. It had been *La Bohème* that night too, she recalled. It had seemed then that Angelo had given her back her dreams, her life even. But now, just as Act Four brought Schaunard and Colline to the garret to disguise tragedy with a scene of great humour, so Olivia was also faced with a depressing case of *déjà vu*. Once she had been able to lift herself with thoughts of another Olivia living out a happier life in some parallel universe, but now she knew that even if there were an infinite number of those existences, nothing could change the very nature of her reality - wherever, whenever, this was what she was destined for.

This time, not even the sight of Marcello putting on a bonnet and shawl and dancing a quadrille with Rodolfo could raise a smile. Nor did the spectacle of Schaunard and Colline duelling with fire irons, or pretending to be a bull and his brave fighter. As she coughed away and wondered if, for once, the audience would get a realistic sounding Mimi, not singing like a lark in her dying moments but heaving up blood through broken notes, she could find no beauty in the luscious resonance of the quartet of voices on stage, no joy in the sound of appreciative laughter from the audience.

It was silenced soon enough anyway. Into the merriment burst Musetta, to tell them that Mimi was dying and had left her viscount in order to be with Rodolfo at the end. Poor Mimi could not even make it up the stairs, and truly Angelo had to virtually carry Olivia to the bed.

David Sutherland shifted in his seat, debating whether or not he should make for backstage, knowing that he had never before, in this production, seen that blood stained handkerchief Mimi was clutching. Aidan did not need the doctor's disquiet to alert him. His honest, child's eyes saw immediately through the characters' sorrow at the realisation that their friend Mimi was dying, to the intense worry that crossed their faces whenever their eyes alighted on the bed where she lay. He too began to twist about in his seat.

'Mummy,' he whispered, 'there's something wrong with Auntie Olivia.'

'It's all right, darling, she's only acting,' his mother responded. 'Now shush.'

Fra mezz'ora è morta - She'll be dead in half an hour, Schaunard sadly remarked to Colline.

Ho tanto freddo! Queste mie mani riscaldare non si potranno mai? - I'm so cold! Shall I never be able to warm these hands of mine? sang Mimi, her ragged voice bringing the glowing words of praise at the tips of the critics' pens to a sudden, confused halt.

'Mummy?' said Aidan nervously.

'Aidan, I've already explained, Olivia is just acting. Now quiet, please,' she urged, but he'd seen her eyes dart to David Sutherland and she did not sound as convinced as she might.

Now Musetta took off her ear-rings and gave them to Marcello, telling him to sell them and bring a doctor. Then she decided to go with him in order to procure a muff to warm Mimi's hands.

Sei buona, o mia Musetta - You're so good, my Musetta, he said with love in his voice and, reunited once more, the two of them went out.

Now Colline took off his coat with the intention of taking it to the pawn shop, though not before singing nostalgically to it of the faithful friendship with which it had seen him through the hard times. All the while Mimi lay motionless upon the bed, with Rodolfo at her side, grief-stricken.

As Colline sang, Aidan grew more and more frightened. It was impossible to distinguish between what he was persuaded was fiction on stage, and the real concern for his aunt that was growing steadily as she lay silent for what seemed an eternity. Finally, though he knew his mother would be annoyed at him for yet one more time breaking the rules by which he was allowed to attend tonight, he had to speak.

'Mummy, is Mimi dead yet?'

'No, she's not,' came the tense reply.

'Did they send for the doctor?'

'Yes, they've gone for the doctor,' Katriona said under her breath, aware that people around them were beginning to get irritated, and wishing that the performance were not in Italian so that Aidan would quit questioning her.

He, however, could not quell his mounting distress as Rodolfo went to see his friends out. He shouldn't have left her. Didn't he know how ill she was? Aidan hadn't liked that man when he'd come to Norfolk with Olivia at Christmas - only interested in the kids if there were another adult there to see him act the perfect father figure - and since then, many a hushed conversation between his parents had been overheard on the subject of 'that bastard.' Now Aidan was beside himself, unable to choose between relief at seeing that Olivia was still alive or terror as she dragged herself up from the bed, crumpling to the floor in a horrible fit of coughing before Rodolfo got to her.

Angelo didn't know what to do, she was supposed to fly into his arms as he ran down the stairs to her, not hit the deck. For a moment he was angered but she was so heavy in his arms when he hauled her up and sat down on the bed, that it was clear she was not putting on this faint. Out of the corner of his eye he could see Petrov looking harassed, so there was at least a silver lining to the prospect of Olivia not coming in with her next entry.

Ho tante cose che ti voglio dire... come il mare profundo ed infinita. Sei il mio amor e tutta la mia vita - I have so many things to tell you... as deep and infinite as the ocean. You are my love and my whole life.

Olivia sang, but to Angelo it was not really her voice, its lyricism was entirely gone. Yet more shocking for him, was the total absence of emotion in the words; they ran through him like the barbs on a serrated hunting knife as he cradled her in his arms, and kissed her cold cheek.

Ah Mimì, mia bella Mimì! - Oh Mimi, my beautiful Mimi, he cried with all the persuasiveness to romance he could muster.

Son bella ancora? - Am I still beautiful? she returned, making Angelo feel like the liar he was.

Bella come un'aurora - Beautiful as the dawn.

Hai sbagliato il raffronto. Volevi dir: bella come un tramonto - You are mistaken. You mean; As beautiful as the sunset.

And then Mimi took off into the past, Puccini bringing back their affair through fragments of earlier arias and duets. The audience were universally pained by the rasping quality of her voice, stirred to greater sorrow by its stark opposition to the earlier beauty with which she had somehow contrived to sing the same melodies.

Che gelida manina, se la lasci riscaldar! Era buio, e la man tu mi prendevi... What a frozen tiny hand, let me warm it for you. It was dark and you took my hand, she reminded him, her voice cracking into nothing as she fell back and was again racked with coughing.

Oh Dio! Mimì! - Oh God, Mimi, sobbed Rodolfo as Musetta and Marcello returned.

'Mummy, I thought they were going for the doctor,' Aidan suddenly blurted out quite audibly. 'Where's the doctor mummy? Why isn't he with them?'

Katriona looked down and saw his eyes bright with tears, trembling like a baby rabbit and realised that her husband had been right to chastise her for giving in to Aidan's pleading to come with her tonight. He was just too young, and besides, even she was beginning to see that there was no call for suspending disbelief for this performance. To stay here and invite outrage with Aidan's constant talking, or to infuriate by clambering to the end of the row just before the end of the opera? It was a tough choice, but saving her son from more distress seemed paramount. She shot David and Dominic an apologetic look and gathered up her terrified son. He was having none of it though and struggled to get free before she could reach the door, then standing transfixed in the aisle as Mimi forced out her last words before drifting into unconsciousness.

Qui, amor... sempre con te. Le mani al caldo... e... dormire - Here, my love, with you always. My hands in the warm... and... to sleep.

Now Musetta began to pray as Schaunard watched Mimi, his face growing suddenly pale.

Marcello, she is dead, he said quietly as Colline came back with money from the sale of his coat and went to Rodolfo's aid, as the deluded hero tried to pull the curtains so as to keep the sunlight from disturbing his sleeping beloved.

'Mummy, he says she's dead. She can't be. Mummy, tell them to the bring the doctor or she'll die mummy,' cried out Aidan tearfully, his voice growing more and more piercing as his vexation intensified, sending a shudder down the spine of each and every patron in the House, for each and every one of them had been yearning to leap from their seat and do the same, so authentic seemed Mimi's condition.

'Mummy *do* something,' begged Aidan.

As Mimi's arm hung limply off the bed as confirmation of her demise, Olivia heard the impassioned cries of her nephew with total shock. All through the scene she had been letting daft, romantic thoughts of how gratifyingly tragic the headlines would be if she were to join Mimi in death at the end of the opera, but now reality hurtled like an arrow through her consciousness, making her aware suddenly of just how close a possibility it was, alerting her finally to what she had been doing to herself.

If you keep this up, not only will you not perform tomorrow night but, if you live, you will never sing again. David Sutherland's voice came back to her now.

If you live.

He wasn't like them - he wasn't a man for being melodramatic, Olivia realised with horror. He was serious, deadly serious.

Thrown from the battlements, guillotined, run through with a Japanese sword; it was all very well to dream of a dramatic, Byronic death but did she actually want to die? Were all the things that she had lost tonight worth this suicide by attrition? Did she want to die when tonight Guy had made a mockery of all those years of guilt and shown Calli to be right after all? Did she want to die and leave Laura to get all the royalties from her recordings thanks to a contract that she should never have signed, and could easily have overturned in court? And did she really, truly want to die for the love of Angelo Verasano, a man who had left her, who was now apparently ready without a second thought to abandon his wife and defenceless little baby, and who would no doubt run off with his next leading lady?

Poor Calliope, a small child to care for and no husband, no coach, no best friend to turn to. Now *that* was a genuine tragedy, thought Olivia.

Coraggio, said Marcello, going to Rodolfo as he slowly became aware of the change in his friend's demeanour.

Then the French horns stabbed into the grim silence in the House, joined by wailing violins as Rodolfo now realised that Mimi was dead.

Mimì... Mimì... he cried, then rushed to the bed to clasp her lifeless body in his arms, consumed with grief.

* * *

There were huge tears of relief cried all round as the curtain parted and the audience rose to greet Olivia. Not for the last time after all, she had already decided, her mind racing with plans for the future.

Never again was she going to let Laura manipulate her like a puppet.

Never again was she going to tread the same stage as Angelo Verasano.

Never again was she going to doubt that the A.P.P. would always be Guy's first priority.

But, above all, never again was she going to let Calliope succeed in her efforts to punish herself for the sins of another. Father Timothy was still there, surely abusing each new generation of girls that passed through that school. Death by any other name, smelled as foul.

Something had to be done, Olivia realised, and should have been done long ago so that Calli could finally be released. She could convince Calli, she knew it. Together they would find the others. Together they would take control of their lives. Together they would finally forgive themselves and each other.

Now, to a roar of approval from the crowd, she extricated her hand from Angelo's, defying her shaking body's call for support as she walked towards the edge of the stage to thank the orchestra, who had foregone their after show pints to stand cheering, with even a defiant timpanist stood in their midst.

Then she stood, tearfully basking in her future, flowers raining down from all sides, bouquet after bouquet being laid at her feet until one caught her eye.

Three dozen yellow roses - the roses of friendship - of true love.

She stooped to gather it to her and pull out a rose for each of the singers who had seen her through the show - Musetta, Schaunard, Colline and Marcello. Then she laughed at the message on the accompanying card.

Olivia,

Life's not an opera. Dinner sometime?

David Sutherland x

'He's wrong,' she thought with a triumphant smile, happy tears flowing as she took one last bow before the curtain descended. 'Life *is* an opera, but it's up to me to write the libretto. It doesn't have to end in tragedy, the villains can lose out, and the doctor *can* arrive just in time to save the heroine.'

- CURTAIN -

Made in the USA
Columbia, SC
17 August 2017